D0048129

Praise for **Scarlett Cole**

"Scarlett Cole's characters pull you in from the very first page with real emotion and sizzling chemistry. Don't miss this action-packed thrill ride."

—Cherry Adair, *New York Times* bestselling author

"Nonstop action and heart-pounding romance—*Under Fire* is a must-read for romantic suspense fans!"

—Cynthia Eden, *New York Times* and *USA Today* bestselling author

"Fantastic characters, scorching sexual tension, and nonstop action make this one of my favorite reads this year! Highly recommend!"

—Laura Kaye, *New York Times* bestselling author

"Sizzling-hot romance."

—*RT Book Reviews* on *Under Fire*

"Scarlett Cole truly knows how to get readers invested in her characters and in the story. Her writing is excellent, and I'd love to read more from her."

—*The Romance Reviews*, Top Pick

"There is categorically no better writer than Scarlett Cole for ratcheting up the conflict, anxiety, and heart-palpitating thrills that she can."

—*Romance Reviews Today* on *Under Fire*

FINAL SIEGE

Scarlett Cole

St. Martin's Paperbacks

This is a work of fiction. All of the characters, organizations, and events portrayed in this novel are either products of the author's imagination or are used fictitiously.

FINAL SIEGE

Copyright © 2018 by Scarlett Cole.
Excerpt from *Deep Cover* copyright © 2018 by Scarlett Cole.

For information address St. Martin's Press, 175 Fifth Avenue, New York, NY 10010.

ISBN: 978-1-250-12846-1

Our books may be purchased in bulk for promotional, educational, or business use. Please contact your local bookseller or the Macmillan Corporate and Premium Sales Department at 1-800-221-7945, ext. 5442, or by e-mail at MacmillanSpecialMarkets@macmillan.com.

Printed in the United States of America

St. Martin's Paperbacks edition / February 2018

St. Martin's Paperbacks are published by St. Martin's Press, 175 Fifth Avenue, New York, NY 10010.

10 9 8 7 6 5 4 3 2 1

To my copy editor, John Simko.

*Your comments and changes always
make my books better.
And I apologize for still not
grasping the correct way to use a comma and
for failing to remember to capitalize T-shirt
in every book I write!*

ACKNOWLEDGMENTS

To my husband, Tim. Without you buying me a laptop and a domain name and telling me to start writing, I don't know that I would have taken the leap from business executive to author. Without your unwavering support and constant belief that running a home and parenting was a team effort, I don't know that I would have been able to stick to it. I know you hate soppy stuff, but believe me, marrying you was one of the best decisions I ever made. I love you, and our crazy life.

To my minions. It would be impossible to list the reasons I love you. But the fact you know how to give great hugs and make the perfect cup of tea means we're raising you right. Thank you for being my greatest cheer squad!

To my military heroes. Thank you for continuing to be a source of experience and humor. I wish I could write half of what you tell me.

To my STARS. A thousand thank-yous for keeping me sane. I love each and every one of you.

To Beth Phelan. Thank you for continuing to demonstrate day after day why you are the most fantastic agent a girl could ever have. Without your support, I'd be lost. Thank you!

To Lizzie Poteet. We didn't make it all the way to eleven, but this makes eight together. Thank you for having faith in me. I miss you already!

To Alex Sehulster. Thank you for stepping in as my editor and for making the transition of this book seamless. I can't wait to see what else we can do together.

To the team at SMP. Thank you for everything you do for me and my stories. Being in print is a dream come true, so thank you for making it so I can hold my babies in my hands! And thank you for another fantastic cover.

To Andrew Feinstein. Thank you for writing *The Shadow World: Inside the Global Arms Trade*. It inspired Delaney's character, and was a book I wasn't expecting to find so riveting.

CHAPTER ONE

Malachai "Mac" MacCarrick pulled the knife from its sheath with barely a whisper. During his years as a Navy SEAL, most of his ops had been black in nature, with silence a prerequisite for staying alive. He and this knife went way back, a gift from someone special who knew and understood his appreciation for a well-made blade sharpened to his exact requirements. Light reflected off the metal, its balance perfection as he turned it in his hand. It had spent most of the last decade in storage in his parents' garage, but in the nine months since he'd left the Navy to start up Eagle Securities he'd enjoyed using it again.

"It's a goddamn chef's knife . . . not an MK 3. Can you bring it into the living room so we can cut the damn cake?" Six, his partner in crime since the day they'd met in kindergarten, and co-owner of Eagle Securities, leaned against the doorframe of the bright kitchen in Mac's apartment. Well, it wasn't technically *his* apartment. He was housesitting for his younger brother, Lochlan, who had not only gotten away with a marginally more bearable Irish name than he had, but had also gotten the lion's share of the brains. He was off in San Francisco, angel investing in some tech incubator, doubling his money in a building that had slides for grown-ups and mandatory massage breaks. Still there were worse places to be than his brother's pad in the luxurious condo building, The Legend, which overlooked the Padres' stadium, especially on a day like today.

Cake. He looked down at the knife. A birthday cake for Cabe, the final part of their triumvirate. Once, though, they had been four. The memory of Brock stabbed at him as surely as if he'd pierced his heart with the knife in his hand. You never got over killing a friend, no matter what the circumstances.

He cleared his throat and locked the memory down tight as he had for the last fourteen years. Thinking of Brock would also mean thinking of Brock's sister, Delaney, and there definitely would be no coming back from that.

"On it. Did you talk to Lou about heading out again so quickly?" Mac asked. Lou had come into Six's life last summer when they'd taken on the job of protecting her from criminals who wanted to steal a formula she'd been working on and turn it into a weapon for chemical warfare. Somewhere along the line they'd fallen in love with one another.

They were quite the pair, the outgoing warrior and the cripplingly shy scientist, and it hurt Mac to watch them at times. He'd once had what they had—and he'd lost it through his own recklessness.

"Yeah. She isn't thrilled we're heading into Syria, but she gets it. Gets me, I guess."

Mac handed the knife to Six and then grabbed a beer from the counter before heading into the living room that overlooked the ballpark. The rest of the crew was spread around the apartment. Gaz, and Jackson, stood laughing by the open balcony doors as Miller complained for the thousandth time about his nickname, Lite. March in San Diego was a little hit and miss, but today the sun beat down on the patio where Sherlock, Buddha, and Ryder were looking out over the stadium toward the Coronado Bridge. On days like this, when the water sparkled blue and he was surrounded by his friends and coworkers, he focused on the good that had happened in his life instead of the bad. They didn't sing "Happy Birthday"—because they were a group of grown men for fuck's sake. But Louisa stepped out of Six's shadow to place a single candle on the cake and instruct Cabe to blow it out. When Cabe rolled his eyes, she playfully smacked him on the shoulder and pointed to the candle. Honestly, Cabe was probably doing them all a favor by putting off the moment when he'd have to cut that cake. Louisa had baked it herself, and knowing how dedicated the vegetarian was to healthy eating, Mac was pretty sure it would be sorely lacking in butter, eggs, and sugar. All the good stuff his mom crammed into her cooking, Louisa wouldn't use. So, the cake was destined to taste awful.

"Come on, make a wish!" Louisa insisted. It was impossible to guess what Cabe *would* wish for, really. An hour-long sit-down with Warren Buffett? A first edition of *The Art of War* . . . in Chinese, if such a thing still existed.

Mac had spent most of his life mediating between Six and Cabe since the day he'd had to break them up as they'd fought over a tattered copy of *One Fish, Two Fish* in kindergarten. For all their love for each other, they were so different. Cabe was as cerebral as Six was spontaneous. At the same time, though, their differences also made them a great team. With Cabe's intense focus, Six's ability to roll with just about any situation, and Mac's resourcefulness, they were a force to be reckoned with.

It was a very rare day that the entire team was home at the same time. Since setting up Eagle Securities nine months before, they'd quickly developed a reputation as exceptional special ops contractors, putting them in demand both domestically and internationally. At first it had been a crazy rush of excitement when the contracts had started to come in and they could step away from the security training they'd set up as a sideline. But trying to stay ahead of the resources required and keeping up with scheduling had quickly become a logistical nightmare. Though they periodically hired outside contractors to keep up with the demand, their ultimate goal was to attract the best ex-special-forces skills possible and add them to the team. Interviewing and screening candidates took time. And truth be told, all three of them would much rather be out in the field than stuck behind a desk asking people where they wanted to be in five years. But it had to be done, so despite the demand for their expertise, they were on a three-day break to rest up, refocus, and take care of administrative shit that was piling up around them.

Mac's cell phone rang, and he looked down at the screen. *Germany.* His chest tightened. The largest military hospital outside of the U.S. was in Landstuhl. Over the course of his career, calls from Germany had either been the best kind of news—that everyone had survived their missions intact—or the worst kind, in which he'd find out that someone was injured. Or fallen.

"Hello," he said, stepping back into the kitchen.

"Am I speaking with Captain Malachai MacCarrick?"

He tried to place the voice. Female. American. Plus, he hadn't been called "Captain" in a while. It was almost strange to hear. "Speaking, although I've left the service."

"This is Meredith Dean from the Landstuhl Regional Medical Center. I'm calling on behalf of one of our patients. A Delaney Shapiro."

Mac's mouth went dry at the mention of her name. A name he thought about a thousand times a day but never said out loud. An image of her laughing in the surf, the tiny diamond stud she wore in her nose sparkling in the sunshine as she grinned at him, crashed into his brain. "Is she okay?" he asked, trying to stem the flood of memories that threatened the edge of his usual control. Memories of their first kiss, of the first time she'd let him slide his hands over her soft, tanned skin. The day she'd let him take her virginity in a motel room on the way to Napa for a relative's wedding. The moment she'd slapped him in front of her brother's coffin fourteen years ago and told him she never wanted to see him again.

And she hadn't since.

"Ms. Shapiro has sustained significant injuries, but in moments of lucidity, she has asked if you are here yet. We have been unable to reach her immediate next of kin."

He strode to his office, grabbed his passport from the safe, and shoved it into his back pocket. "Tell her I'm on my way. I'm coming from San Diego. I'll be on the first flight I can get."

He hung up the phone and threw enough clothes for a few days into his backpack. Clean underwear and socks, always-packed toiletry bag, three T-shirts, two pairs of jeans, and a couple of hoodies, because if he remembered correctly, March in Germany was cold.

He hurried to the living room and signaled to Cabe and Six.

"What's up?" Cabe said, eying the backpack on the bed. "We got a job?"

"I gotta go," he said. "Delaney is in Landstuhl." He unplugged his chargers from the wall and shoved them into the front pocket of his pack.

"What the hell?" Six tugged his hand through his hair. "The place or the hospital? What happened?"

For the first time since his phone had rung, Mac allowed himself a moment of panic. "Hospital. I don't know how she ended up there. All I know is that she's been asking for me when she's lucid. I'm sorry guys, it means we're going to be short for—"

"Shut up," Cabe said. "You need to go. And we've got your back. Don't worry about tickets. I'll find you a flight while you're on route to the airport. I'll text you details, okay?"

Mac nodded and gathered his wits. He shoved his jacket into the top of his backpack as he had no intention of checking anything. He wanted to walk off that plane and head straight to the hospital. "Thanks, guys. I'll let you know what's what as soon as I get there."

Cabe stood and slapped him on the back in a hug. "Take care, man."

Six did the same.

"Lock up for me?" he said to Six as he made for the door without waiting for a response.

Delaney needed him.

He finally had the chance to make things right.

Even though her eyes were closed, Delaney could tell the light above her head flickered. And it was making the pain in her head so much worse. With the last of her energy, she attempted to force her eyes open but couldn't. It felt like her eyelids had been glued together. Had she been in an accident? Her heart raced. Nothing made sense.

Every part of her body ached. Her chest felt like it was on fire when she breathed. And the one time she'd tried to move her leg to relieve the ache in her lower back, pain had seared up her calf. Voices came and went, some not speaking English and none of them familiar.

Fear. She couldn't control it. It consumed her. Somewhere in the back of her mind she knew that staying alert was the only way to get out of a difficult situation, but she was so tired. Exhaustion threatened to suck her back under, but she was determined to push through.

"Delaney? Hey, *Buttons*, can you hear me?" A man spoke to her. Knew her name. Sounded familiar. *Who was Buttons?* She tried to turn her head toward the voice. Anything that would let the person know she could hear him, whoever he was.

She clung to the voice, but it became garbled. Soon, she could no longer hear it. Then she felt . . . nothing.

She had no idea how much time had passed before she finally heard the voice again.

"How long will she be like this for?" The voice sounded clearer. Less . . . muffled.

"It's the combination of the painkillers and medication she needs right now, Sir, and the legacy effect of drugs they used on her. She needed rest. They said she was very lucky to be rescued." A different voice. A woman. And titles, like *Sir*.

"I want to know who brought her in. Can you get me that information, please?" The man was controlled. Insistent. Firm.

"That's not information I am able to provide, but it'll be my pleasure to find somebody who can talk with you." Footsteps moved away from her.

"Goddammit, Delaney," the man muttered. "What the hell were you doing?"

Someone took her hand. The man, she assumed, given how close to her ear his voice was. Close enough that she could feel his breath on the side of her face. Something about his touch felt familiar but it was impossible to process anything more than that. She tried to move away, to tug her hand free of whoever held it.

"Delaney, oh my God. Can you hear me? Squeeze it again if you can hear me, Buttons."

This time, instead of pulling away, she willed her fingers to move.

"Nurse! She just squeezed my hand."

She gave opening her eyes another try, finally prying them apart. But the bright sunlight in the room and the flickering fluorescent were more than she could stand. She closed them again and tried to speak, but her mouth was drier than the desert.

The desert.

She heard a click, and the room darkened mercifully. Somebody had shut off the light. Memories raced back. Something beeped next to her, the noise feeling like nails driven into her eardrums. *Stop it, please! Someone!* She reached for her face and felt a tube near her nose, trying to tug it away. *Where the hell am I?*

What had happened? The jarring groan of grinding gears, of a broken or misused clutch, sounded through her head. But she couldn't figure out why it was relevant.

"Delaney, stop it. You're going to hurt yourself." The man's voice was right next to her ear. He held her by the wrist. They'd been held before. With rope. *Oh, God. Why was I tied up?*

She was going to be raped. Or worse, killed like in those awful videos. Frustration battled with fear as her body wouldn't respond to the most basic of demands. What had they given her? Something to subdue her. A drug of some kind. Her head spun with all the possibilities, but her body lay useless. She couldn't die, not without trying to live.

"Help," she tried to shout as the beeping sound increased. But she could barely speak. Hands pressed her shoulders to the bed. "*No!*" But her body still wouldn't respond. Tears burned the corners of her eyes as defeat settled over her.

"Please," she whispered. "Don't do this."

"Nothing's going to happen to you, Delaney. You're safe."

The accent. It was American. That had to be a good sign. She forced her eyes to open again. "Help me."

"Buttons, I got you, okay? It's Mac. I'm here."

Through the tears and the halo of sunshine, she tried to take in the blurry outline. "Mac?"

"Yeah. It's me, Delaney."

Mac. Dear God. What the . . . She closed her eyes, but held onto biceps that were firm and strong. Her anchor.

"Hey. It's okay, sweetheart. You gotta wake up. I know you hate waking up, but I need you to."

She opened her eyes again, concentrated on focusing, as he wiped her cheeks with a tissue. "What . . . happened? Why are you . . ."

What had she done? Everything hurt and her headache pounded in rhythm with her racing heart. Why was Mac there? Had somebody called him?

Rescuers. There had been rescuers. She gasped, then exhaled. Air escaped her lungs so quickly she feared they'd permanently deflated. She'd been taken, shoved to the floor of a truck. Her source had told her that those men could be trusted. They were supposed to be willing to share their side of the story. God, she was going to vomit.

The hut. She could still smell the dirt into which she'd been thrown down face-first. In the spot where she'd been left for what felt like days, hours blending together. When finally the guys with guns had burst into the house in which she'd been hidden and had told her in calm American accents that they were there to get her out. They'd lifted her broken body, and the pain had been too much. Passing out had been blessed relief.

"Mac," she whispered, and tried to stop the tears and the uncontrollable shaking of her body. She shrugged his hands off her shoulders, and scrambled to the other side of the bed. Even as he held his hand in the air, the universal sign of surrender, a part of her wanted to reach for him, to let him hold her the way he had when she'd sneak into his dorm room at night.

Her head spun in confusion as she pressed her fingertips to her temples. She couldn't do this again, couldn't grieve for him all over again. Not on top of everything else.

"Delaney, sweetheart. You're safe." Those eyes of his that always reminded her of the dark blue ocean at sunset reassured her she was. She'd dreamt of them. Missed them.

God, the anger she felt toward him now was only a fraction of the love she'd felt for him all that time ago. Until he'd killed her brother when they were both twenty years old.

Delaney jolted and swallowed, trying to get some moisture back into her mouth, and failing. "Where am I?" she gasped as she attempted to hide her confusion. She had a thousand questions right now, but getting answers was what all her years as an investigative reporter had trained her to do best.

"Landstuhl Medical Center in Germany. What happened to you? Where did they bring you in from?"

Germany? "Water," she gasped.

"On it," Mac said, jumping to his feet. Delaney took one deep breath after the other to regain control.

What was he doing here? How had he even known where she was? And if he'd found out she was here, wouldn't her mother also . . . She glanced around the room, though she knew better. Her mother was no doubt still at home, self-medicating with a large bottle of Southern Comfort.

With a grunt of effort that caused a sweat to break out on her forehead, Delaney attempted to push herself up into a seated position. Her ribs screamed in agony, and her wrist buckled beneath her.

"Wait, Delaney. What are you trying to do?" Mac placed a glass of water with a straw on the table next to her hospital bed as a doctor and nurse joined them.

"Here," Mac said, reaching for her gently. He took her weight and slid her up the bed, then held her with one arm while he adjusted the pillows behind her head. His arm felt warm, safe. And much larger than she remembered.

When he lowered her back onto the pillows, she took in the face whose contours she'd once known better than her own. She reached out her hand and trailed her fingertips along the angular jaw that always used to be clean-shaven, although now it was covered in a dark scruff that gave him a certain appeal. The freckles across the bridge of his nose that a buried piece of her was relieved to see he'd never grown out of, even though they reminded her of summers spent surfing and hanging out with him on the beaches of Encinitas. Hair the color of dark chestnut, as thick as ever. It stood up in all directions, which should have looked foolish but instead made him more handsome . . . and more of a man . . . than she could deal with.

But it was his eyes that got her. They always had. The ones that had always seen her as they'd grown up together—he as her brother's loyal best friend, she as the younger sister who went from being an annoyance he'd had to deal with to . . . well, back then he would have said to the woman he was going to marry. Those were the sweet words he'd often whispered to her after they'd made love in the back of his truck.

When he leaned into her hand, she snatched it away quickly. "Meds," she said hoarsely by way of explanation. Perhaps more to herself than to him. His sigh told her he'd missed their connection just as much as she had. But it was pointless getting nostalgic.

Mac offered her a sip of water, and she took it, the ice-cold fluid soothing her parched throat.

She looked away, unable to bear the pain that welled up inside her. She'd loved him with every piece of who she was, but she'd been sure that she couldn't stay with him without being reminded of losing Brock. And yet, no matter how far she got from Mac, the agony of Brock's loss had never left her.

The pain of being beaten and thrown onto the dirt floor while being held hostage was second only to the breakdown of her family. The loss of her brother had been horrifying enough, but the death of her father—a heart attack not three months later brought on by stress—had caused what was left of her family to implode. Mac had taken two people she loved from her.

"Better?" Mac handed her the glass.

Her hands shook as she took it from him, the adrenaline pounding through her veins. Against her better judgment, she turned to look up at him. "You can't be here," she whispered. "Not like this."

There was a scrape of metal as Mac lifted a chair and placed it next to the bed. "Yeah, well, for all the ways I thought I'd see you again, I never quite imagined this, Buttons. There'll be time for chitchat and shit later. But for now, I want to know how the hell you ended up here, and like this."

For the first time in more than forty-eight hours the tight band that had locked itself around Mac's chest loosened.

His Delaney.

He shouldn't think it, shouldn't let himself believe that she was his even for a single minute, but he couldn't help himself. When she'd touched him, he'd felt it. Even better, had *seen* it. The look that had always been there when she'd trailed her eyes over his face, like he was everything she wanted. Once upon a time it had made him feel a million feet tall. And those lips he'd kissed a hundred thousand times, and had dreamt of kissing a hundred thousand times more after they'd split. *Shit,* he was a mess that she was so close and wouldn't let him so much as hold her hand, to reassure her she was going to be okay.

But there was finally a pinkness to her cheeks, even if

it was offset by a yellowed bruise around her eye. That some asshole had brought his fist to her face was almost enough to have him pulling all Eagle operatives onto the first jet available to a place to which he'd vowed never to return.

He'd waited patiently as nurses, followed by two doctors, hurried into the room. The nurse politely asked him to give Delaney some privacy, but he bluntly refused. Until he understood what exactly had happened to her, until he was certain she was safe, he wasn't going to let her out of his sight for a millisecond.

Plus, he'd missed her. And he'd waited two grueling days on a plastic chair for her to open her eyes.

As a concession, he stepped out of the medical team's way and watched as they went through their checkup on her progress.

She was tolerating having him around—at least for now. It was hard to believe it had been fourteen years since she'd slapped him in front of Brock's coffin. Not that he could blame her. And so, while everyone around them mourned Brock, he'd mourned the loss of both his friend *and* Delaney. He'd lost a future he'd wanted more than any of his swimming scholarships. One he'd cared about more than the military career he'd ultimately undertaken to fulfill Brock's dreams. One he still mourned.

Mac looked over to where Delaney lay in bed. Occasionally, she would nervously nibble on her bottom lip, something she'd always done when she was uncertain or unsure. The first night she'd kissed him, when she'd stepped up onto her toes and surprised him in the hallway of her parents' home and he'd told her that as much as he wanted to, he couldn't—*Guys don't kiss their best friend's sister*, he'd said—she'd bitten down on her lip just like that. He'd kissed her back, then, just to stop her from doing it again. Or so he'd told himself at the time.

Her chocolate brown hair was still long, but dirty, and he knew that it would bother her once she processed everything else that was going on. Those eyes in which he'd once seen his future reflected back at him, one that involved late-night surfs and kids and travel and forever, darted from left to right as she took in the people talking around her. Occasionally, she'd look toward him, seeking him out for a fleeting moment, but then her shoulders would rise and fall as if sighing, and she'd look away.

Banking the exhaustion he felt, and affronted by how long the medical team was keeping him at arm's length, he stepped back to the foot of the bed so he was squarely in her line of sight. He needed her to know he was there for her, even if she needed time to get used to the idea. She'd repeatedly asked for him, after all. Even if she'd been too out of it to realize what she was doing. At some point, he'd need to figure out the logistics of getting them out of the hospital and back on American soil as quickly as he could. He hoped to convince her to let him help her once they were home, but even if she wouldn't, he wouldn't be far away. At least for now, while she recovered. He'd worry about needing to get back to work at Eagle Securities later.

"I'm advising we keep you here for at least a few more days before you even consider moving," the doctor said. "But we can review again in the morning."

Delaney blanched. "It's important that I get back to work."

There were logistics to consider. Delaney was going

to need clothes, travel papers, and probably some heavy-duty pain medication prescriptions to get her home.

"Perhaps Mr. MacCarrick can help get you set up to work here." The doctor looked in his direction, but Mac made no acknowledgment. Mac had no clue what kind of work was so urgent, but he was going to make sure Delaney's health was front and center first.

As the room began to empty, he moved his chair closer to the edge of the bed. "You doing okay, Delaney?" He reached for her hand, taking in her scabbed and bruised knuckles, the short unpainted nails, but she pulled it out of his reach and placed it on her lap.

"They wouldn't answer my questions," she said, her voice as rough around the edges as if she smoked twenty a day—though he knew for a fact she hated cigarettes. Plus, there was something to her tone—helplessness tinged with frustration. "I wanted to know what happened to my interpreter, Farzam. He traveled from Tajikistan with me." She looked straight at him, her bloodshot eyes wide. "They might tell you if you asked."

Of course they wouldn't tell her. They probably wouldn't tell *him*. Everything would be need-to-know only. But he'd play along and try to find out what was going on if it helped her stay positive that she was doing something. And he'd ignore the look in her eye, the one that told him she hated having to ask him, to rely on him for anything, even though it cut through him. "Where were you?" he asked. "I'll see what I can find out."

A look of doubt crossed her features, like she didn't believe he'd do everything he could to help. Which hurt. Or maybe it was because she didn't trust him with the information, which hurt twice as bad.

"Kunduz."

A Taliban stronghold. Holy shit.

Taliban and Afghan forces were constantly battling for control of that city, a critical transport hub with a porous border into Tajikistan used for smuggling opium and heroin to Europe through Central Asia. It was always going to be one of the first places under attack—a situation he'd experienced firsthand.

Train, advise, and assist—that was all he and Cabe and the rest of his brothers had been supposed to do when they'd been out there. But there had been too much heavy resistance, and the Afghan Special Forces had been surrounded by insurgents. Damn, it was the closest he'd ever come to panic on a battlefield, but of course they'd had to engage. They'd have been dead within the hour if they hadn't. By the time backup air strikes had eventually come, two good men were dead.

He tried to push the memories away as he sat back in his chair, crossing one leg over the other. "Want to tell me what you were doing there?"

Delaney reached to push her hair off her face, but winced and dropped her arm. It hurt him that she was in so much pain. He'd do just about anything to switch places and bear it for her.

Without thinking, he leaned forward and tucked her hair behind her ear. It was still as soft as silk and he wished he could wrap it around his hand as he kissed her.

"Where are my things?" she asked, looking around the room. "Did anything make it here with me?"

He gestured to a chair with the folded pile of clothes and small purse that the nurse had shown him when he'd first arrived. For now, he'd ignore the fact that Delaney had totally avoided answering his question. It could wait a few minutes more. "That's all they brought in with you."

"Damn." She coughed and took a sip of water. "Don't suppose there's anything in the purse?"

He shook his head. Whatever she'd once carried in it had been taken—he'd gone through it and wasn't going to apologize to her for doing so. Silently, he'd prayed that she wasn't stupid enough to have been carrying anything with too many personal details. "You're going to need travel papers, emergency ones, but those can be arranged."

Delaney shook her head. "What's the date?"

"What's the last date you remember?" Mac asked.

"*Sneaky.* Answering a question with a question." She picked at a thread on the utilitarian bedding. "The journalist in me hates that."

The corner of his mouth twitched as he watched her slim fingers twirl a loose thread of cotton around. "Well, the SEAL in me hates that you were in the crosshairs of a violent insurgency and won't tell me why that happened, so . . ." He let the sentence hang between them.

She looked toward him and narrowed her eyes. For a second he thought she was going to smile, could have sworn he saw a ghost of one whisper across her lips.

"I arrived in the village on Monday. What was that? Like the twenty-fourth, maybe twenty-fifth. Of February." Delaney wrinkled her forehead and pressed a hand to her temple. He could tell the effort hurt. "We walked into the hills the next day, and that's when . . . well, when I was taken . . . maybe a couple of days in house . . . hut . . . whatever. So, I guess it's Friday or Saturday."

It worried him that she was a few days off, even though it was to be expected. "It's Monday. You lost a bit of time. The doc said the people who took you gave you something that knocked you out."

It was warm in the room, but Delaney pulled the blanket up under her chin as she yawned. "That explains why I couldn't open my eyes properly," she said, snuggling into the pillows.

He was losing her to sleep, and Lord knew she needed it. But there was one thing he needed to know before he let her slip into it. The chair scraped the floor as he stood and went to perch on the edge of the bed. He reached out without thinking and moved another stray piece of hair from her forehead. Delaney pulled away from him, and he remembered that she wasn't his anymore. Hell, he didn't even know if she was somebody else's.

"Delaney . . . how badly did they hurt you? Did they . . . ?" *Shit.* He couldn't even bring himself to say the word. No matter what had happened to her, he'd be by her side, but he needed to know what he was up against.

"They beat me, that was all," she mumbled, her eyes closed as she drifted toward sleep. Her hand slipped into his, and warmth trickled through him. He knew he shouldn't read anything into the actions of an exhausted woman, but it gave him hope. She'd be embarrassed in the morning if he told her what she'd done. But at some subconscious level, she needed him.

"I felt so alone, Mac."

Alone.

As her body relaxed into sleep—the deep, heavy sleep that Delaney had always loved, sleep so restful she would struggle to get out of bed in the morning—he traced his fingers along her heart-shaped face, along her jaw while holding her hand tightly.

"I'm here, Delaney," he whispered before placing a chaste kiss on her temple. "You're not alone anymore."

CHAPTER TWO

There were too many other things to worry about without thinking about Mac and his questions. She needed to get well, get a flight, and get home. She needed to pick the story up where she had left off. Because it was a good one. And because she'd always felt a responsibility, in Brock's absence, to do something good for her country in his honor. She needed to fly back to Afghanistan to pick up her leads before they went cold. Plus, she couldn't let what happened to her fester mentally. A scared investigative journalist was a dead investigative journalist—or worse, an out-of-work one—something most people would never understand.

Mac had been torn. He hadn't wanted to leave her to go shopping, no matter how many times she'd told him she'd be fine, but she needed things to travel home. So, he'd made a list and told her an hour ago that he was going to get them.

She'd been torn too. She didn't want him buying her underwear, yet the thought of him running his fingers over the fabric as he picked something out for her made her shiver as she recalled the one time he'd snuck into the Victoria's Secret dressing room with her. He was bound to come back with little shorts and a lace bra, something he'd liked her seeing her in, instead of the practical cotton she craved against her skin. The thought shouldn't make her want to cry but it did.

She'd gone through enough, and didn't have the energy to deal with Mac too.

Tears pooled in the corner of her eyes and she let them fall in a moment of weakness. She wiped them on the back of her hand.

"Here. Use this." A tissue appeared in her peripheral vision.

How had he gotten everything done so quickly? It was stupid, but she'd been looking forward to a little time alone and now he'd caught her at her weakest moment.

None of this was his business—where she'd been, what she'd been doing, how she'd get home. None of it was his problem, or his thing to fix. Nothing about her had been *his* since the day he'd gotten Brock to jump off that goddamn cliff. Since he'd driven Brock north, in his car, and encouraged him. Her brother hated heights, had since he was a child and their parents had taken them to the top of the Empire State Building. She knew that, her parents knew that, and Mac had known it. It had crushed her when Becca, an old school friend, had told her she'd seen Mac and Brock in heated discussion on the walk up to the cliff top. And it had killed her to read the inquest testimonies of witnesses who said it appeared Brock hadn't really wanted to jump.

Every time she heard Mac's voice now, she also could hear it *then*—goading Brock, threatening to push him if he didn't jump, laughing as he ran past Brock to jump off first. In her mind, she could still see Brock following him, slipping on the edge of the cliff before he could launch himself out toward the water, and hitting the rocks below.

Everything he was now, no matter how patient, and helpful, and kind he was now . . . it was all synonymous with who he was then. The two parts of him inseparable.

She watched Mac place several shopping bags at the foot of the bed and begin to pull things out. With military precision, he folded a hoodie that looked as soft as the thick blanket she kept on the sofa at home. He pulled out pajamas next and handed them to her.

"I know you prefer to sleep naked . . . well, at least you used to," he said gruffly. "But I figured you might want something to sleep in that isn't the same size as my camping tent."

She did, desperately. The hospital gown had the mobility of stiff cardboard and gaped when she walked to the bathroom. Gingerly, she made her way to the edge of the bed. The pain was a little worse today, but only because she'd begun to refuse the painkillers. They muddled her head, and she need to clear it to get through this. She stood, and her vision spun a little. She reached out to hold onto the bed until it settled.

"Let me help you, Buttons," he said, using the nickname he'd given her the first night they slept together, after it had taken him an age to undo all the buttons that had run down the back of her dress.

"I got this," she said, letting go in the hope that her legs would be more stable than they had been that morning. Carefully, she reached behind her to undo the ties, but her ribs ached as if someone had their foot on them.

"For heaven's sake," Mac said, marching to her, holding a multipack of underwear in his hands, "I've seen you naked already." He ripped the pack open roughly and pulled out a pair of simple cotton panties. "I know you like thongs, but this was all I could find in your size, and I figured they may be more comfortable. You know, cotton and all." Mac dropped to his knees. "Put your hand on my shoulder and put one of your legs through."

Embarrassment filled her from her toes to the flaming heat in her cheeks. But she did as he asked, willing to admit that bending forward to do it herself would probably bring on an epic case of the spins. And because he'd brought her cotton, not lace. She tried to ignore the way his hands slid up her thighs and the way that even though she hated him, her body still remembered him. It came alive as he tugged the panties gently over her hips.

"Never thought that if I got to see you again, it'd involve putting clothes *on*," he said, and looked up at her instead of at what he was doing, saving them both from further embarrassment.

She wanted to tell him that the familiarity was just making it harder to be around him. But she couldn't speak. Couldn't find the words to explain to herself, let alone to Mac, why his actions where overwhelming her. And she was pragmatic enough to know she couldn't have gotten changed alone. Not right now.

He grabbed the pajama bottoms off the bed and repeated the steps he'd already taken with the underwear. *Damn*. His warm fingers brushed against her spine as he pulled the ties open. She wasn't ready for him to see her. It was too intimate. As if sensing her discomfort, he eased the T-shirt over her head from his position behind her, and she quickly shucked the hospital gown and placed her arms through the openings. The soft fabric dropped over her breasts as his hands came to rest on her shoulders.

"Delaney. Let me help you. Please."

He had always been an overwhelming presence. Larger than life, physically and in spirit. So had Brock.

That was what made it hurt so much more. The memories of Brock and Mac being practically inseparable. Teammates on the school swim team, they'd done everything together. Hell, Mac had even dragged Brock's lifeless body to the shore, swimming against the tide. She began to shake, and the memories just kept crashing in.

Mac slid his arms around her, but all she wanted to do was run, get somewhere quiet where she would be safe. She didn't need Mac, she could stand on her own two feet. Be strong enough, brave enough to get through this.

"Delaney, sweetheart. You're safe. It's okay."

But she wasn't. Her thoughts bounced faster than she could keep up with them, from the abduction, to Brock, to the story, to Mac and the way he felt so strong and capable behind her, like all she needed to do was lean back and trust him to catch her.

She breathed harder and faster, yet she felt breathless. Just as her knees gave out from beneath her, Mac scooped her into his arms, sat down on the bed, and pulled her close.

"It's panic. Adrenaline. Shock," Mac said. "Focus on us. Focus on being here now. Look around the room, find five items and name them out loud to me."

"Window," she said, her voice trembling. Why couldn't she control how she was feeling? Mac pulled her closer, his body offering her the warmth she sought desperately.

"Chair . . . clothes . . . coffee cup." Some things hadn't changed. Mac still drank too much caffeine.

"One more," Mac reminded her.

Her breath was steadying, she felt less . . . fearful. Which was stupid to feel in the first place because she knew she was safe in the hospital. A military hospital at that. One she really wanted to leave. She looked down at his hands, taking in the charcoal gray Luminox on his wrist. He'd upgraded from the blue Swatch she'd bought him with her weekend job money. "Watch," she said sadly. She'd been the one who'd wanted to move on. Who'd needed to.

She put her hands on his wrists and pushed them apart. As reassuring as his body felt against hers, she needed to shake off whatever had just happened. Climbing off his knee, she suddenly felt a pang of disloyalty to her brother.

"I have some calls to make this afternoon," she said. She owed her boss, Benjamin Streep, a call.

Mac stood from the bed and went back to the bags of items he'd bought for her. "Don't let me stop you," he said, pulling out a hairbrush and some elastics.

She hadn't asked him for those items, but he'd bought them for her anyway. "In private," she said, folding her arms in front of her chest. It probably sounded snippy. She'd be showing gratitude to anyone else who tried to assist her. But it was Mac, and she couldn't let him win her over. It had taken two years to even begin to get over him the last time. She didn't think she'd survive if she had to go through it again.

Mac looked at her pointedly for a moment and then nodded. "I'll be outside," he said, unplugging his phone from the charger and handing it to her.

She watched his wide shoulders as he walked out into the corridor and bit down an irrational fit of jealousy as he struck up a conversation with one of the young nurses. He wasn't hers—and she didn't want him—so it shouldn't matter who he spoke to.

Delaney grabbed the little notebook Mac had bought her and a pen he'd loaned her and dialed her boss. It wasn't lost on her that despite her telling Mac she could do all this on her own, so far she wasn't. She'd had to borrow his phone yesterday too, to text her boss at Honedia, an online news outlet that focused on "pure news." A mash-up of the words "honest" and "media," the name of the company had been her idea, as had the idea it become a not-for-profit organization. Ultimately, though, she wanted to be its editorial director. Which meant following this story that was big enough to get her a Pulitzer. Definitely not something Mac would approve of.

Which was why she didn't want him around while she tried to figure out how to get from Germany back to Kunduz.

"Please, let me help you get comfortable," Mac urged, hurting for Delaney as she winced again. For all his medic training, he felt ill-equipped to ease her pain. "This was a really bad idea. We should have waited a little while and flown out in a couple of days."

Their first flight, from Germany to New York, had been a little easier on her. The plane hadn't been full, and they'd shared three seats between the two of them. Plus, she'd taken enough pills to knock herself out.

But shortly after takeoff for flight number two, which had been delayed for four hours thanks to a freezing March New York snowstorm and was packed to capacity, the pilot had announced it was going to be a bumpy ride as they battled the conditions. As turbulence shook the plane, Delaney sat by the window, her forehead rested on the glass, her arms clutched around her ribs.

"I'm not your responsibility," she said through gritted teeth, a slight sheen of sweat on her brow. "I could have gotten home on my own, you know." She'd been frustrated since the boss of her news company had ordered her to head straight back to the U.S. He'd been frustrated because she wouldn't tell him exactly what she'd been working on.

"I'm sure you could have, Buttons, but you'd be more comfortable if you rested on me." He began to lift the arm of the seat, but she placed her hand on it and grimaced.

"I'm fine," she said, but he knew she didn't mean it. They still had three hours left on the flight. She popped two more pills from the strip of painkillers and flipped the lid off her water.

Mac watched as she knocked them back. When had Delaney become so stubborn? There had been a time when she'd been more . . . what, *easygoing*? Now she was impossible. Independent. And *not his responsibility*.

She'd been saying so ever since he'd been handed her empty purse. She'd repeated it as he'd dealt with emergency travel papers, and when she'd needed a credit card to pay for a flight, and when she'd needed a phone to call home.

She'd said it when she'd decided to check herself out of the hospital against doctor's advice. And said it endlessly when she'd needed help putting on the clothes he'd bought for her.

But what bothered him more than the stubborn need

to do it all by herself was how she refused to look him in the eye and wouldn't let him in one inch. It had been physically difficult for her to accept his help, even though he was standing right in front of her willing to give it.

Even though she was in pain, she'd spared a smile for everyone at the hospital and now did the same for everyone from the airline who'd accommodated their need for extra legroom for the ankle boot she needed to wear. She'd thanked the doctors who'd cared for her, thanked the cabdriver, and had even thanked the gate agent who'd allowed them to preboard.

But to him . . .

"Tell me again what your colleague in . . . what was it called again? Goddamn, these meds are making me loopy. I can't focus," Delaney snapped.

Mac overlooked her irritated tone. "The United States Naval Special Warfare Development Group. It's a mouthful, so we call it DEVGRU."

"DEVGRU. That's it. Tell me what your colleague said."

Her voice hitched at the end, that slight catch that told him she was in pain. When she wasn't busy being polite, when she let the mask drop, he could see real frustration beneath it. He'd seen it clearly for the first time two days ago after she'd called her boss. Whatever he or she had said to Delaney, she'd been like a bear with a sore head ever since. He'd tried to eavesdrop on the call from the hallway, but that nurse, Sara, had gotten between him and the doorway and refused to take a hint. On a different day in a different situation, he might have been on board with a hot young nurse hitting on him, but now that he had Delaney in his line of sight, no woman could ever be hot enough, smart enough, or funny enough to take him away from his mission. He'd stayed by her side at the hospital until they'd threatened to call security to kick him out at the end of each day.

When he hadn't been with her, he'd been calling in favors from friends to understand where exactly she'd been found.

"They said that you'd been lucky there were still special ops teams based in the Middle East Theatre working on solidifying the Afghan military's position in Kunduz against a credible intelligence threat. Since they'd been watching all the routes in and out, you'd been in their sights from the moment you were taken."

Delaney shook her head. "I know I should be grateful, and I am, but how come it took so damn long for them to come get me?"

It was a fair question, and a difficult one to answer for someone not military who didn't understand the politics the military were constrained by. Negotiations over military action every time. Permissions required to use lethal force. Scoping, planning, and executing hostage retrievals took time.

"These things always take time, Delaney. It's not as simple as showing up and knocking on the door."

Plus, when his contact told him that she'd been taken by a new splinter group who had not yet declared their name, a cold sweat had formed on his skin. Those unknown groups were the worst, as their affiliations, numbers, and access to weapons were complete unknowns.

After he'd learned who she'd been up against, he'd researched the organization Delaney worked for. He'd wanted some kind of confirmation that they would have the funds required to protect her when she returned to the U.S., even if it was temporary until the risk had been properly assessed. But he'd been disappointed. Honedia was not the wealthy company of some oligarch. While he'd not found the reassurance he'd needed, it had come as no surprise that Delaney was held in high regard at her job.

Delaney pulled her shoulders back in a stretch, and he tried not to fixate on how her T-shirt pulled across her breasts. Thinking about how she'd matured as a woman had been keeping him awake at night. She'd captivated him since the summer they'd gone camping when she was sixteen and he was eighteen. He'd tried not to look at her tight body packed into a neon pink two-piece— she was his friend's *sister*, after all. Plus, the age difference had made him feel skeevy. As they'd sat around the campfire at night, listening to Six play his guitar— badly—he'd been drawn to listening to her talk about books. She had a melodic voice and a funny way of interpreting what she'd read. Plus, she wasn't reading chick shit. She told him about biographies of great world leaders and documentaries on migration . . . things he found interesting. Just when he had himself convinced she was mature enough for him as he listened to her explain how English Prime Minister Winston Churchill had won the Nobel Prize for Literature in 1953, though, Cabe had thrown him a pointed look of warning. That fucker always did see *everything*.

Now, he could look at her. And did. He took in how her pretty pink lips had filled out into a plum-colored pout. She'd always been slim, but she'd curved out in all the places he loved. Clearly, she was still athletic and adventurous. She'd always been up for hikes and early-morning surfs. And he couldn't get enough of those eyes. Too dark to be amber, too spectacular to be brown, they were a shade that was impossible to describe. Sometimes, drinking a glass of cognac, he was reminded of them, but only fleetingly. In the cold light of day, it didn't compare.

Honey brown. That's how he'd often thought of them. Sweet and warm.

They studied him now with emotions he couldn't separate. Pain, for sure. Hate, because of Brock. And occasionally a flicker of what he used to see there, something that told him they could still set each other's worlds on fire.

They were also glistening with the tears she refused to cry.

Mac turned in his seat to face her. "You might be able to take this," he said carefully. "But I can't. Watching you is hurting me. Let me help you get comfortable for these last few hours. I *know* you could do this alone, I don't doubt that for a second. But please don't make me watch you do it."

Delaney sighed and swallowed deeply. "Fine. But don't read anything into this."

She'd been saying that a lot too. But how couldn't he? How could he read nothing into the fact she'd asked for him? And how could she ignore the fact that he'd boarded a plane with a moment's notice and jetted halfway around the world to look after her?

Mac got busy rearranging their space so she'd be more comfortable. He hadn't mentioned that he'd trained as a medic but he applied his knowledge to make sure she was properly supported. When he'd said something about the SEALs in passing, she'd shut him down immediately— and he'd realized why. The SEALs had been Brock's dream. It was why they'd all enlisted after his death. But it was also why they'd been on the cliff that day. Brock had wanted Mac's help. He'd had never been good with heights, and he'd known he'd need to overcome that fear to be a SEAL.

He shook his head to clear the memory of that day, lifted the seat handle between the two of them, and helped her sit close to him before encouraging her to turn slightly to face the window. Delaney groaned as she leaned against him and the seat, and he felt the tension dissipate from her body. With his arm around her and her hair teasing his cheek, it was hard to remember where he was. They'd never had their own place, but on the occasions they'd had the opportunity to sleep together—on a road trip or when she'd come to visit him in college—she'd always fallen asleep in his arms. He hadn't wanted to spoon with any woman since. It reminded him too much of her.

"I'm not sure I can be here, with you, like this," she said so quietly he almost missed it.

"Just rest, Delaney." Out of age-old habit, he pressed his lips to the top of her head. "I know there's a lot going on in that head of yours. But I'm here. Be angry at me when we land. Go back to hating me if you need to. But get some rest."

The words hung between the two of them, and he could have sworn she'd closed her eyes.

"Thank you, Mac," she said quietly.

He smiled into her hair at the whispered words. "You're welcome, Delaney. Now just sleep."

He could tell the moment she did as he asked. His arms burned as he held her steady, but he wouldn't let her go for the world. He'd lost her once, and even if he wasn't destined to get her back ever again, he needed to help her. He needed to show her he was still the man she could depend on. Perhaps helping her through this would go some way toward helping him with his own demons.

As he settled as best he could in a middle seat made for a man half his size, he decided he'd do what he did best. Plan.

If Delaney Shapiro thought that after they landed she'd walk out of his life as quickly as she'd waltzed back into it, she was in for a fight.

"No. Absolutely not. That is the dumbest idea I've ever heard." Delaney put her hands on her hips, searched the curbside pickup area of the airport, and then stared back at Mac.

He looked at her patiently, like she was a spoiled child having a hissy fit and who, given another moment, might calm down on her own. All of which was significantly closer to the truth than she wanted to admit. Her foot throbbed, and the ankle boot the hospital had given her to wear weighed a ton. Her ribs still hurt, and she was bone tired. She wanted food, a shower, and a bed, and quite frankly didn't care which order they came in.

She looked out again to where cars were entering the pickup area, jostling with one another to pull over while avoiding cars trying to pull out. It was stupid to search for Cabe when she had no idea what kind of vehicle he'd even be in. The beat-up old Chevy in which he'd driven away from Brock's funeral with Six and Mac in the back had been on its last legs even then. There was no way it was still on the road.

She hadn't spoken to any of her brother's friends in so many years, and crashing into them at this stage in her life was almost too painful to bear. Her heart could barely hold all the memories of their adventures, and the shell she'd built around that time in her life was far more fragile than she'd ever want to admit.

"Coming home with me is a *great* idea," Mac said. "Lochlan's place has a pool. You can rest up. Rehab a little."

Delaney shook her head. "I don't need to go to Lochlan's to rest up and rehab. I can do that anywhere." Allowing Mac to talk her into waiting for a ride from Cabe suddenly seemed like a really bad idea. "You know, I'm going to go back over there and grab a cab," she said, tipping her chin in the direction of the queue of people waiting in line.

Mac folded his arms across his chest. "One. You can barely stand on that foot, and that is an exceptionally long queue with only a handful of cabs. Two. You don't have any cash right now. Three. Stop being ridiculous and just wait for Cabe."

He was right, and it irritated her. As did the way his T-shirt stretched across his biceps. She was still raw from waking up in his arms on the plane. At first she'd savored it, and then she'd remembered.

"I'll come with you to your place."

She shook her head. "Not an option."

Mac ran his hand across his stubble. "Give me one good reason why not."

"Because I don't have a place. My lease was up before I left and included a steep hike, so I moved my stuff into Mom's storage locker." Unable to face what had been their family home in Encinitas and its memories of her husband and son, her mom had sold it and moved to the city.

"Not sure your mom is ready to see me yet?" Mac said with a grimace.

"*I'm* not ready to see you yet. Why can't you get that?"

The corner of Mac's mouth twitched, the beginning of a smile, but she wasn't going to let it affect her, even though it gave her butterflies—contradictory little fuckers.

"Do you have a place lined up? If you do, you could call your landlord and see if you can get the keys early." Before Delaney had left, she'd couch-surfed between acquaintances' homes, but she couldn't imagine any of those friends taking in a longer-term, semi-invalid houseguest.

She could possibly call her ex, Stephen, who was a screenwriter like her father had been, worked odd hours, and lived off coffee. But it wouldn't be fair to him. Despite his wanting to stay friends, they'd barely spoken since she'd broken it off with him eight months ago after realizing that they'd been on a high-speed path to marriage. Nothing had been wrong with Stephen. He'd *done* nothing wrong. She'd left him because he wasn't Mac. No, she couldn't stay with him. He would read too much into her request.

Delaney shook her head to clear it. The painkillers had made her foggy, and the first thing she'd do once she was settled, preferably flat in a bed, would be to get rid of them. But what bed, and where? She couldn't think of any other options. Her career wasn't conducive to girlfriends and brunches, and she'd grown up in a world of men. Her wit often bordered on acidic and her lack of interest in the latest OPI nail colors ruled her out of the seen-to-be-seen set of San Diego. Plus, her go-to conversations were human rights violations in North Korea and the lack of understanding between the terms "refugee" and "migrant," neither of which went down particularly well at dinner parties.

And she'd barely been out of the surf long enough when she was younger to make time for friends. She hadn't set foot in the water since the day Brock died because it had felt too much like a final goodbye.

"I spend so much time traveling," she finally said to Mac, "that it isn't worth paying rent for a place."

"So, where the hell were you thinking of going?" Mac said, his voice filled with exasperation. She kept a poker face but smiled inside. Mac hadn't lost his patience easily when they were younger and she imagined that his military training had only refined his self-control, so seeing even the tiniest hint of frustration felt like a moral victory.

"Does Six still live in Encinitas?" she asked. Out of her brother's friends, aside from Mac she'd been closest to Six, who had always treated her like his own kid sister.

Mac shook his head as if she was missing something unbelievably obvious. "He does. With his girlfriend, Louisa. Who just moved in with him." He folded his arms across his chest, making his biceps pop. *Asshole.*

A black truck pulled up alongside them and Cabe stepped down from the cab. "Bit of a drastic way to get back in touch with us all, Delaney. Next time, just text," he said, pulling her into a gentle hug. "How've you been? We've missed you."

God, she'd missed these men too. Even through her anger, their absence had left a gaping hole in her life and her heart. It was part of the reason she'd gone clear across the country to study in New York. Anything to get away from all the reminders.

"I've been better." Gently, she hugged him. The guy had always been athletic, but now he felt like solid muscle. "You filled out!"

Cabe laughed, and Mac frowned at her for a moment before shaking his head and stepping to the truck to throw his pack into the back.

"Not sure you can do the kind of stuff we do and not bulk up a little," he said with a shrug. But she knew Cabe well. He'd always been humble and committed. She'd been focused on the worst of that day for so long that she hadn't remembered all the good about them.

Cabe opened the cab door and was about to help her inside when Mac swept her into his arms and boosted her onto the seat.

Cabe shook his head at Mac. "You always were a territorial asshole."

Mac slammed the door shut.

"So where are we going, Delaney?" Cabe asked once they were all in the truck, Mac thankfully riding shotgun instead of sitting next to her.

"My mom's," she said at the same time Mac said, "My place."

Cabe looked between the two of them. "This is new," he said. "You two used to be so in synch it made my teeth hurt."

He'd always had a cute grin, but right now she wanted to punch him in the teeth. "My mom's," she repeated, and rattled off the address.

As Cabe pulled out of the airport, Delaney tried to ignore Mac's pointed stare as well as her instincts to reach out and smooth the crinkly lines between his eyes like she always used to. He'd aged well. Too well.

"Austin," a Blake Shelton song that she liked came on the radio. Guilt tripped through her. She'd gotten out of San Diego as quickly as she could. Only unlike the girl in the song, she'd never called and there wouldn't be a happy ending. In thirty minutes, she'd be out of Mac's life again for good.

She settled back into the seat. For all she was driven—*hardwired*, people had even called her—to chase the story, she was happy to be home. For the first time in nearly two weeks, she took a restful breath and let the rhythm of the truck lull her to sleep.

"Cabe! This isn't what I . . . What the hell? I'm flagging a cab."

Mac looked over at Cabe and grinned. The mild-mannered Delaney he'd once known was now a whirl-wind, and he had to admit he liked it. He watched as she tugged on her ponytail and looked up at his apartment unit. She shook her head before giving them both the evil eye.

"I said my mom's. Not here," she shouted.

Cabe slapped Mac on the back. "Good luck with that," he said as Delaney got out and hobbled slowly toward the Gaslamp Quarter and Sixth Street. "Don't remember her being this stubborn," he added as he climbed back into the truck.

When they were younger and Mac would ask her where she'd like to go for dinner or how she wanted to spend the afternoon, the answer had always been the same because she trusted him to pick something they'd enjoy. "*I'm easy. Why don't you choose?*"

Mac kind of liked the spine she'd developed. He had a feeling *this* Delaney would tell him exactly what she'd like to do. He let her hobble a few more paces before he jogged to her side.

"Don't be a stranger, Delaney," Cabe shouted through the open window as he passed them.

Delaney growled in response.

"Look," Mac said. "Don't make this hard, Buttons. It's getting late. We're tired. I'm offering you a safe place where you don't need to deal with anything or anyone you don't want to. Why don't you at least stay tonight and see how you feel in the morning? I'll leave you alone if that's what you need, but just quit being so stubborn."

Delaney stopped and looked at him. "*That*," she said, pointing her finger toward the retreating taillights of Cabe's truck, "was a hijack."

He shrugged. No point in correcting her when she was right. Cabe had agreed with him that it was in Delaney's best interests. "Maybe it was, but you're here now. So just come inside."

She looked out toward the busy main street where taxis were driving by and then looked down at the ground. "Fine."

When she stomped by as best she could with that boot on her foot, he bit back a smile. Step one of his plan was to simply get her inside his home. He led them into the lobby and pressed the elevator button that would take them to his floor. Everything else would fall into place once they'd had some food and rest.

Mac cracked the door to the apartment open and was hit with the smell of something delicious cooking. His mouth watered as he let Delaney walk in ahead of him.

Of course the guys would want to see Delaney. Even if it was getting late and all he wanted after being cooped up in a plane for the best part of a day was a long hot shower. Preferably with Delaney, but clearly *that* wasn't going to happen. She'd been way chattier and friendlier with Cabe in the few minutes she'd been awake on the drive than she'd been with him the entire time he'd spent with her since the hospital room in Germany. It was as though she'd forgiven them for being there the day Brock died, but not him. Cabe, though, had already been in the water when Brock had fallen, as had Six. It hurt that she singled him out so completely, even though he knew he deserved it.

"*Delaney!*" Six walked toward her and scooped her off the ground for a hug. She whimpered in pain, and he quickly put her down.

"Shit," Six said. "Dumb move. But it's been too long, Shapiro."

Delaney rubbed her hand along her bicep. "I'm beginning to see that," she said.

"Yeah, well. I'm gonna head out because I have to pick Lou up from her lab on the way home. But let's get together when you've had a chance to get better and get over jet lag." When Six kissed her on the cheek, she didn't flinch the way she did whenever Mac came anywhere near her.

Delaney headed to the main balcony.

Through the open doors, pop music roared from the stadium—some band Mac had never heard. By the sound of it, he was quite grateful that he hadn't.

"Veal in marsala sauce and roasted vegetables," Six said to him. "They're just keeping warm in there, so eat them sooner rather than later. Oh, and Louisa went shopping to fill the fridge. There's a whole bunch of stuff you need, but feel free to throw out the tofu. It's like eating soft cement. I put some white wine in the fridge and a red on the counter."

"Thanks, brother," he said. Mac walked Six toward the door. "It's been quite the week. Ready for Syria?"

"Yeah. Planning's done. We have all permits. Gave the

guys out there a heads-up that we are going to be flying in. Some of the team needed immunization updates. So, all good. Wheels up Thursday. Then in theatre for ten days."

Theatre had always struck Mac as an odd choice of word to describe their ops location.

"I'll be in on Monday. Just going to take the weekend to get Delaney set up." He looked over to where she leaned over the balcony, her face to the breeze blowing off the bay.

"You doing okay?" Six asked.

There was no point pretending that he didn't know what Six meant. "I'm still in the game, but it ain't pretty," he said, slapping his friend on the shoulder. "Thanks for bringing dinner."

Six studied Mac for a second. "Yeah. Well. I get why you need to take care of her, but look out for yourself too."

After Six left, Mac wandered into the kitchen. Lochlan's apartment was growing on him, but he'd never be able to afford it. As soon as his brother came back from San Francisco permanently, he'd need to find a place of his own, but for tonight he was going to pretend the apartment was his, and Delaney was his, and everything in his life was exactly where he wanted it at age thirty-three instead of in a mess.

He opened the bottle of red and poured two large glasses. He checked out her ass as he walked out onto the balcony, knowing there was probably a circle of hell he could be sent to for it. It was cool outside, but she didn't seem to care.

Mac handed her a glass. "Six left us stocked. Thought you might like some of this with dinner."

Delaney reached for the wine and took a sip. "Thanks."

"You know who's playing?" he asked.

Delaney shook her head but didn't say anything further.

Mac sighed. It never used to be this way between them. For the first time since they'd been reunited, the thought crossed his mind that they might never return to how they once were. "I'll go finish up making dinner."

As he served the last of the vegetables, she stepped into the apartment and slid the door closed. He grabbed two forks and placed them on the other side of the breakfast bar.

"I'm tired," Delaney said, looking down at the food and not at him. "I think I'm going to eat in my room, if you'll show me where I can crash."

Carefully, he reached across and took her hand. It had always seemed incredibly small when he held her that way. "Don't," he said, his words getting stuck in his throat. "Don't run. That's not you, Delaney."

"You don't know who I am anymore, Mac." She looked up at him, and the hurt in her eyes stopped his heart.

"You're right. I don't. I know who you *were* though. And the girl I knew back then had more courage than the entire football team."

He held his breath, uncertain of whether he'd misjudged her. Perhaps she had changed in ways that weren't for the better. He'd probably acquired habits she wouldn't love either.

When the scrape of the bar stools along the tiled floor echoed through the apartment, his heart started to beat again. Quickly, he finished the rest of the preparation. Napkins, water, some bread and olive oil.

They sat in silence as they devoured their food, the long flight having left them both hungry and at odds.

"I'm sorry," Delaney said quietly as she reached for a piece of bread and began to rip it into pieces. "I don't know which way is up right now, Mac."

Without overthinking the action, he gently spun her stool and stood between her knees. "I know it's not easy, coming back from something like you have." There was no value to telling her how he'd once been on the brink of capture, being beaten by three insurgents, when Cabe had quite literally saved his life. Yet with all his training, he'd be a fool to pretend that he hadn't had jitters the night before his next mission. By morning, though, they'd been gone, buried under years of training.

He pulled her into his arms and buried his disappointment when she didn't wrap her arms around him. Instead, he pressed his lips to the top of her head, savoring the feel of her against him.

At the very moment he'd been about to release her, she slid her hand around his waist and dropped it into the back pocket of his jeans. It was something she'd always done when they walked along side by side.

Mac swallowed deeply and clenched his jaw to stop deeper emotions from bubbling to the surface. She'd have to make the decision to let go of him. If this was the last time she was going to let him hold her, it was going to have to be long enough to last him for his lifetime.

"Why did it have to happen?" she said quietly.

He didn't have to ask to know which *it* she was talking about. It always came down to Brock. He felt the same. If only he'd been able to swim faster or hold his breath for longer, been a better friend. Guilt ate away at his gut, leaving him feeling raw.

"Can I talk to you? About that day?" It was time to break his promise to Brock. Brock wouldn't want his secret to come between the two of them. He wouldn't want to see Delaney hurting like this after all the years, and they'd been good enough friends that he was sure Brock wouldn't want this for him either.

Delaney shook her head. "I don't think I can." She pulled her hand from his pocket. "Not today. It's too much. Look, I really am tired. I'll see you in the morning," she said as she stood.

He watched her walk to the bedrooms, not caring which one she decided to sleep in. It didn't matter because he wouldn't be there with her.

CHAPTER THREE

"You and I both know that it isn't enough to go forward with the article. There's no value in an incomplete story."

Delaney rolled her eyes, grateful that her boss, Benjamin Streep couldn't see her right now. Not least because not all her bruises had faded yet, even though it had been two weeks since she'd been abducted.

"But you haven't talked to the media yet about your own experience. About the kidnapping," he continued. "Would you want to do that?"

Delaney tapped her pen against the dining room table, then threw it down. After a weekend where Mac had been nothing but helpful and attentively present, he'd finally gone back to work, and it was time for her to do the same. She'd collected all her notes and books out of storage, bought a new laptop online so she could access all her files from the cloud, and began to organize all the new information she'd found on her trip. Endless calls to her contacts in Afghanistan had not revealed the fate of her interpreter, and she was out of people to call on the new phone she'd purchased the day before.

There was no end to what she'd do to bring home the story. It burned inside her. But what had happened to *her* was private. Just thinking about what had happened made her feel sick to her stomach and gave her nightmares that kept her up half the night. She'd barely been able to make it through all the military debriefings and the statement the military police connected to the hospital had asked her to make. Taking the sleeping pills she'd been offered by doctors for her injuries might have helped with the fear along with her pain, but having been around her mother, Delaney had learned that numbness wasn't anything she sought.

"No. I'm not for sale. And it's too much of a distraction. It'll get in the way of me figuring out the real story: Someone in the U.S. is providing funds and weapons to insurgents." *Fake it until you make it.* She needed to sound as hungry for the story as she'd ever been, even if pursuing it terrified her. "If only I'd been shown that delivery like I'd been promised when we set up the meet. How could it have gotten so messed up? My contacts were solid."

There was a pause on the other end of the line. Not a good sign. Benjamin Streep was a thoughtful man with the strictest moral code of any person she'd ever met. "You can't go back."

"Don't be naive, Benjamin. I *have* to go back. We need proof. Shipping documents, flight manifests, photographs of weapons at the place where they begin their journey and again at their destination. More sophisticated weapons runners than these guys have lathered, rinsed, and repeated for twenty goddamn years without anybody being able to pin them down because compiling the evidence was complex. It's the same here. We need more than a bunch of factors that all point in the same direction—we need concrete irrefutable proof. We need to reveal the identity of whoever is doing this when there is no room for them to deny it."

Damn. Why had she gone off like that? Pain? Meds? Emotional hangover? *Nice job, Delaney.*

"Delaney," Benjamin said calmly. She hated that tone and knew what was coming next. "You aren't going back. At least not yet. Give yourself time to heal. You know this company isn't about racing to distribute the story. We're where people come for unbiased facts. If there's one thing the last election taught us, it's that the media distorts the picture. We want to change that. I don't want you working until you're healed."

She *needed* to go back, though. And soon. It was like wiping out on her way down a black diamond slope—if she didn't return to the mountain right away, the fear would grow. It would wrap its invisible arms around her and pin her down so that she'd never leave San Diego ever again. In the past, thrill had always won out over fear. But after what had happened in Afghanistan—after that dirt floor—something had shifted. As much as she needed to go back to chase the story, win a Pulitzer, and have the courage and reputation of famed investigative reporter Nellie Bly, a part of her was scared.

Delaney rubbed her wrists where the fading scabs and red marks from the ropes itched as they healed, reminders of how close she had come to losing everything.

"You need to let me get back in the saddle," she said. "If I wait too long . . ." She left the words hanging.

"I get it, Delaney. I do. But I care more about you than I do anything else. I'll speak to you in a few days. And give some thought to whether you want to use our outlet to tell your story."

The phone beeped, telling her that Benjamin had hung up.

Shit.

That crappy call out of the way, there was only one more item on her things-I-don't-really-want-to-do list. And one decision to make. Go visit her mom, and decide where she was going to live.

She looked around Lochlan's impressive apartment. Over the weekend, Mac had given her space, which she hadn't expected. They'd taken turns cooking, and she realized she'd forgotten just how good Mac was at it. But when he'd dropped a comment about how spending months eating field rations had only developed his love for good food, she'd been reminded of Brock and his dream of being a SEAL. They would always get back to that. Always. She couldn't stay here any longer.

She grabbed a hoodie that Mac had loaned her. The clothes he'd bought for her in Germany had been enough to last the weekend, but they were in the wash and she needed to grab some supplies from the things she had in storage at her mom's.

The very idea of visiting her mother and her glorious world of Technicolor drama made Delaney nauseated as her cab hustled north through the Gaslamp Quarter. Though it was a cooler March day, the area was hopping. She felt a pang of envy seeing people with light jackets eating on patios. She tried to imagine *having* people to brunch with, but couldn't. Occasionally she regretted all the hours she'd put into her studies, her constant pursuit of her career. Perhaps if she'd looked up every now and then, she'd have more friends today.

As she stepped out of the taxi, a silver sedan slowed on the opposite side of the street. For a moment, it felt as though the driver wearing a baseball hat and dark shades was watching her. But that was stupid. Paranoid. A blowback from what happened to her . . . not unexpected.

Her fingers hovered over the buzzer when she stopped in front of her mom's unit. She hadn't called to let Reba know she was home or what had happened.

Pushing away thoughts of running back to Mac's apartment, she pressed her mom's apartment number.

"Hello, Reba here," her mom answered with a drawl, one as fake as the Kate Spade knockoff Delaney had picked up on a Tribeca street corner on her last trip to New York. Born and raised in California, Reba affected the accent of someone born and raised in northwestern Louisiana. Nobody had ever had the heart to tell her mom that it sounded phony.

"Hey, Mom. It's Delaney."

"My baby's home," she cried. "Come on up."

The buzzer sounded and the door clicked. She took the elevator to her mom's floor and walked to the door, each footstep filled with dread over how her mother would react to her injuries.

The door was already wide open. When her mom, whose eyesight required glasses but whose vanity prevented her from wearing them, finally focused on her, she gasped. "Oh, my sweet Delaney," she said, hurrying forward to put her hands on either side of Delaney's face. The stack of bracelets she wore jangled loudly. "What in heaven's name happened to you?" The sickly sweet scent of jasmine embraced her.

"Car accident." The lie slipped out of Delaney's lips with practiced ease. As soon as she'd found out that the hospital had been trying to find her next of kin—her mother—she'd told them to stop. Most of her adult life had been spent minimizing her mom's tendency to over-react. There was nothing to be gained by telling her the truth. "I came home to see my own doctor and recover."

Reba clucked as she led them back inside. "Very wise. Those Afghanistani, Afghan . . . Afghani . . . whatever, doctors couldn't be qualified."

"Mom! You can't say stuff like that. For a start, it's *Afghan.* "Afghani" is the currency. And the doctors were all great, and I'm healing fine." Great, she was defending imaginary Afghan doctors she hadn't seen. "I just came by to say hi and pick up some clothes from your storage."

"No you don't, Delaney. You will take a seat, and you will tell me about what happened. Coffee?"

"Please," Delaney conceded as she took a seat at the bar. "And I'm fine. It was nothing. It could have happened here," she said, gesturing toward the apartment balcony where a series of car horn blasts thoughtfully helped back up her story.

"Where are you staying?" her mom asked, popping a cartridge into the coffee maker, then reaching for a mug from a shelf.

Delaney paused, uncertain how her mom would take the news. "I'm staying with Mac."

Her mom stopped mid-reach. "Malachai MacCarrick?" If the words were any more brittle, they would have shattered into a million pieces on the kitchen tiles. She turned around slowly.

"Yeah. He's helping me out."

Her mom grabbed a glass instead of a mug and wandered over to the ornate silver tray of alcohol that sat on the antique dresser.

The fact that her mom poured herself a beyond-generous measure of Southern Comfort was all Delaney needed to know.

Mac hit the elevator button and watched the illuminated numbers fall toward G. Finally home. According to his watch and phone and computer, it was Wednesday, but he wasn't convinced. In some ways it felt like only ten minutes had passed since he'd left San Diego on Monday; in other ways it felt like weeks since he'd quietly opened the door to Delaney's bedroom at five a.m., in no mood to get on a plane to Washington, and had whispered goodbye to the air. Seeing her sleeping like the dead, her hair spread all over the pillow and her body sprawled on top of the sheets, had made him smile. Many things about her had changed, but some things had stayed very much the same. He'd wished he could climb into bed with her to see if something as simple as physical connection could bring them closer.

Leaving her to go finalize the contract for an upcoming piece of work had felt wrong. Now that he was back, he was anxious to figure out if they had any chance of a future. It had taken every ounce of his self-control to give her space last weekend. He could tell that if he'd pushed her, she'd run. Would she even be upstairs now, or would he find a note on the counter? Would he find only empty hangers swinging in the closet of the spare room?

When they were younger, they'd had so much in common. A love of surfing. Travel. Lazy afternoons stealing kisses and waiting for her parents or his college roommate to head out for the day, or even half an hour, so they could explore each other's bodies. Though he could be quick if he needed to, he always preferred to take things slow. Very.

His phone rang as he entered the elevator. He smiled as he looked at the display. "Hey, Mom."

"You never write, you never call . . ."

Mac laughed. It was the way his mother had greeted him on the phone since the first call he'd made from college. Over the years, it had taken on truth. He'd be gone at a moment's notice, and to places in the world that weren't known for their cellular reception. "I'm just getting home. Can I call you back later?"

"You can do one better. Bring Delaney over to dinner. I'm sure the situation between the two of you is complicated, but I've missed that girl." His mom and Delaney had always gotten along, which had made him happy.

"How did you know about Delaney?" He hadn't said a word, mostly because he didn't want his mom to start meddling in a "When are you going to give me grandkids?" kind of way.

"I saw Cabe's mom at the Encinitas library this morning. Cabe told her that he picked you and Delaney up from the airport. Is there anything you want to tell me?" Her voice went up at the end.

Fuck. It was like being twelve again. My mom saw your mom and she said . . .

"I was helping her out, Mom."

"I didn't know you were back in touch."

The elevator jolted as it came to a stop and the doors slid open. "Listen, Mom. It's complicated. I'll call you back, probably tomorrow."

She chuckled on the end of the line. "The best things always are. I love you."

"Love you too, Mom."

The travel plan he'd left on the fridge had said he wouldn't be back until tomorrow, but the meeting he'd attended on the use of contractors to protect foreign dignitaries had ended early, so he'd hauled ass to get to the airport and get back.

As he let himself into the apartment, his ears were assaulted by weird-ass hippy-shit music, all chimes and pan pipes and waves crashing. Silently, he dropped his bags to the floor, slid his shoes off, and opened an extra button on his collared shirt. Following the teeth-grating spa tune, he headed for the living room.

There, in a sports bra that stretched across incredibly toned shoulders, and a tiny pair of shorts stretched equally spectacularly over her ass, was Delaney, attempting to contort herself into a position he thought would be very useful in bed. For a moment, he leaned against the corner of the wall, and simply watched. His dick stirred in appreciation.

She stood tall, trying to place the foot she'd hurt flat on the floor. Her ankle clearly was still bothering her.

His eyes roamed back to her narrow waist and the round cheeks of her ass. His brain filled with visions of walking up behind her, his chest to her back, and nudging her forward until she could bend comfortably over the back of the chair. He imagined lowering the shorts down her tanned thighs. In his mind, she was naked underneath. If he kept up these thoughts, he was going to have a full-on erection. She'd always been able to arouse him. He'd been her first, and in appreciation of that, he'd never really pushed her to . . . experiment. But now . . .

Delaney reached her hands high into the air, then leaned forward, legs straight, until her hands touched the floor. God, she had a great ass. She obviously worked out more than she used to, although she'd always been fit. But, damn. She winced and fell forward.

"Goddammit," she cried, rubbing on her ankle.

Mac hurried forward and scooped her into his arms. "What the hell are you doing?" he said, irritation replacing appreciation.

"Mac? You aren't supposed to be home until tomorrow."

He placed her down on the sofa and she rubbed her ankle. "Why isn't your foot strapped up?" It was a little over two weeks since she'd been injured—not enough time for everything to heal. Mac crouched down in front of her and reached for her foot.

Delaney snatched it away. "I'm fine. I know what I am doing."

He didn't need to look up to know she was pouting—it was in her tone—so he focused on checking out her foot despite her protests. "I'm a trained medic, Delaney. And this should still be strapped up."

"Fine," she said. "I just wanted to stretch out. I feel like an old lady right now."

He looked up at her and her indescribable eyes met his. He tried hard to ignore her golden tan, smooth skin, and the way her breasts defied gravity in the black and neon green sports bra. "Nobody would accuse you of that," he said, unable to resist running the tip of his finger along her thigh.

Her eyes flared a little at the contact. Then she sighed and placed her hand on top of his, stopping the movement. As quickly as the moment had begun, it was gone. "Fine, I'll strap it back up," Delaney said, attempting to stand.

He placed a hand on her shoulder. "Let me get it. Where is your bandage?"

She nodded in the direction of the large dining room table that was covered with papers, files, and books. Considering that everything she'd brought back from Germany had fit in a small backpack, it looked like she'd been busy. There was a pile of delivery boxes on the floor, and a new laptop sat on the table. "I'm sorry. I would have cleaned up if I had known you were coming home today."

"Don't worry about it," he said, getting to his feet. "It's about time the place looked lived in." It was true. He was organized. Meticulous. Resourceful. Didn't need much. With Delaney's mess lying around, it looked a little more like somebody actually lived there. Mac found the bandage on the table and returned to his spot on the floor by her feet.

He carefully bound her ankle with an ACE bandage that was a little wider than he would have liked. He wrapped it around her ankle twice to anchor it. There was still a little swelling, so he checked it wasn't too tight.

"Try to keep your toes upright for me, Buttons," he said, running it under her foot and giving it a gentle tug to pull it into the correct position. Her toenails were painted a pretty peach.

"I could have done this myself," Delaney said, leaning forward. The floral smell of her shampoo hit him in the gut as her hair brushed the side of his face. "So, medic, huh?"

Mac fastened the bandage and placed her foot back on the ground before joining her on the sofa. "Yeah," he nodded. "So, yoga, huh?" he said, looking her up and down.

Delaney chuckled. "Yeah. Maybe a little too soon. I'd

only just started when you arrived, guess I need to wait a little longer."

The bruises on her face had faded, but he couldn't resist running his thumb along her cheekbone. "You look better," he said. Too good. Good enough to lean forward and kiss. Right now, she looked like she was thinking the exact same thing. "But don't overdo it."

Carefully, Delaney stood. "I should go get changed."

"Come out with me tonight. To meet up with Six and Lou." He was sure the idea of going out with him alone would feel too much like a date.

She looked out of the window toward the harbor, fine lines gathering between her eyes. She was clearly undecided.

"He's going away on a job soon. It's not pretty, and they could probably both do with the distraction," he added quickly, although he knew that both Six and Lou handled Six's departures like pros. Right now, he'd say whatever he needed to if she agreed to go out to dinner with him.

"Fine, but you need to give me five minutes to get changed. I feel stupid in workout clothes when I can't even work out."

"Whatever you need," he said as he stood. He should change, too. Probably shower. If Delaney was still the girlie girl those pretty toenails told him she was, he'd probably have time.

He watched her as she walked . . . no, sauntered . . . through the apartment.

If he was going to survive tonight, he'd better make the shower a cold one.

Delaney shut the door to her bedroom and carefully leaned back against the cool surface. It chilled her heated skin as goose bumps appeared on her flesh. Mac was the only man on Earth who could move her, stir up emotions she'd buried so deep, with the simplest of touches. The kindest of gestures.

She thought about the way his fingers had wrapped the bandage around her skin with the sparest movements. And the smell of him. It wasn't his aftershave, but something more . . . damn . . . She didn't know the word . . . worldly, mature, older.

Walking gingerly now that she was out of his line of sight, she pulled open the door to her closet where she'd hung the few items she'd retrieved from her mom's. Bringing anything more would have made it too easy to settle in. To stay. She couldn't do that to herself—or to Brock.

In Mac's absence, she'd done the unthinkable. She'd snooped around the apartment, especially Mac's room. Not that she'd found anything of major interest at first. There was no obvious sign of any women in his life, but there was a twelve pack of condoms with four missing. It shouldn't have hurt to realize he was having sex with other women. Of course he was. It wasn't like she'd been living like a nun in the time since she'd last seen him. But somehow, underneath all the hatred, she'd still always thought of him as hers. And had never found anyone who made her *feel* the way Mac did.

Then she'd seen them, three photo frames on the windowsill. And her heart had burst into a million little pieces.

The first photo was of the four of them—Cabe, Six, Mac, and Brock—all lined up at some swim meet. All young, tanned, and ridiculously good-looking. The second was of the same group, minus Brock—taken recently by the look of Mac's hair—outside a building with a huge Eagle Securities sign. But it was the third that stopped her in her tracks. It was a photograph she'd never seen, but she knew immediately when it had been taken. It was a close-up of her taken all those years ago on the morning after she'd lost her virginity to Mac in a motel room on their way to her cousin's wedding in Napa. God, she looked . . . in love. Happy. Like she'd just had the best sex of her life. She was leaning against Mac's beat-up truck, the motel sign in the background, wearing a pretty sundress and Mac's gray zip-up sweater that dwarfed her. The wooden frame was dented and scratched, which told her it had traveled. All these years, he'd kept it.

Now that he was home in the living room not ten feet away from her, she couldn't pretend she hadn't seen it.

The sound of water hitting the tiled floor of the bathroom down the hall made her jump. The idea of a naked Mac under the hot spray made her heart race even faster. But the thoughts were traitorous. She owed Brock more than this.

She slipped out of her workout clothes that she'd only had on for ten minutes and pulled out a pair of her favorite jeans. Paired with a white T-shirt and navy jacket, they would have to do. The days of the girly sundresses were gone. Her white sneakers were the most comfortable for her foot. For a moment, she considered shaking her hair loose, but she decided to keep it in a ponytail. Mac had loved it when she wore her hair down, and she didn't want to do anything to encourage him.

With a quick flick of mascara and a splash of peach lip gloss, she was good to go. As she stepped out of the room into the hallway, she almost crashed into Mac. He gripped her biceps to steady her. "Jesus Christ," she gasped. "Do you really need to sneak everywhere?"

He grinned as he looked down at her T-shirt and then back to her face. "Occupational habit," he said. "You look great."

So did he, but she wasn't going to tell him that the navy T-shirt fit him to perfection. "This isn't a date." It was blunt, but it was the truth. Her heart dropped a little, though, when his grin slipped momentarily as he shook off her barb.

"I know. But I'm still going to let you know that the pretty girl I once dated grew up into a spectacular woman. Let's go," he said, offering her his elbow.

She took it, but only because her ankle throbbed like a bitch after her yoga experiment. If his arm was firm and muscular, she tried not to dwell on it, and when he offered to hail a cab to take them the block and a half to the Mexican restaurant on Fifth Avenue, she refused.

As they approached the restaurant, she saw Six was tucked away at the back of the patio, despite there being better tables available.

"Why don't we sit up here?" she said, pointing to a larger table with a great view of the street.

"Lou doesn't like crowds. You'll see."

"Delaney," Six said, coming to his feet. "You're looking a whole lot better than the last time I saw you." He pulled her into a hug gentler than the last one he'd given her, and she grinned.

"I've showered . . . I think that might be it."

Six laughed. "Let me introduce my girlfriend, Louisa North. Lou, this is Delaney."

Lou had long brown hair and bangs that partially covered her eyes. She looked a little nervous, on edge even, until Six ran a hand over her shoulders and the two of them sat back down. "I'm pleased to meet you, Delaney," she said, tilting her head to the side so her hair parted. "Six has told me so much about you." Louisa looked at Six and smiled softly. As fascinating as it was to watch Lou, it was the look on Six's face that made her heart stutter a little. Six looked at Lou as if she was . . . well, his everything.

She recognized that look. Mac had stared at her that way too, once.

It wasn't long before the table was full of tacos and tequila. As time ticked by, she became more fascinated by Six and Lou. They were so different. Six was loud, and just as funny as she remembered. And Lou was so . . . reserved. Her interactions with everyone around her were so limited. But as the evening grew late, and the alcohol took effect, she loosened up a little. Delaney was fascinated to learn about the research laboratory she was in the process of establishing. The woman clearly had brains. And ambition. Something Delaney truly admired.

Delaney did her best to keep Mac at a distance, despite the way he always offered her the plate of food first, their fingers brushing often. His hand kept ending up on the back of her chair, and more than once he twirled his fingers in her ponytail like he used to before snatching his hand away, as if remembering that they were part of each other's pasts, not their present.

"Hey, I'm gonna hit the washroom," Mac said, standing.

"Me too," Lou said.

"Want me to go with you?" Six asked, moving his chair so Lou could climb out of the corner.

"Nah. I'll be fine with Mac, right?"

Mac slung an arm around Louisa's shoulder. "Better with me than that asshole."

Six threw a packet of sugar at Mac and laughed. "Fuck you," he said playfully.

"I really like her," Delaney said as Lou and Mac walked away. "You did good, Six."

"I did better than good," he admitted with a bashful grin that looked a little out of place on the most confident man she'd ever known. "What about you? No boyfriend back here waiting for you?"

It was a personal question, but she shook her head anyway. "No. It takes a certain kind of man to deal with what I do for a living."

"Mac told me you do undercover investigative reporting. Is that what you were doing out in Afghanistan?"

It didn't surprise her that Mac had shared where she'd been. "It was. But Mac shouldn't . . . he . . . it's my business."

Six took a toothpick out of the pot on the table and began to chew on it. "Here's the deal, Delaney. We were all worried sick about you. Mac especially. And we care. Even if you don't want us to. Not just because of Brock, although Lord knows that would be enough on its own. But we care about you too."

Delaney sighed and ran a finger down the condensation on the outside of her glass. "I know you do. But that was all a long time ago."

"And yet somehow, when you were in trouble, you asked for him. And, just like Cabe or I would have done, he came running. Because *he* cares."

"But that's the thing. I don't even remember asking for him. And I don't know what to do . . ."

Six sat back in his chair and glanced back toward where Mac and Lou had disappeared. "He came because he still loves you, Delaney. He—"

"Don't say that." Her heart couldn't take it, didn't want to imagine a path back to him. "He killed Brock. He—"

"Stop that, Delaney. I let you say it back then because it was what you needed to believe. But you and I both know it's bullshit. 'Misadventure' was the verdict. Not 'murder' or 'manslaughter.' You want to know why Mac outranks Cabe and me? Why he earned more medals than Cabe and me? Because he has lived every moment of his life in atonement for that day, a day we all wish we could go back and change."

Delaney exhaled. "I can't talk about this. Not with you. Not now." Out of the corner of her eye, she saw a silver sedan parked up on the other side of the street. Was it way too much of a coincidence that she'd seen one outside of her mother's when she'd first gone to see her? Discreetly, she tried to get a read on the occupant, but it was dark, and his headlights were on.

Six turned and followed her line of sight. "What?"

She shook her head. "Nothing. I'm seeing ghosts. Listen. I appreciate you mean well, but . . ."

Six straightened up in his chair, and Delaney saw Mac and Lou headed back toward them. "He's loved you all these years, Delaney. I am outta here in thirty-six hours on a high-risk job. I know what the stakes are, so does Lou. So, we live our lives by *our* rules *every* day, so there are no regrets. I know what you put on the line to do what you do. Mac does too. But if he has no chance with you . . . ever . . . because you can't stop telling yourself that narrative about Brock . . . well then, you owe it to him to tell him that, move out, and leave him alone. But if that's not the case, please don't waste another moment. Life is too short to not love someone with every cell in your body, and anybody with half a brain can tell you two still belong together."

Delaney was quiet for the rest of dinner and didn't think to argue when Mac pulled out his credit card and paid for her food. What Six had said weighed on her mind. Not just the part about Mac's feelings for her, but the part about him being off to do a high-risk job.

She hugged Louisa goodbye, even though the funny and intelligent woman seemed a little uncomfortable.

Six pulled Delaney into his arms. "I'm sorry, I didn't mean to lecture you," he whispered in her ear.

Delaney sighed. "You were right, Six. But don't worry about me, *or* Mac. Be safe. Please. I only just found you again."

He nodded. "I always am," he said, standing tall. "Even more so now I have someone to come home to." His eyes moved to where Mac was hugging Lou.

Lou and Six hopped into a cab, and she and Mac walked the short distance home. Six's words lay heavy in her heart and gut. She hated the idea that he was off somewhere that wasn't safe, yet she fully understood what drove him to do it.

"You okay, Delaney?" Mac asked, dropping the keys to the apartment on the marble kitchen counter.

Was she? She felt a little . . . raw. "I'm not sure," she replied honestly.

Mac walked toward her and stopped in front of her before pulling her into a hug. When his lips brushed the top of her head, she let him, anxious to find some kind of comfort . . . of . . . *something* . . . to ground her.

When Mac's lips moved to her temple, she tried to remember why she hated him so much. Why she'd moved across the country to avoid him.

As they traveled along her cheek and down her jaw, she made a feeble pretense at moving away from him, but his arms held her steadily in place, which was a good thing because her knees felt weak, her breath flighty.

But when they reached her own lips, when his mouth brushed against hers, it was impossible to deny that Six had been right about her having to make a choice.

But whether she was supposed to leave or stay, she still didn't know.

CHAPTER FOUR

She was sweeter than he even remembered.

As her lips opened for him and her tongue tentatively moved against his, Mac wondered how the hell he'd gotten so lucky a second time around. When he'd boarded that plane to Germany, he'd just wanted to help her, to get her home safely. But this was more than he could ever imagine. More than he'd allowed himself to hope for. At least, not this fast. He'd imagined spending the next few months gaining her trust, her confidence. Seeing her around—though hopefully not on the arm of some guy whose face he'd have the urge to break.

But, no. She was right here. Letting him kiss her, letting him hold her, letting him run his hands down that ass he'd seen in tight Lycra and finding it just as firm and tight as he'd imagined.

Hell . . . she was coming on to *him*. And he wasn't about to say no. Instead, he slid his arms around her waist and pulled her closer, savoring the way her body felt pressed up against his. It felt different, better. They'd both changed, but with her back in his arms, everything clicked into place. The way her lips moved, the flavor of her, the way she sighed against his lips. The way she gasped as he touched her.

When her hands slid into his back pockets, he moved his own to her face and cupped her cheeks gently. "Delaney," he breathed.

Mac didn't know what had come over her, or him, but there was no way he was going to stop running his lips over each and every part of Delaney for as long as she'd let him. He pressed his lips to her forehead.

As he'd waited for Lou outside the restrooms, he'd seen Delaney shake her head as Six had said something to her. Her face had fallen, Six's eyes had caught his, and he'd leaned across the table toward Delaney to say something intently that had made Delaney jerk back in her seat. By the time Mac had returned to the table, though, whatever had been happening had ended. For the rest of the evening, Delaney had been less talkative than Lou even, which was saying a whole lot.

He'd been frustrated that Six had upset her, but given that the guy was shipping out soon, bringing it up had felt wrong.

Her hands reached up and gripped his wrists, only this time she wasn't pulling him closer. She was tugging him away. "I can't do this," she whispered. "I'm sorry."

For a moment, he could have sworn that tears pricked the corners of her eyes, but she blinked them away quickly.

"This isn't going to solve anything," she said.

He was torn. Fight her pulling away, but possibly lose. Or let her go, let her have her distance for now, and follow the old battle strategy adage of lose the battle to win the war.

He lowered his arms but took her wrists in his hands.

"Yeah, it's not, Delaney. But it's a start. And I'll take a start over an end any day of the week."

"I don't know what *that* was. But this"—she slipped her hand from his and gestured between the two of them—"you and I . . . together physically . . . was never the problem. Our history is much bigger than that." She stepped out of his reach and looked over at the table that contained all her work. "I've lined up some apartments to go look at tomorrow. I'll pick the first one that's available. Good night, Mac."

As much as he was sure he could convince her to fall back into his bed physically, she wasn't ready emotionally. If he got her there before she was fully open to him again, he'd lose her for good. He knew it. So for now, he could be a patient man.

"I'll go look with you tomorrow," he said as she reached her bedroom door. "Drive you around."

Delaney shook her head. "Thank you, but I'm really not your responsibility, Mac."

There it was. *Again*. She didn't want to rely on him. And it fucking hurt. Like the bullet wound that had required seven stitches in his thigh five years earlier. Although he wasn't so sure that his heart could be put back together quite so easily.

When the door to the room clicked shut, he dragged his fingers through his hair and ran a hand along his jaw. *Damn*. For a moment, he stayed rooted to the spot, looking at the solid piece of wood with ultramodern handles that stood between the two of them and hating Lochlan's goddamn apartment.

Sulking about it wasn't going to solve anything. He walked to the fridge and grabbed another beer. Yeah, he'd probably had more alcohol than he needed and would probably have the makings of a hangover in the morning, but right now he didn't give a shit. Of his options, getting drunk and passing out was the least offensive. The others, kicking down Delaney's door and picking up where they left off until she saw sense, or jerking off alone in his bedroom while he thought about the woman getting naked across the hall, felt stupid and immature.

He wandered over to the dining room table where Delaney had set up office. He ran his fingers over a book, *The Shadow World,* by Andrew Feinstein. He picked it up and flicked through the chapters, seeing names, campaigns, and weapons he recognized. It was the sort of book Cabe would love reading. A billion pages long. Delaney had used sticky notes, underlined sections, and folded page corners all the way through. Of course she'd read it from cover to cover.

Her notes were so orderly. Long gone were the little hearts with which she used to dot her *i*'s. Maybe, like the hearts, *he* was something she simply didn't do anymore.

A click sounded from the hallway, and the small band of light under her bedroom door disappeared.

Even though he was wired and horny as hell, he made his way to his bedroom. He paused by Delaney's door, fighting the urge to knock and go sleep next to her.

When he got to his own room, he placed his half-drunk beer on the bedside table and shucked his clothes before crawling into the sheets naked. He'd hoped the extra beer would help him sleep. But as he closed his eyes, visions of Delaney in her workout gear filled his mind. As if on autopilot, his dick grew hard. He slid his hands under the cool covers and gripped himself the way he liked.

Firm, with a long stroke from base to tip. Memories began to blend. Of her sitting next to him on their surfboards at sunset when they were younger, and a lewder version of her bending forward in her workout clothes. He imagined her riding his dick in that neon sports bra. She'd be wet; she always had been with him. She'd grab her hair in both hands and pile it on top of her head as she slid up and down.

His breath caught in his chest and he clamped his lips together. The last thing he needed was Delaney knowing that he was jacking off across the hall from her. But, he needed the release. It was ten days since they'd reunited. A hell of a lot longer since he'd had sex. He focused on the way she'd looked, the way her breasts had pressed up against his chest as they'd kissed in the living room, the way her ass had teased him. Years of deployment had given him a great imagination, and he imagined her breasts bouncing. Breathing heavily, he felt the moment he was about to come, could tell by the way his abs tightened and his balls were ready to explode.

In his head, Mac called out Delaney's name as he came. He gasped for air and slowed his strokes until his breathing and emotions returned to normal. Once he'd cleaned up, he crawled back into bed and finally gave in to his exhaustion.

His alarm sounded what felt like mere moments later. He reached his arm out of the covers and fumbled around for his phone. His head swam. Four hours' sleep. *Shit.* Work. He needed to get his shit together.

Twenty minutes later, he'd showered in cold water to chase away the heavy head, gotten dressed, and was in the process of savoring his first cup of coffee.

Six would be leaving in twenty-four hours and taking

some of the guys with him. It was a trial, a test run for a much larger piece of work. They were to provide covert coverage for a CIA paramilitary team in Syria who were reporting on the uprising. It was a hugely lucrative contract. The kind they dreamt of. The kind that would put their special ops firm on the map. It was ironic how the SEAL in him had hated the fact that contractors outweighed actual U.S. military on the ground in many war zones, but here he was, ready to form his own chain of command as a contractor. At least now he got to pick which jobs to work on, ones that would make a difference, instead of deploying his men at a moment's notice to go fix things that had been screwed up for so long, nobody knew how to put the pieces back together, or how to withdraw. But it weighed on him that Six's heading out had been partly his call. After all this time and training, sending another man off into conflict never got any easier emotionally, even though he had long ago gotten his head around doing just that.

Part of Mac wanted to suggest that he, Cabe, and Six all go out together, but they each had their own teams, and their own jobs to do. It was the luck of the draw—or in this case, their scheduling—that this time it happened to be Six.

Which was why they'd all taken up Mac's mom on her last-minute invitation to come to Encinitas for a barbecue later that day. To make things feel normal. As normal as seeing Delaney venture out of the bedroom, her hair a mess, an old baseball jersey sliding off one shoulder. It was like old times–ones he should let stay in the past instead of trying to drag them into the present. When she grabbed the coffee out of his hand on the way to the table, he let her. She wasn't a morning person.

She pulled out a chair at the table where she'd set up her things and took a sip. The coffee was hotter than Hades, and Delaney winced. "Since when do you take sugar?" she asked, her face screwing up in a grimace.

Mac poured her another cup and took it to the table, placing it next to her laptop. "Since ten years ago and an R and R break in Turkey. Waitress in an out-of-the-way guesthouse. I casually called her *Sugar*. I got sugar in every cup of coffee after that. Couldn't get her to stop. By the end of the trip I was hooked."

Delaney raised an eyebrow as she handed him back his drink, and he did his best to ignore the way the baseball shirt slid a little further off her shoulder.

"So are you back at work then?" he asked.

She nodded as her eyes scoured whatever she was looking at on her laptop. Without answering, she reached for the notepad and quickly scribbled a name.

Victor Lemtov.

He reached across the table and grabbed the paper from her. "Of Los Feliz?"

Delaney snatched the paper back. "You know better than to go looking over my notes." She said it so primly, and by the way she looked up at him, eyes narrowed, he knew he was looking at Delaney the journalist. "I'm sure we aren't talking about the same person, but why don't you tell me a little about the Lemtov *you* know, just to be sure." Casually, she leaned back in the chair and held her pen at both ends.

Mac tried hard to remind himself that this was her job. And that his initial response—a fear strong enough to want to tell her to stay the hell away from Lemtov—was an overreaction. But Lemtov had been involved in the attempt to abduct Louisa. The people with whom he was associated had wanted her to re-create a drug she'd created that had the power to paralyze its victims while leaving them completely conscious.

"He's a Russian criminal. Not connected to the mafia directly that we can tell. But definitely growing." If he was involved in what had happened to Delaney, Mac should call their CIA contact, Andrew Aitken. He'd been able to get all the correct authorizations for Eagle Securities to work as contractors before. Maybe they should get them again.

Delaney tapped the pen on her palm. "Define 'growing.'"

Mac took a breath. "He's on the FBI's radar. Just not high enough to warrant the resources for a serious investigation."

"Makes sense," she mumbled under her breath and then returned to her screen.

"Why?" Mac asked.

"Oh, nothing," she said without looking up.

Mac stalked around to the other side of the table and crouched down, waiting patiently until Delaney turned to look at him. "You don't get to "oh nothing" me, Delaney. Not after the shape you were in when I saw you that first day in the hospital."

"What I am doing has nothing to do with you. . . . I'm not—"

"You say *'your responsibility'* one more time, I'm going to lose my fucking mind."

"I've been doing fine without your help for years, and—"

"You weren't fine in that hospital, Delaney. And you've had nearly a week to move out, but you haven't. Not that I want you to, but you know you're safer here while you figure out which way is up. So, do us both a favor, and tell me what the hell you are looking into, so I'm not flying blind."

Of all the arrogant, conceited . . . Gah!

"Listen," she said, getting to her feet then regretting it the moment her ankle twinged. "I must have been off my damn mind on meds when I asked for you. I probably asked for my mom too. And Brock. And Kanye freaking West for all I know. You just happened to be the one they could track down because of your military record or something. Second, I'm a journalist. I don't reveal shit until I am goddamn ready. And I have appointments today to look around at condos. So, do me a favor and get out of my way so I can go get ready."

Slowly, Mac stood until he towered over her. She'd always found his height incredibly attractive, but now it just seemed too overwhelming, and she needed him out of her space. "I don't care who else you might have asked for," he said, "because I was the only one who came. I don't want you to leave, but I know we can't just pick up where we left off all those years ago, so you moving into your own place at some point makes sense. As for Lemtov, he was involved in trying to abduct Louisa last summer. He was arrested as part of a takedown that we led, and he was released on bail while he awaited trial. But the case is weak. An old man's word against his, with no proof or money trail. You have no idea who you are looking into, and I do. So, stop being so stubborn."

Louisa? During dinner, Six had alluded to the fact that they'd met while she was a client. She'd tried to get more details then, but the three of them had clammed up. She'd give anything to know what Mac knew now. Curiosity, the craving for truth, burned deep in her gut. Fear receded.

She wasn't so naive that she'd refuse high-quality help.

"I believe there is a weapons dealer funding the insurgents in places like Kunduz," she said.

Mac folded his arms across his chest. "Well, that's nothing new. There have always been runners out of Eastern Europe, going back as far as the collapse of the USSR."

Carefully, Delaney returned to the dining room chair, and slowly rotated her ankle under the table. Even though it was still strapped up, it throbbed like a bitch. "Yes, but this appears to be funded within the U.S. The Kunduz delivery I had arranged to see traveled from the U.S. via Russia. Big weapons dealers insist they are purely providers of logistics. One major dealer's defense was basically that a cabbie can't be arrested for dealing coke if a dealer is caught taking a taxi to the airport."

Mac scoffed and pulled out another chair. "Sounds like a technicality. They're flying in and out of the world's deadliest hot spots. Coups. Dictators. Mass genocide. They sure as shit aren't shipping barley."

"Yeah. Obviously. But the people who are financially funding with cash are also the ones supplying the weapons, and they are getting away with providing the weapons due to the dual purpose clause when shipping products to embargoed areas."

Mac's brow furrowed. " 'Dual purpose clause'?"

"It's an exemption put on things that could be weapons or could be items required for other purposes. *Gah* . . . okay. I'm not doing a great job of explaining this." Delaney searched for a better explanation. "Here's an example: A basic helicopter can be used for managing extensive livestock movement or spraying crops. So it can be imported as agricultural equipment. But the moment it gets there, it's repurposed into a military vehicle and weaponized. It can work the same way with chemicals that can be used for a beneficial purpose but it is repurposed for chemical warfare."

She'd been so freaking close to proving it. Her informant had taken a snapshot of the inside of the container while it was being processed for shipping. Pressurized canisters of chemicals and what she had been assured were second-grade weapons. She had shipping notes and plane manifests. All she had needed was a positive sighting of it at the other end of the journey. But she hadn't seen it, in fact, she'd been grabbed only hours before the scheduled arrival, too much of a coincidence in her opinion. All she could prove was that it had landed in Russia. She had no evidence that it had ever arrived on Afghan soil.

"So what does Lemtov have to do with this?" Mac finished his coffee in four large gulps and put his cup down on the table.

"Honestly," Delaney said, "I don't know. I just got an email saying I should check him out. I don't know the sender of the email, but I have a strong suspicion that if I try to trace it, it will bounce around for a little while and then seem to come from some place I've never heard of with a population of ten people and seven sheep. None of who give a flip about some random guy named Victor Lemtov. But I intend to trace the shell company that shipped the goods out in the first place. Maybe the two are connected."

The alarm on Mac's phone began to ring, reminding him it was time to leave. "Shit," he said, turning it off quickly. "I have to go. We have to do some final planning with Six's team. Look. I can help. With this. Can we talk more later?"

Delaney nodded. Hopefully she'd have more to tell him when he got back. "For sure. Tell Six to bring his ass back in one piece."

"You got a secret thing for Six's ass," Mac said with a wink as he grabbed his wallet and keys of the kitchen counter.

"Most definitely," she said casually taking a sip of her coffee.

"Look, my mom is having a barbecue this afternoon. Six'll be there and you can tell him yourself. Come with me. Mom'd love to see you, I know."

Delaney looked at her computer. She had a mountain of work to do. And seeing Mac's family again felt a little too close to home. "I don't know, Mac . . . I don't think that's the best idea."

"Just think about it. Please."

"Okay. I'll see how far I get with all this after I get back from apartment hunting," she said, gesturing to all the piles on the table.

He shook his head and returned to her side. "Be careful," he said before pressing a kiss to the top of her head.

She watched as he walked to the apartment door. His ass was way better than Six's, but she'd keep that thought to herself.

After a quick shower, Delaney took the time to blow-dry her hair and decided to wear it down. Dressed in her best, and only, pair of black pants—though they didn't match her white sneakers and bandages—and a cream blouse, she grabbed her purse and left the apartment.

Her plan was to start with cheap and cheerful apartments, but if she couldn't find any that met even her own
low standards, she'd start surfing the web for people looking for roommates. It wasn't exactly that she didn't have
money. She'd always been cautious about spending, and
because she'd been away a lot on assignment, her living
expenses hadn't been too high. But setting up home had
always felt a little bit like . . . giving up. Sitting in a beautiful home with a comfortable bed and soft sheets, it
could be too easy to come to the decision that months on
the road following leads and stories was a thing of her
past. And then what would she do? Join the local knit-
ting circle, or a book club, maybe? She laughed at the idea
of a bunch of women sitting around discussing her choice
of books on the international arms trade.

Most of the apartments she was looking at were farther north than Mac's incredible centrally located
apartment, so she took a cab. The first was in a nondescript building in a half-decent neighborhood. Inside, a
giant notice declared the elevator out of order. Thankfully the apartment was on the third floor. Half walking,
half hopping, and leaning heavily on the railing, Delaney
made her way upstairs. The hallways were tired, but
decently lit.

Delaney knocked on the door and was greeted by the
agent and the strong smell of urine. "Sorry about this,"
the agent said, wafting her hand in front of her own nose.
"The previous owners had pets and were evicted. I'm
sure it will come out with a decent carpet cleaning."

Without setting a foot inside, Delaney knew it
wouldn't, but she hobbled around the apartment making
noncommittal "hmms" and "ahhs." She didn't want car-

pet, especially ones that stunk of animal pee. She wanted hardwood. Easy to clean.

Her luck didn't fare any better in the second or third ones, both of which were worse than the first. Depressingly, the smell of cat urine won out over a moldy bathroom and an apartment that had only one window.

The fourth apartment was the winner—if you defined "winner" as the "best out of four," rather than anything close to what she really wanted. But the neighborhood was cute, the small apartment was bright thanks to large windows in the main living space, and it was a little closer to her mother's and Mac's than the others. Not that proximity to Mac had anything to do with . . . well, with anything. Or anything to do with the kiss they'd shared, which had been a complete shock. All she remembered from their relationship was the sweetness, the tenderness, not heat like he'd laid on her last night.

Using her ankle throughout the day had done the opposite of what she'd anticipated. It had loosened up. And while she was convinced it would ache by the time she took her sneakers off tonight, she used the opportunity to walk the several blocks back to Mac's. The air was fresh—straight off the bay, as her mother would say. And it was nearly the first day of spring. It had been over three weeks since the abduction had taken place, and this was the first day she'd felt . . . normal.

She resisted stopping at the Ghirardelli store on Fifth Avenue, because as much as she could inhale the whole shop, she'd been sitting on her ass way too long. The scale in Mac's bathroom told her she'd gained five pounds. She also ignored the pizza place on Island, even though it smelled so damn good. Her stomach rumbled, but there were plenty of healthier options in Mac's fridge. Which, come to think of it, she should probably give him some money for.

Tugging her phone out of her purse, she stopped to make a note of it. When she looked up, she noticed in the glass of the pizzeria a stranger standing on the other side of the street glancing around curiously. The first time that she'd seen the silver sedan outside her mom's, the driver had been wearing the same black ball cap. It was a reach to assume they were the same person, but she wasn't foolish enough to take chances.

Delaney began to walk again, testing her ankle a little as she picked up pace. She took a right onto Sixth and breathed a sigh of relief at the sight of tourists and locals alike packing the street and going about their business. She still felt like she was about to puke, but panic wasn't going to help. She headed toward the Gaslamp Marriott that stood proud at the bottom of the street. It was less than half a block to the condo from there, but she knew there would be more people milling around there than the condo reception. Braving a look behind her, she could see the man in the cap still on her tail.

Sweat began to form on her brow, and her ankle stopped cooperating and began to throb horribly. Despite the pain shooting up her leg, she began to jog. If he showed any signs of catching up with her, she would sprint straight into the hotel. But he didn't. She glanced over her shoulder one last time and saw that he appeared to be hanging back. When she turned for the ballpark and saw the apartment entrance, her heart raced even faster.

She rummaged around in her purse as she ran, pulling out the key card that would allow her inside. To safety. The entrance was within sight. Delaney powered her legs.

"Delaney," a voice called out, but she kept running. "Delaney, wait up."

As hands grabbed her shoulders, she screamed.

"What happened?" Mac said calmly as he placed the bowl on the floor and carefully lifted Delaney's sore foot into the iced water.

Delaney was spooked, and he needed to keep calm, no matter how churned up he'd gotten at the sight of her running away from something that had terrified her. Hell, she hadn't even recognized his voice. Something had set her off.

As soon as she'd recognized him, she'd hugged him tightly, but then had hurried them inside while looking over her shoulder. Which meant she was one foot in the here and now with him and one foot in whatever had set her off.

He wanted answers, but the way Delaney was biting her lip told him he wasn't going to get any. "Please, Delaney. You look pale. And your skin is clammy. Trust me, whatever this is isn't going to go away by itself. You need to talk about it."

"It's stupid, Mac. Nothing. I was seeing things. There's a car that I've seen a couple of times. And the driver, well . . . I guess I'm seeing ghosts. It's probably nothing."

Ghosts or real, it had scared the shit of her. A few minutes later and he would have missed the whole thing. He'd never been more relieved to have left work early to make sure he had time to persuade her to join him at his mom's barbecue.

And given she'd been talking about Lemtov the previous morning, he wasn't so sure that what had scared her *was* nothing. "Talk it through with me," he said, calmly. "Step by step. When, where . . . as many details as you can remember."

Delaney laughed nervously. "You know, it's probably some guy who lives the next block over. That's why I keep seeing him."

"Let me be the judge of that." Plus, Mac had means. Contacts. People who had access to cameras—through legal channels or through a little bit of hacking. Once Delaney told him the details, he'd go back and retrace her steps. And quite possibly find and kill the guy, even if scaring the shit out of her was all he was guilty of.

"Honestly, Mac. I need you to tell me it's nothing, not build it up into something more. I saw the car twice, and then I saw him wearing a ball cap and aviators on the street behind me today. I thought he was following me home, but he dropped back. I was freaked is all."

Fine. He could work it backward from the point where he'd picked her up. One way or another he was going to get to the bottom of it. Except that tomorrow he was going to Washington to complete the contract he'd finalized on his last trip there. Some high-ranking Saudi diplomat who wanted additional security for family members. This kind of security detail wasn't their preferred type of work, but it could lead to something more through the contacts he'd make. For the first time in his life, he wished he could blow off a job.

Whether he liked it or not, he needed to leave, but that didn't mean he couldn't task one of the others staying behind to look into what had happened to Delaney.

She was right that she needed him to help her calm down, not spin off into a conspiracy theory. At least until he had more proof one way or another.

"Give me the basics, and I can take it from there. It's

just a precaution, and you're probably right. What you've been through would cause anybody to see the worst in a situation. And sometimes that's a healthy thing. But let me check, okay?"

"Fine. The first time I saw the car was Monday when I went to see my mom. As I got out of the cab, he drove past, but slowly, like a really bad drive-by."

"Your mom still in the same place?" Mac asked, even though he knew the answer. He just wanted her to keep talking.

"Yes. I saw the car again on Wednesday when we were having dinner with Six. And he was on foot when I saw him today by the pizza place over on Island. He followed me down Sixth, but I lost him."

Mac made a mental note. Should be easy enough to catch a CCTV of him. Heck, he'd gone to school with the head of security at the hotel on the corner of Sixth and Island, and he was sure they had exterior cameras. That would be an easy favor to call in.

Mac checked his watch, and stood. "Let me get you something to dry off with." Thinking over what she'd said, he made his way to the bathroom. It really could be all some stupid coincidence, but why would this guy, as opposed to any of his neighbors, stand out? He grabbed a towel, returned to the living room, and tapped her leg.

Delaney lifted it out of the water, and Mac gently rubbed it dry. "I'll get someone to take a look, get a plate, run a name and address. You are probably right that it's nothing, but I'm off on another job tomorrow afternoon, so you'll be on your own. First sign of any problem, just call the police. Stay in public places. You know the smart things to do. I'll be back Wednesday. It's only a quick one."

She nodded. "I should be fine. I get the keys to my new place tomorrow, so I'll be busy getting things from my mom's and unpacking. I'll be gone before you get back."

His stomach dropped. Tomorrow felt like way too soon for her to go. Hell, they'd been back on American soil less than a week. It was less than three weeks since she'd been taken. She wasn't properly healed yet.

"Why don't you wait until I get back? I can help you move in," he said as persuasively as he could, given that his heart was beating a mile a minute. "You shouldn't be doing heavy lifting on that foot."

Delaney smiled and placed her hand on his cheek. "Don't," she said softly. "Don't make this hard. I need to go. You have work to do. I need to start getting on with my life. I've been here a week. It's time you got your place back." She looked over to the dining room table where piles of books and papers continued to grow like weeds.

"What time do you get the keys tomorrow? I should at least go over and check the security, so that you—"

"No. You don't need to. I've done fine without you all these years, Mac. It's time to go. I can't tell you how very grateful I am that you flew all the way to Germany, which I'll pay you back for if you'll let me know how much."

How much? Couldn't she see he didn't want his stupid money back? Or his place back. He wanted *her* back. The old her. The new her. All the different hers there were going to be in the future.

"I don't give a shit about the flight. Does your new place at least have a doorman?" The idea of her going into a new apartment before he'd had the chance to check up on the guy with the silver sedan made him feel uneasy.

"Look, I—"

"Does it?" he demanded.

Delaney shook her head. "No, it doesn't. But it's got a buzzer entry, and I'm not stupid."

Mac got to his feet and began to pace. *Yes, you* are *being stupid. Stay here instead of being stubborn. You never used to be this way. You are impossible. You're—*

"Maybe I should just go to Mom's tonight." Delaney got to her feet and headed toward the bedroom.

He grabbed her wrist softly. "Goddamn, Delaney. Give me a minute to catch up before you go marching out of here."

She stood looking at him, her eyes wide, her cheeks pink. He tugged gently on her arm, and she moved closer to him. She was leaving him. Again. And he knew he wouldn't be able to force her to stay. All he could do was check that where she was going was safe. And that her transition there was smooth.

"I know you don't need me," he said, his voice gruff as he looked at the way her hair fell in loose waves over her shoulders. "I know you probably don't even want me there. But I need you to let me, Delaney. Because I won't rest if I don't know you are safe. I've worried about you for the last decade but haven't been able to do anything about it. Just . . . just let me do this. Let me worry. Okay?"

She stopped when her feet butted up against his, when she had to look up to him. For once she looked at him like she used to, like he was a good man and she was grateful for him. "Okay," she replied quietly. "But then we need to draw a line underneath this . . . reunion . . . whatever."

"Do we?" he asked, watching her eyes watch his lips.

"Yes," she whispered.

He placed a finger under her chin and lifted her face to his. With his eyes on her, he brought his lips to hers, at first keeping the pressure light and gentle. They were so unbelievably soft, the only part of her that time hadn't hardened. Her eyes fluttered shut as the kiss turned demanding. God, he wanted to devour her, slowly, over the next several hours.

Gently, he slipped his hand around the back of her neck and threaded his fingers through that long mane of hers that felt like silk. He knew that at any moment she could push him away, but he was determined to take whatever she'd give him. He slid his hand along the dip in her waist, allowing his thumb to brush over the side of her breast until she stepped up against him. When she groaned, he remembered how she sounded when she came. She slid her hands along his face into his hair, and he remembered how she used to grip it when he'd drop to his knees in front of her.

His actions were becoming more urgent, as were hers. He wrapped his arms around her and pulled her tight against his body, knowing she could feel how hard he was getting. He'd worry about her moving out later. For now, he wanted nothing but her.

Dragging kisses along her jaw, he nudged her head to the left so he could kiss her behind her ear.

"Mac," she gasped, as his lips brushed the side of her neck. She'd always loved it when he kissed her there. "Mac, please."

Her words were ones of caution, not encouragement. He kissed her one more time against her pulse and then raised his head to look at her. Her lips were more ruby than plum, and the color in her cheeks was high.

"I'm sorry," she said. "That was my fault. I shouldn't . . . I mean . . . we can't."

"Don't tell me you didn't want that. You were right there with me and we both know it. . . . Consent is the most important thing in the world to me. Don't make out like you didn't want this, Delaney."

She looked down at the floor. "Don't you understand?" she said. "It's never been about not wanting you. It's everything you remind me of."

Mac took a deep breath. Now wasn't the time. "We need to go," he said, knowing that Six had gone to Louisa's lab to collect her and that Cabe was already on his way to Encinitas.

Delaney raised an eyebrow. "I said I'd think about it. But, I can't go with you after that, Mac. It's not fair. To either of us."

"I already told Mom you were coming. I know, dick move, but I want you there. And she missed you. A lot. Please don't disappoint her, Delaney." It was a low blow, and he knew it—bringing his mom into it. Delaney and his mom had always gotten along famously. His mom had hurt almost as much as he had when the two of them had broken up.

"Cheap shot." With a sigh, Delaney grabbed her purse. "Fine. But keep your lips and your hands to yourself, Mac."

"Whatever you say, Buttons," he said. But deliberately didn't make any promises.

CHAPTER FIVE

As Mac pulled up outside the familiar house on Third Street, Delaney saw a familiar-looking young woman whose dark hair was pulled up into a messy bun. "Is that Aoife?" she asked. She'd always been envious of Mac's large family and had wondered what had become of his younger siblings, Lochlan, Aoife, and Niamh. She couldn't remember the last time she'd seen any of them.

"Yeah, she works in San Francisco as office manager for Lochlan's tech incubator," he said, rolling his eyes at Aoife as she waved excitedly at Delaney and then stuck her tongue out at him. "Despite appearances, she's really clever."

Delaney laughed. Beneath the gruffness, she could hear the admiration and love he felt for his sister. They'd always been thick as thieves, the four MacCarricks who used to fight over who had the most difficult name. She'd always thought that Niamh had been given the short straw.

"What about Niamh?"

"She works for a consulting firm out of their L.A.

office, so she won't be here today. She went to work there straight out of school. Graduated from Berkeley with a whole bunch of whistles and bells. Dean's List, rocket-high GPA, magna cum something. They're all so smart that it makes me wonder if I was adopted."

"I don't know. From what I hear, you did okay for yourself, *Captain*."

Mac killed the engine. "Not the same kind of smart."

"Well, if you didn't all look so freaking similar, you might be able to persuade me to agree. You and your brother are the most alike." Lochlan had been in her class at school. "Do you remember the time Lochlan shoved grass down my shirt and you kicked his ass?"

Mac looked over at her, a grin on his face. "Wasn't the first time I'd kicked someone's ass for you, and given that you haven't changed, I doubt it's going to be the last."

"So not funny, Mac," she said, slapping his arm and not knowing whether to be offended or laugh, though it was hard to not respond to the humor in his eyes.

Sylvie, Mac's mom, appeared on the driveway. The petite woman in a pretty denim sundress and light sweater didn't look a day over forty, even though she was well into her fifties. Delaney still couldn't quite believe she could have given birth to four children, especially one who'd turned out to be the size of Mac.

"She's desperate to see you. Wouldn't be surprised if she made you a cake." Mac took her hand. "Thanks for coming with me, Delaney. I'm not the only one who missed you."

Gently, she pulled her hand out of his. "Well, better go say hello then." She opened the door and dropped down out of the truck.

Every now and then, she was reminded of just how

wonderful it had been to grow up in Encinitas. There was something in the air, something that made her feel calm, something that took her back to the time in her life when all that mattered was mascara, a cute bikini, and Mac. Her mother had always said that if they could bottle the air by the ocean, they could sell it as an elixir of youth.

Brock had loved surfing . . . and so had she. But she hadn't been in the water since that day. In the ocean, she saw Brock everywhere. In the swagger of a young surfer, arms out of his wetsuit, carrying his board down to the water's edge. In the crash of a wave. In the glimmer of the sun hitting the surface of the water. She took a deep breath and wondered if it would be okay to slip down to the beach just to be closer to Brock for a few moments. She hadn't visited his grave because she'd always been sure he would have rather been cremated and had his ashes spread in the ocean.

"You okay?" Mac said, walking around the truck. She realized she hadn't taken a step since she'd gotten out.

"What? Oh, yes. I'm fine . . . memories . . . you know." She shrugged, needing to lighten the moment. She couldn't break down right now, no matter how strong the memories were.

Mac's mom hurried over and pushed Mac out of the way to pull Delaney into her arms. "Delaney. Oh, my child." Sylvie stepped back and gripped Delaney's arms with unexpected strength, given her size. "You always were such a wee thing, but look at you now. I'm so glad you could make it."

Six walked out of the back garden wearing a pair of board shorts, a football in one hand and his arm slung casually over Louisa's shoulder. "'Bout time you got here," he said.

"He beat me here by minutes, right, Mom?" Mac said with a laugh.

"That he did, Malachai. But long enough for Six to get antsy as he always does, so I suggest the four of you go down to the beach and kill some energy for a couple of hours. We'll grill later, and you and I can catch up properly." She patted Delaney's hand.

"You want to go, Delaney?" Mac asked.

"I don't have a suit," she said. It had been a deliberate omission. The idea of going down to the water she'd loved so deeply terrified her. Intellectually, she knew it was an overreaction. But to be forced to confront the memory of Brock in a place that had meant too much to all of them was almost more than she could deal with. More than half the time she'd ever spent with her brother was on that damn beach.

"We look about the same size," Louisa said. "The boys can get a head start, and we can head over to our place to hook you up."

Delaney looked to Mac, who nodded. "Come on, it'll be fun to blow off the cobwebs on the beach."

There seemed to be no escape, and Delaney forced herself to smile in agreement.

"We'll head to the entrance off the bottom of your road," Mac said to Lou. "I'll be the one kicking Six's ass in a beach workout. He's looking a little flabby around the gut right now."

"Fuck you." Six laughed. "Sorry, Mrs. MacCarrick."

"You only 'Mrs. MacCarrick' me when you already know you're in trouble. Now be gone. The pair of you. I'll send Cabe along when he gets here."

Mac pulled his T-shirt off and tucked it into the back of his shorts, and the three of them watched the two men go. It was difficult to ignore they were both perfectly fit and attractive specimens.

"Hard to believe one of them would scream every time Count Duckula came on the TV, and the other thought balloons held the spirits of dead people and would cry when we popped them," Sylvie said.

"Okay. You have to tell me which one of those was Six," Louisa said with a laugh.

"How did I not know this story?" Delaney asked, desperate to focus on anything other than the ocean.

Sylvie mimicked zipping her mouth and throwing away the key. "My lips are sealed. Now the two of you go too."

"Come on, we're over on E Street," Louisa said without looking at her. "I'm betting Six was scared of Duckula. Dead spirits in balloons is way too cerebral."

Despite the tightness in her chest, Delaney couldn't help but laugh, and remembered Mac having told her not to be offended that Lou rarely looked at people when she spoke. "I'm trying to think back to see if I can remember a party or something where one of them freaked out, but they're a bit older than me."

"Six told me how you guys all grew up together. He told me about your brother and dad too. I'm sorry about that."

It was odd to talk about them with someone she didn't really know. Someone who didn't know or remember her brother. "Yeah. Shit happens sometimes, right?" It was glib, but she was already feeling too surrounded by their past. They turned onto E Street and crossed over the train tracks, heading up the steep hill that led to the library.

"It does. My dad committed suicide when I was younger, so I get it."

Delaney's heart hurt. "Oh my God, that's awful. I'm sorry."

"Yeah, well. Sorry. I'm clearly not great at small talk, am I? Straight to the whole death-of-family-members thing. I should have started by asking if you like cross-stitch or something," Louisa said as they reached the top of the hill and a cute yellow split-level set back off the road. The lot was lushly planted with palms and shrubs.

Delaney couldn't help but laugh. "For the record, no, I don't. And I don't mind. I'm a journalist, so I love it when someone cuts straight to the heart of something. Wasn't this Six's grandparents'?" Delaney asked as Louisa let them inside.

"It was. Now it's Six's. Well, ours. I had a house closer to the city, but it never felt like home quite like this one does, although we've done some pretty extensive renovating. I'll get you a suit. Make yourself at home."

The layout of the house felt unfamiliar, though she'd been there when she was younger, traipsing after her brother when he'd gone to visit his friend. Perhaps it had been changed in the renovations Louisa had mentioned. One wall of the living room was covered in black-and-white photographs, many, she assumed, taken by Six on his travels. But some were of people, and one in particular caught her eye. It was one of their summers spent camping.

God. They all looked so young. Six had always been the biggest. Even back then he'd been a couple of inches taller than the others. Her brother had long wild surf hair back then. Not quite dreadlocks, but not quite curls. Just always salty and windblown. Just his presence had made her feel safe as a child, and his loss . . . well, there were days when she wondered whether she'd ever fill the hole his death had left inside her.

Mac had his arm slung casually over her shoulder. It was the summer they'd gotten together, but before they'd kissed for the first time. They'd looked like a couple long before they'd become one. Like they were predestined. Or maybe she was reading too much into a photograph of two horny young people.

"One of Six's favorites. He always says this was the summer before you all grew up. Here," Louisa said, handing her a cute blue-patterned bikini that would be perfect under her capris and T-shirt. "You can change in the bathroom at the end of the hall."

Once she was changed and her underwear was stowed away in her purse, they walked down to the beach carrying a bag full of towels. Louisa told her more about the research facility she was setting up, which required countless permits and licenses, not to mention all the hiring that needed to be done and building work that was still underway. Delaney empathized, her own work often constrained by bureaucracy. By the time they hit the beach, Delaney realized that beneath the cool exterior and sometimes blunt phrasing, Louisa was extremely bright, and considerate, and funny.

"I'm seriously going to test the Count Duckula thing," she said. "While you were changing, I found this company that makes custom decals. I ordered a whole bunch of Count Duckulas to stick on the windows for when he gets back."

As they reached the wooden stairs to the beach, she looked out and could see Mac and Six tossing the ball between them. Cabe had joined them. From the looks of a small group of girls setting their towels down near them, they had a growing fan club. She bit down on the little bubble of jealousy, hoping to burst it, but she couldn't. It lingered. She hated that she felt that way about Mac.

"How do you get your head around Six going away?" she asked. "I mean, my brother was planning to enlist, and I was terrified."

Louisa held onto the railing as she descended the uneven, sand-swept steps. "I tell him that if he doesn't come back, I'll kill him myself," she said, but the sad chuckle that accompanied her words wasn't overly convincing. "It's who he is. And to be honest, I wouldn't want him any other way. So I just deal with it."

"Well, I'm no expert, but I've known Six a *really* long time, and I get the impression he'd do just about anything he could to make sure he made it back to you." Delaney stopped on the last step and took off her sandals. Stepping down onto the sand felt momentous.

"Thank you," Louisa said, kicking off her own shoes. "You okay, Delaney?"

Was she?

It was all too familiar. Easy breezy days spent together on the beach. The sun reflecting off the water as if someone had tipped a container of diamonds onto the surface. The smell of salt in the air. Sand that threatened to be warm under her feet, and a gentle . . . energy. Something that made her want to sit down on the sand and just look out over the water for five minutes to find that stillness she'd been chasing since the day she'd woken up in that hospital in Germany.

"Yeah. I'm fine," she said, wanting to be as she stepped down onto the beach.

Hoping that one day she really *could* be.

The Santa Ana winds were making it tough to play ball, forcing them to pass harder and run faster. Not that it was a problem for the three of them. Mac had played ball on this beach with Six and Cabe since they were kids. Plus, he had Delaney to impress.

Yeah. He'd turned into *that* guy.

The one who'd do bicep curls before hitting the beach.

His game was on point. He was in the best shape of his life. And Delaney was head down with Louisa, as she had been for the last hour, chatting up a storm.

"Face it. That two pack of yours is not that impressive," Six said, tipping his chin in the direction of the girls.

Mac laughed. "I'm not sure. That group of girls behind us seem to think it is."

Six shook his head. "Yeah, but they ain't Delaney, right?"

"What are you two pussies talking about?" Cabe said as he walked toward them.

Six threw a sweaty arm over his shoulder. It was gross. "Mac's getting all pouty because Delaney hasn't been checking him out all afternoon."

"Am I the only guy who's still got a dick left?" Cabe asked. "You guys are only half the men you once were."

"Fuck you," Six and Mac said in unison.

"Don't worry, Mac, my friend. I'm your wingman. Watch this." Six walked toward Lou and Delaney, who stopped talking when his shadow breached their towels. He couldn't hear what Six was saying, but he could see the girls fall into fits of laughter. The way Delaney looked up at Six, shielding her eyes from the sun, told him she was responding to whatever Six was orchestrating. Why the hell couldn't she relax like that around him?

"If you guys are doing couple shit, I'm heading back to your mom's." Cabe slapped him on the back. "See if I can't talk her into letting me grill."

"You know Dad's not going to let you."

Cabe picked his T-shirt and towel up off the sand and slipped his sandals onto his feet. "He burns the shit out of meat, Mac. You'd have thought he'd have figured it out after all these years. What kind of American man is he?"

"Says it's the Irish in him and that he can't eat meat that looks as if a good vet could resuscitate it."

"Yeah, well. I'll let your mom know you're about half an hour behind me."

Mac walked to where the three of them stood as Six reached for Lou's sunscreen, poured some into his hands and began to rub it onto her shoulders. He wondered if Delaney needed any help with hers seeing she had gotten Lou to do it when they'd first arrived at the beach.

As if by magic, Delaney reached for her tube, just as he joined them.

"Will you do my shoulders, too?" Delaney asked, just as Six's hands started to stray lower and lower, his hands slipping beneath the waistband of Lou's bikini.

"Ask Mac," Six said as he pulled Lou back against him and playfully nuzzled the side of her neck making her giggle.

Delaney looked away, a grin on her face until she caught his eye.

God, she looked good in that bikini. The way the top

hugged her breasts, holding them high and round, had set him off thinking about how much fun it would be to tug on the strings and watch it fall away. Discreetly he adjusted his shorts. When she'd first arrived at the beach and stripped off her clothes, he'd had to dive in the water, which was thankfully the wrong side of warm.

She handed him her tube of sunscreen and he took it from her. The liquid was cool as he poured it into his hands. He flipped the lid closed then rubbed his hands together, his heart pounding in anticipation of touching her smooth skin again. Skin that had always felt so good pressed naked up against his. It was soft and heated as he pressed his palms on her shoulders and began to rub the sunscreen in gently.

It would be so easy, was so tempting, to skim his fingertips down her shoulder blades, to graze the side of her breasts, but now wasn't the time, no matter how badly his dick disagreed. As he ran his fingertips along the side of her neck, she'd shivered, and for a moment she leaned into him as he pressed his fingers into her tense muscles.

"Mac," she murmured almost dreamily, then shook her head before shrugging his fingers away.

Six hauled Louisa squealing over his shoulder in a fireman's lift. "Don't say I never do anything for you, Mac," he shouted as he walked into the ocean. With a scream, Louisa hit the water, and came up fighting. It was funny watching the shy brunette try to get her revenge on his giant of a friend. He couldn't help but laugh when Six pretended that she'd landed a shot and fell back into the water.

"They both know she can't win, right?" Delaney said, a soft smile on her face as she came up next to him.

"No one can beat a SEAL in the water," he said. "It's our second home."

They stood in silence, watching their friends play.

"It's been a long time since I've been in the ocean," she whispered, almost as if to herself.

"Want to go in?" he said. He wasn't sure how'd he be able to control his reaction to her if she came any closer to him on land. Subtly, he stepped back an inch. Yeah, the bikini looked just as good from the rear as it did from the front. And, *damn*, he wanted to drop to his knees behind her, grab her ass, bite it, kiss it, pull those cheeks apart and—

"I haven't been in the water since Brock."

The words stopped his thoughts in their tracks.

The coroner had said that the head injury hadn't been what killed Brock. There had been evidence of salt water in his lungs, which meant he'd been still breathing when he'd hit the water. All because Mac hadn't got there quickly enough.

He grabbed Delaney's hand. "I'm sorry, Buttons."

Delaney didn't pull away. If anything, she gripped his hand tighter, and he interlocked their little fingers like he used to out of habit. "He's everywhere, here," she said. "There are wisps of him wherever I look." She sniffed and cleared her throat. "Cookouts, parties, early morning swims in the summer."

Looking back to when his mom had suggested the beach, he should have realized that the look that had passed across her face wasn't one of reservation. It had been fear. "We can go," he said, turning his back on the water in a feeble attempt to block it from her view. "Let's go get our things."

But she tugged on his hand as he began to lead them

back to their towels. "I think I'll regret it if I don't at least put my feet in the water that meant so much to him. To all of us." Her eyes shone with unfilled tears.

"I didn't bring you here to make you sad, Delaney." A tear escaped, and he caught it with his thumb as he cupped her cheek. "I just thought you might enjoy a little R and R, given everything else that is going on."

Delaney shook her head gently. "I know. I even thought to myself when we pulled up in the car that it might be nice to come down to the beach alone for a few minutes to . . . you know. Talk with him, I guess."

"You want to walk into that water, I'll walk with you. You want to do it alone, I'll wait right here for you. As long as you need, Delaney. I've got you. Even though you don't need me or want me to have you. I'm not going anywhere. Not today at least," he added, along with a smile that was a long way from genuine. There hadn't been the shift he'd hoped for in their relationship, and just saying those words out loud to her forced him to acknowledge that their relationship was like the sand shifting beneath his feet.

Her ponytail fell over her shoulder as she turned to look out toward the water. They stood like that for a minute. Then two. He held her hand, rubbing his thumb over her knuckles.

"Walk with me," she said finally.

He gripped her hand more firmly as they walked toward the edge of the water. Being March and the tail end of the Santa Ana winds, there was little real surf and just a whole bunch of choppy swell. As they neared the water's edge, her grip on his hand tightened. Her fear became palpable . . . like her legs were trying to carry her forward, but her heart was holding her back.

In his head, he reamed off all the stats he could tell her to reassure her that she'd be safe with him. That it didn't matter if she got into difficulty because he'd nailed the five-hundred-yard swimming when he signed up to become a SEAL, beating any other candidate by twenty-two seconds. That it didn't matter how far away from him she got because he'd nailed the two-and-a-half-mile swim of every triathlon he'd ever entered. That it didn't matter how far under she went because he could hold his breath underwater for almost seven minutes by practicing static apnea. But then he remembered that the very reason he'd been driven to learn all those things was the same reason she was terrified of the water.

Brock.

The memory of not having been quick enough in the water and the knowledge that Brock would never get to live out his dream of becoming a SEAL had fueled Mac, had driven him to achieve a level of performance that few SEALs achieved.

"You want to go a little bit farther?" he asked, their toes inches away from the water. He noticed she'd taken the bandage off her foot. It had to be aching with the walking she'd done and the time she'd spent on her feet. The cool water would help.

Delaney took a deep breath, and he let her lead the two of them into the water until it just brushed her ass. She let go of his hand and wrapped her arms around herself.

"You okay?" he asked. The water was cool, but he was used to it. He looked over at her and saw that she was shaking. Not with cold. It was too sudden, too violent. Without thinking, he stepped up behind her and wrapped his arms around her. "You're okay, Delaney," he whispered in her ear. "It's a brave thing you're doing."

A splash of wetness hit his arm, and he looked over her shoulder to see tears running down her face. "I miss him, Mac," she said. "Every single day. We did everything together. He taught me to stand on a surfboard. He let me tag along with you guys even though it irritated you all. He stood up for me when Mom was in one of her moods. I just . . ."

Mac wrapped his arms tighter around her, hoping that he could warm her up, ground her. He wanted to be whatever she needed because he wanted her back, and because it was his fault she was shivering in the water she once loved, filled with fear of it.

She placed her hands on his arms, forcing him to hold her even tighter, and he felt the jagged sobs as they reverberated through her body.

"I'm sorry, Delaney," he crooned over and over. "I'm so sorry."

They stood for a few more moments until her sobs subsided. She gently pushed his arms away and turned to face him. "I know you are, Mac. But sometimes sorry just isn't enough."

The sound of Elvis singing about being unable to help falling in love drifted down the hallway through the wide-open door of her small bachelor apartment. From where she sat on the floor by the single window in the living room, she could see just about every corner of the room, but she was happy to be in her own space—even though Mac was acting like the host of a home renovation show, first demolishing her doorframe and rebuilding her a new one, and now installing new locks on the door.

He was due to leave directly for the airport shortly, in

fact, he should have already been on his way, but he'd pushed back his flight so he could help her.

As she looked past the boxes piled around her to Mac, who was humming along to Elvis as he worked, she felt a huge amount of guilt. Yesterday had been awkward, and when she'd finally stopped crying on the beach and given her eyes thirty minutes to return to normal—because, God knew, she was one of those unfortunate ugly criers—they were late back to the barbecue. Mac's family had looked at the two of them sympathetically. She hated sympathy more than just about anything else. Mac had tried to distract them, telling his family some stupid story about a training exercise where Cabe had lost his pants. And Cabe had retaliated with a story about Mac involving a pissed-off BUD/s trainer and a day spent being sugar cookied—which she now knew meant running into the ocean fully clothed, only to run straight out and roll around the sand.

Despite his attempts to create a diversion, she still hadn't been ready when Sylvie had asked whether she should read anything into the two of them being there. Delaney had quickly and vehemently denied it, and when she'd realized that Mac had paused what he was saying to listen to her answer, her heart hurt like she'd stabbed herself in the chest. It was beginning to matter to her what Mac thought. But it *couldn't* matter. She'd never survive his permanent presence in her life.

Everybody had been so happy to see her, and for a moment, she'd allowed herself to remember what it felt like to be enveloped in a huge family filled with love. Aoife had sat next to her, begging Delaney to tell her about all the unusual places she'd visited. And Mac had been right about his mom. She'd made Delaney a cake. In a steady hand, she'd iced *Welcome Home, DELANEY* on the top. Delaney wasn't sure how to interpret it. Did she mean welcome home from Germany? Because that she could deal with. But if she meant welcome *home* . . . well, that was something else entirely.

It had been painful to realize that her decision to step away from Mac after Brock's funeral had cost her every single one of the people sitting around her in perfectly matched lawn furniture.

As the light had begun to dwindle, she'd seen Six and Lou head home, but not before Mac had hugged his friend, gripping his shoulders tightly as he said something that was obviously important. Six had looked down at the ground and then over at Lou, who had been too busy hugging Sylvie to notice. Mac had followed his gaze and said something to Six that had him standing an inch taller. Then Six had put his hand out for Lou, and she'd slid under his arm.

Something about the way Mac had watched the two of them walk up the street to their own home had her swallowing deeply. She could see the concern for his friend, who was off to a place that was volatile, and hostile, and constantly evolving. But she had also seen something else. Something she'd felt too after a day spent with the couple.

Longing.

To have what Six and Lou had found.

To not be alone.

"You okay, Delaney?" Mac said, putting the screwdriver down on one of the boxes. He'd asked her the same question on the drive home when she'd curled up against the window, not to create distance between them, but so she could fall asleep and escape the questions running around in her head. Over coffee when they'd returned home from his parents' house, he'd challenged her logic on moving out. He'd not meant to go back over the topic he'd already agreed was a good thing, but goddamn, something about the tears in her eyes on that beach had broken him. And he wanted to protect her, be there for her now more than ever. And when she'd explained that this was the only way forward, he'd insisted on helping.

"I'm fine." She repositioned her laptop on her lap and studied the map on the screen. Major drug routes from Mexico into America. Meth from Asia. Cocaine from Colombia, Venezuela, and Brazil. Something told her that if she followed the drugs, she'd find the money, and if she found the money, she'd find the weapons supplier. And she'd woken up with a sense of urgency. What if her abduction wasn't opportunistic? What if someone had betrayed her? What if trouble hadn't followed her back from Afghanistan? What if it had been in the U.S. all along?

Mac sat down on the floor next to her and looked at the screen. "If you could put a fraction more energy or enthusiasm into the *"I'm fine"* sentiment, I might be more inclined to believe you," he said.

"Yesterday took a lot out of me," she answered honestly. "All of this has. My editor doesn't want me to return to work for a week, but I need to do *something* before my brain atrophies."

"Most other people would do something like make up their bed or fill the fridge on the day they move in."

"I was just thinking the same thing," she said, finally finding the courage to look at Mac straight on. His eyes had always been intense. When she'd been younger, she'd sit in his arms and they'd just look at each other. Really see each other. Like they were doing now. She forced herself to hold his gaze.

"I probably haven't said this yet, but I'm proud of you, Delaney. What you do. How smart you are. The confidence you have. I've wondered a lot through the years about the kind of woman you'd become and—I've got to be honest—this wasn't it."

Delaney laughed. "How did you think I'd be?"

Mac rubbed his hand over his stubbled jaw. She knew he'd been up early to see Six and the team off and lock up their large warehouse building so Six had one less thing to worry about, but she couldn't argue that the scruff looked good on him.

"I don't know, you were always so . . . well, not *settled*, exactly . . . but I never got the sense of wanderlust. So, I guess I figured you'd be married, two kids, picket fence. Teacher, because you were always smart."

Delaney leaned her head back on the wall and closed her eyes. Maybe those had been her dreams once. Married, but to the man sitting next to her. Not quite a picket fence, but maybe a family home in a nice neighborhood. And probably a teacher, maybe a professor. But life had thrown her a curveball, and she'd spent the last decade trying to catch it.

"I love my work," she said, squiggling the touchpad on her laptop to bring her screen to life again so she could enter her password. "I guess there's always been too much to do. And then the election happened, and I knew there had to be a more honest approach to media. That's how I came up with the idea behind Honedia."

"It's your company?" Mac asked.

Delaney shook her head. "No. Well, not exactly. I didn't have the experience or know-how to set up a news organization. But I knew some people who could. Plus, it's a bipartisan nonprofit organization. We all agreed the truth shouldn't come with a price tag or political control—which I know sounds so obvious, but it's part of our basic tenets."

Mac leaned forward and rested his arms on his knees. "Are you a shareholder then?"

"No. While it's technically possible for a nonprofit to have shareholders, we don't. We have a board of directors, which I'm on. We have months when we barely break even because the expenses of wrestling down the truth can be huge."

"Like you out in Afghanistan?"

"Yeah. And who knows where the investigation might take us. It might spread further afield, it might have government reach if we can prove any of the illicit activity is sanctioned. So now I'm checking out known drug and gun routes to see if there are any similarities with the patterns I am looking at."

"Like this?" he said, pointing down at the boat routes. "We have a new shipping client out of Uruguay. They were telling us what they are seeing. The late-night runs, the illegally registered vessels, the piracy . . . just how bad it is. How come you're looking at this?"

"It's just a theory I have. What's the most basic thing arms dealers need?"

Mac turned slightly. "Money."

Delaney smiled. "Yep. I might have to triangulate this to make sense of it all, but if an arms dealer needs money, it's got to be gained illegally, whether through weapon sales or some other illegal business—"

"Like money laundering from the sale of drugs," Mac said excitedly. "Makes sense."

"If this dealer isn't one of the big boys, it has to be someone relatively new. Viktor Bout, allegedly one of the biggest arms dealers, is estimated to be worth billions, way more than the collective gross domestic product of Sierra Leone and Liberia, two of the countries his weapons helped destroy. Before he was sent to prison, he could have bought a giant nuclear installation made of pure platinum, if he wanted to. But *new* dealers, those without Bout's reach who are just making the connections by stealing the jobs away from the big boys, they're going to need cash. They're going to need to buy supplies up front and get cash for them after the sale."

"So if you can find the income trails to see where they lead, then overlap it with access to aviation, and flow of inventory—whether it's weapons or drugs . . ."

Delaney nodded, getting excited by the potential of the conversation as she always did. "Exactly, I can look for points of convergence."

Mac stood up and returned to the doorframe, picking up another piece of the lock. "Sounds a lot easier than it probably is though, right?"

She tried to ignore the way his T-shirt pulled tight around his bicep as he screwed whatever he had just picked up into the frame. "Yeah. But I think it might be worth doing. And it's mostly research-based, so I can rest my ankle. I would have thought it would be better after almost three weeks."

"Why don't you get it X-rayed? Check that they didn't miss something in your initial exam." He closed the door and checked that the lock closed properly.

An email notification popped up on her screen, and she clicked it out of habit. "Yeah, I might do that if it doesn't feel better after the weekend."

"You know the difference between 'concealment' and 'cover,' Delaney? If you do go out?"

Delaney shook her head. "Not really. Well, I mean probably not in the context you mean."

" 'Concealment' is hiding. Like, behind a curtain. No one can see you, but if they realized that was where you were hiding, they could easily shoot you or grab you. 'Cover' is making it impossible to get at you." He looked at her fiercely. "Remember the difference."

She nodded, understanding what he was trying to tell her. To stay safe. "When do you leave?"

Mac glanced her way. "As soon as I'm sure you've got a decent set of locks on this shit-tastic door."

For a moment, she wondered if what he was going to do was dangerous, but didn't ask, because that would lead to worrying. Or worse, caring. Instead, she glanced down at the email.

Stay the fuck out of shit that doesn't concern you. We thought you'd learned your lesson in Kunduz. Obviously not. Don't make us finish what we started.

The words brought her to an abrupt halt, as did the image. Of her. On the ground in that godforsaken house she'd been taken to. Mac was still talking, but his words became a buzz in the background. She hadn't googled herself since she'd gotten back, but she knew from her boss that there had been some news coverage. The email had come to her *Contact Me* address from the company website rather than her personal one.

Forcing herself to control her racing heart and focus, she swirled the cursor over the email address.

It was probably from a burner email that wouldn't be able to be traced, but she'd send the threat to the Honedia's tech expert anyway. In their line of investigative reporting, it wasn't unusual to find information that needed tracking and tracing. It wasn't the first time she'd been threatened, but somehow this seemed more menacing.

Her immediate reaction was to tell Mac, but he was going off on a job, and she didn't want to worry him unnecessarily when she could run it by Honedia's tech and legal teams first.

"I'm done," Mac said, closing his toolbox with a bang.

Delaney slammed the lid of her laptop. "Thank you," she said, clambering to her feet in a way that she knew looked ungainly.

"Hey, are you sure you're okay?" Mac asked, reaching for her elbow to help her. "You look a little gray."

"I'm fine," she said, brushing his arm away. "Just stood up on my ankle a little funny. Thanks for doing this." The door now looked like it could give Fort Knox a run for its money.

"Anytime." Mac looked down at his watch. "Shit, I've got to go, Delaney. Listen, you have my number if you need me."

Sadness filtered through her fear, and Delaney hated it. "You're going to be safe, right?" she asked as he unlocked all her new locks and opened the door.

Mac cupped her cheek. "Always, Buttons. I'll see you when I get back."

"I don't think that's wise," she said, but she couldn't help leaning into his palm. She needed something. Some warmth, some connection to ground her after the shock of the email, after seeing herself in that photograph.

Mac leaned in and pressed his lips to hers. "It wasn't

a question," he said as he walked down the hall. "It was a statement. And lock your doors."

Delaney leaned back on the sofa that she'd repositioned to face out of the large window and closed her eyes. Shell companies should be outlawed. Or at least limited to one or two tiers of deception.

She wasn't sure what time it was. Or when she'd last eaten a normal meal, although the extra-large bag of barbecue crinkle-cut chips she'd made her way through had filled the hole in her stomach.

It had been three days since Mac had left for his job to who knew where. If she thought about it for too long, she'd start to panic. She'd get texts from him at odd hours of the night, not that she'd see them until morning. Part of her would be frustrated that he was thinking of her in the small hours—because that was when he was on *her* mind. She didn't want to believe that it was some giant cosmic sign that they thought of each other at the same time of day. The other part of her would just be relieved he wasn't hurt.

So she'd thrown herself into her work. The net she had cast was wide. She had a bunch of feelers out, trying to work backward from the airfield. Her contact there had told her that the guy who'd brought the shipment had told him that it had been a long series of pickups. Some of the containers had come from an old warehouse on the outskirts of San Diego, and another set had been transferred from a truck outside of El Centro about twelve miles north of the Mexico border.

She'd been picking at the San Diego lead like an annoying scab. Her phone vibrated, but she ignored it. Her mom had clearly been drinking, given her earlier texts already riddled with spelling mistakes. She'd been over to visit Delaney's new place the day before, and the disappointment had been etched on her face as clearly as the spidery veins that covered her cheeks from all the alcohol she'd consumed.

It vibrated again, and as she checked her phone, she noted it was nearly time for dinner.

4 across. A society ruled by men. Moral authority and control of property exclusively in male hands. A_ _R_ _ _A_Y

Mac!

Since when do you do the crossword? And it's androcracy.

Just got off my shift. Too wired to sleep.

He'd sent her messages like this the last few days. She'd tried to keep her distance. Until now. And now she needed to know why he was wired.

Where are you? Are you safe?

There was a pause as little dots flashed at the bottom of her screen. *Washington. You worried about me, Delaney?*

Now it was her turn to delay answering. *Washington?* After she'd been worried he'd gone to a war zone or something, like Six.

The only thing likely to kill you in Washington is dying of old age trying to get anywhere in traffic.

Sorry I worried you. It's confidential but I didn't realize not telling you was an issue.

Delaney tapped the side of her phone before she responded. *I wasn't worried. But good to know you are safe.*

There was another lull, this one so long that she put

down her phone and went back to work. Investigating every shell company she found was driving her insane.

Hey. Do you remember those lilies that made you sneeze?

Did she ever. Her prom. She'd loved the corsage he'd bought her. Embarrassingly, the night had been spent with her sneezing and Mac apologizing while demanding she throw the damn thing away. But she hadn't been able to. Despite the watery eyes, she'd thought it was the most beautiful thing in the world.

I do. She didn't expand. The unexpected trip down memory lane hurt her heart. Especially when she remembered that the first time Mac had come to her house officially as her boyfriend was to ask her to the prom. For years, Brock had warned all his friends to stay away from his baby sister. He'd even tried to tell her to walk away from Mac, explaining that it wasn't that he didn't think the world of Mac, just that he wanted more for her. But that night, when Mac had officially asked her in front of her parents, Brock had finally accepted the two of them, reducing her to a puddle of tears.

You'd hate being here then. Attached was a photograph of a large, luxurious hallway with a large table. On it was a giant vase of gorgeous lilies.

It shouldn't have made her laugh, but it did. He was right, her sinuses would have exploded.

The phone rang in her hand, and she answered it. "You're right, I'm glad I'm not there," she said with a laugh.

"Well, that's charming," her mother said.

Crap. Delaney looked down at the phone. She'd fully expected it to be Mac, and now she was stuck. She stood up and wandered to the window. "Sorry, Mom. Thought you were someone else."

"Was it Mac?" There was a needle-sharp edge to her voice that reached through the phone.

"Yes Mom," Delaney said as she twirled the plastic rod that opened and closed the blinds on the window. "He fitted some new locks for me today."

"That was good of him." Reba's voice went up and down, as if she were unable to decide whether she was shocked, surprised, or angry.

"He was being overprotective."

"I'm serious, Delaney Shapiro. You remember Annelle?"

Annelle was her mom's least favorite character in *Steel Magnolias*, so if she was about to get a lecture, it wasn't going to be a good one. "Not today, Mom." It was her standard answer when her mom was drunk. Debate was futile, and her mom wouldn't remember making the call in the morning anyway.

"Listen to me. I'm your momma," Reba slurred. "Annelle arrived and was nice enough, took to the church too hard, then had to back off to become a good person."

Delaney rolled her eyes. "Spoken like a good Presbyterian."

Her mom tutted. "You know what I mean. Malachai was a good boy. Then Brock . . . I guess what I mean to say is, maybe we've all been too entrenched in our positions. And he gave you security as a gift," her mom sniffed.

Oh, God. Please don't let her start crying. Delaney couldn't deal with that. Nor could she understand her mom's analogy, but her tone told her there was progress in accepting Mac.

"So, you're happy that Mac is around? And yes, I am grateful for the new locks."

She looked over at the door that now had a reinforced frame and several new security locks, which, given the size of her tiny apartment, made the space feel even more like a prison cell. But at least she could sleep at night knowing she was secure.

"A man like that wouldn't arrange for new locks for someone he didn't care about."

Delaney stepped away from the blinds, walked to the cheap wood bookcase, and continued loading the books and papers she'd transported from Mac's but had left sitting on the floor in the three days since he'd left. "Doesn't it bother you, though, Mom? What happened to Brock? That Mac was up there on that cliff with him?"

As soon as the questions left her lips, she knew it was a mistake. As much as she'd needed to ask them, now was most definitely not the time.

Reba breathed heavily into the phone for a moment, then came the telltale clink of stemware and ice. She'd probably been drinking since lunch. "A mother isn't supposed to outlast her child, Delaney. It ain't natural." The sound of ice clinking got closer to the phone, followed by the slosh of liquid. "I don't know what happened on that cliff, and I'll never know for sure. But the coroner *did* record an accidental death verdict, and from what I heard, Mac has gone on and done very honorable things." Her mother sniffed again, followed by more ice-cube sloshing. "Maybe it's time for us to heal."

"Okay, I gotta go, Mom. Let's do lunch one day this week if you feel like it." *If you can stay sober long enough.*

"I'd love that. I think I may get Brock's baby book out

and flick through it," she said quietly, then hung up with a click.

No goodbye. Delaney wondered whether she should go over and spend the night even though she didn't want to. Drinking and Brock usually sent her mom into melodramatic tailspins, and she sometimes woke up on the floor. Alone and confused, occasionally injured.

But Delaney wanted to be *here*, in her new home. And she wasn't going to judge herself for it. For a decade, she'd done her best to pick up the pieces of her mother and had sat through countless verbal tirades when the viscous, angry drunk came out after the mournful, pitiful drunk had had its say. And it had taken years of therapy to sort through it all. Enabling her mom's drinking wasn't in anyone's best interest.

Delaney wandered to her kitchen and rummaged around in the fridge for a stir-fry. She set some frozen edamame to thaw under running cold water before carefully chopping some peppers and onions. Thank heavens for grocery delivery. She had everything she needed to last a few days. Even though her ankle was finally beginning to feel better, she doubted it was up to an expedition to the grocery store.

A loud knock at her door made her jump, sending the knife clattering over the small counter. Nobody had her address except Mac and a guy Mac had sent over named Ghost who'd shown up that morning with new smoke detectors. Maybe it was one of her new neighbors? After all, nobody had buzzed from downstairs to be let in.

Quietly, she went to the door and looked through the peephole. In the dim light of the hallway, she could see a man in a brown delivery uniform wearing a ball cap that said Lucy's Floral on it and holding a huge bouquet of beautiful purple and white flowers. Her first thought was that it was from Mac. But then she saw it contained lilies, just like the ones they'd been laughing about earlier that always made her sneeze.

"Who is it?" she shouted, though she could see him.

"Flower delivery for Delaney Shapiro," the man said, his face hidden from view, but his body language relaxed. The cap made her think of the man who'd followed her, but in the half-light it was hard to be sure.

CHAPTER SIX

"Ma, I'm telling you. Me and Delaney. We aren't a couple." Mac picked at the last of his fries from the Four Seasons Hotel room service menu, dipping them in ketchup before taking a bite. He felt like he was fifteen again, and he had no interest whatsoever in discussing his love life with his mother.

"I know, Malachai, but you two . . . well, you have a history. And it might be healing for the two of you to spend some time together."

He couldn't bring himself to tell her to leave it alone, though, because Delaney and Brock had meant something to all of them. His mom had considered them extended family. Plus, everything about him and Delaney was muddled in his head. He'd thought the two of them spending time together might rip the Band-Aid off, but after the day on the beach, he was beginning to wonder if he wasn't just picking at a scab.

Mac looked around the double room he shared with Ryder who, along with Sherlock, was currently out with their client exploring the monuments of Washington's

National Mall. For a second, he let his mind wander to taking Delaney away to a luxury hotel like this. Bring her somewhere that wasn't so tightly wrapped up in memories. It might do them both good to simply reconnect as Mac and Delaney, as adults. Create new memories that weren't tainted by—no, that wasn't right—weren't so connected to the past. Or just find out once and for all what might be left of the two of them.

"I know, Mom. But this runs deep for Delaney. It's . . ." *Shit*. What was it? Two steps forward, one step back. "Complicated."

He grinned, remembering putting sunscreen on her back at the beach. The way her skin had felt just as soft and smooth as it used to. It had been the gentlemanly thing for Mac to do, taking the lotion from her and rubbing it in, even if it had taken Six to orchestrate it. And so what if he'd gotten a kick out of the way she'd shivered as he'd gently ran his fingers along the back of her neck? He'd gotten turned on when she'd sighed and moaned his name as he dug his fingers into her tense shoulders. It was so close to the way she'd used to say it when they'd made love. When she'd moved beneath him and fallen apart in his arms. And goddamn, as much as it had turned him on, it had hurt. An audible reminder of what he'd lost.

"I'm sure it is for both of you, Malachai. It was an awful period in your lives. But it made you the man you are today, and I am very proud of you. I care about Delaney, but never more than I love you."

Words stuck in the back of his throat. His mom said she loved him every day, and somehow, even though he was across the country, he could feel the warmth of her words.

"Thanks, Ma. Love you, too. Look, I gotta go. I'll call you tomorrow."

And he would because he'd spent so much time away from her, worrying her to death—although she'd never said a word—when he was in theatre, doing what he had to do. He owed it to her to spare a couple of minutes out of his day just to see how she was doing, even if all he had the time for was a quick text or one of those ridiculous selfies she'd begun to demand . . . something about needing to see he was in one piece while he was on a tour.

Mac pushed away from the table and walked into the shower. It was early evening, and he'd been awake ninety minutes. He'd gone for a run through the city, the change in temperature from San Diego noticeable, but as always he'd been prepared for every temperature combination. Just because he'd trained in freezing weather didn't mean he liked it. Unlike Ryder, who woke late in the afternoon for night shift craving breakfast, he'd craved a burger, fries, and a side of onion rings. It would have tasted a whole lot better with an ice-cold beer, but he'd never drunk on duty. Ever.

Night shift on security detail was the most insanely boring one. Especially when the people being protected had young children. Everyone was locked down tight nice and early, meaning the hours dragged. He almost envied Sherlock and Ryder their daytime shifts.

He wandered into the bathroom and turned on the shower, waiting for a moment for it to become hot. When he stepped inside, he let the water pound down on his head, which was foggy, even after getting outside for a while. He'd buried his feelings for Delaney so long that he'd managed to convince himself that he'd find a girl who wasn't Delaney and settle down. But seeing her

again had shattered that illusion. Seeing her had reminded him that while he'd dated some great women,
they had been muted when compared to Delaney. No, if
he'd settled, he'd only end up resenting any situation that
didn't include Delaney.

Plus, he had a secret. Something he hadn't told the rest
of the guys. He wanted kids. Not in an abstract at-some-
point-I'll-have-them kind of way. But in a real wake-up-
tomorrow-to-a-home-with-kids-in-it way. He'd put it off
for his career, and he'd put it off to start Eagle, but he didn't
want to wait too much longer. Being around his client's
family the last few days had only reinforced that.

By the time he'd finished up in the shower and gotten
dressed, he'd managed to stop his thoughts from racing.
He headed up to his client's rooms and began his final
walk around the Royal Suite, one of the largest and most
expensive in the hotel, before Sherlock and Ryder brought
their client and his family up to the room—though
"room" was too weak a word for the huge space. It was
almost bigger than Lochlan's apartment, certainly more
luxurious, and according to the website, cost nearly
twenty grand a night. The suite's entrance hall had been
converted into a temporary security office, with monitors connected to external cameras showing the deserted
hallway. He would spend the next ten hours in that office once his client returned. The vase of lilies he'd photographed to send to Delaney taunted him. She'd barely
responded after he'd sent it, leaving him kicking himself
for having dragged them both back into the past. What
he really needed to be doing was pulling them into the
future. But now wasn't the time to think about any of that.
He was on duty, and he needed to put everything else out
of his mind.

Thankfully, his job was made marginally easier by the hotel, which had invested in bulletproof glass in all windows. He checked the library and noted that his client's personal staff had already gotten the fire going. Fifty degrees was warm for Washington in March, but compared to the over one-hundred-degree heat his clients had left behind in Riyadh, it probably felt like an icebox.

He stepped out onto the balcony and looked out over Georgetown's M Street. An entourage of black limos was turning toward the hotel. It would take seven more minutes to get everyone out of the vehicles, through the elevator, and up to the room. Mac stepped back inside and locked the balcony doors. Quickly, he made his way through the formal living room and media room, checking for any sign of disturbance. The previous night, before Mac had been due to take over from Ryder, their client, Mr. Abboud, had asked Mac to put him through a *special ops* workout in the personal fitness center because, in his client's words, he "was at that level of fitness." Mac had obliged because he'd felt like a workout, but he'd taken great pleasure in kicking the guy's ass, leaving him to crawl away to shower while pretending he was fine. It had made his day when the client had walked stiffly that morning. But he'd also thought about Delaney. About the way she'd looked at him at the beach when she thought he wasn't looking, those eyes of hers taking in his abs. Appreciative eyes were great motivation to bust a gut through his workout.

Some of their military friends had found their way into the bodyguard business, but he couldn't imagine anything less interesting. A couple of others had landed roles on the Discovery Channel. Great shows, but he had no aspirations to fame. He knew that deep down inside he was still chasing Brock's dream of being the ultimate SEAL, the ultimate warrior. At some point, he was going to have to think about his own life and what he wanted out of it. Not the work with Eagle, because he loved that. But more broadly.

Like a wife. And kids. The door opened and his client, his wife, and their two young children entered the suite.

"Mac, Mac, Mac." Rahila, a little seven-year-old girl with dense brown curls and wide brown eyes ran toward him. They had written protocols for this. They needed to be friendly, but not so friendly that it was difficult to do their jobs. But she'd wrapped him around her little finger by asking if he could sit in the back of the limo with her and by drawing a picture of him that he'd taped to his security desk.

"Hello, Rahila," he said, doing his best to respect their positions. With any other little girl, he would have probably tousled those curls or gotten down to eye level to say hi. But this was his client's daughter, and he wanted to remain professional.

She wrapped her arms around his leg as her father came to shake hands. "I apologize, Mac," he said. "Her friendliness knows no bounds." He muttered some words to his wife, who grabbed the little girl and took her away into the bedroom.

"We'll dine in our room tonight," the client said as he followed his family into the room before closing the door.

And Mac envied him that simple luxury. Being able to close the door to the rest of the world and having his family safely with him inside.

Delaney looked at the chain that Mac had installed. She could crack open the door to talk to the guy, but if he was legitimate, he'd never be able to get the bouquet through the gap.

"How did you get in the building?" she asked.

"One of your neighbors kindly held the door," he replied.

Not comfortable opening the door, she said, "Just leave them outside the door, thank you." She could wait until he was down the hall, preferably in the elevator or out of sight in the stairwell, and then unlock the seventeen hundred new locks and grab them, taking them straight to the garbage in the hope of avoiding a coughing fit.

"Sorry, Miss Shapiro, but I need a signature for them."

Damn. Was that normal? She tried to think back to the last time she'd been sent flowers, and she was pretty certain she hadn't been asked to sign. "One second."

Her spidey senses had been messed up since Kunduz. She'd been seeing things everywhere that she shouldn't have read into but had. But this felt wrong.

"Do you have any I.D.?" she asked to kill time while she grabbed her phone.

"Normally don't need any, ma'am." He sounded almost amused by her question. He probably thought she was some eccentric recluse. "Usually the flowers say it all."

Quickly, she googled Lucy's Floral and found it to be a real shop on Fourth by the Hard Rock. It could all be stupid paranoia on top of coincidence, but something in her gut niggled. And if she refused to accept the delivery, what was the worst that could happen? The bouquet would be returned to the shop, and she could take a cab to retrieve it tomorrow and apologize for her overreaction.

She dialed their number as she continued to watch through the peephole.

"Miss, I have a few other deliveries to make today, and I'm already behind," the man shouted, while keeping the brim of his cap down.

"Hello, Lucy's Floral, how can I help you today?" The woman sounded tired. Delaney glanced at the clock. After six. Wouldn't the store be closing soon? And why would someone be delivering so late?

Delaney stepped away from the door and covered the mouthpiece of her phone. "I might be being over-cautious, but there is a man in a brown uniform saying he is delivering from Lucy's Floral. Could you confirm he is who he says he is, please?"

She took a step back toward the door, and jumped when the man knocked loudly a second time. "Miss, please." His tone was frustrated. "I'm gonna have to go if you don't answer."

"That's odd," the woman said. "I thought all the deliveries had been done for the day, but I only work late afternoons until closing. What is your name?"

"Delaney Shapiro."

A neighbor down the hall opened his door and shouted something in the delivery man's direction that she couldn't make out. As the delivery guy began to turn to look in the neighbor's direction, everything fell into a weird kind of slow motion.

At the same time she heard the woman on the end of the line confirm that they had no delivery scheduled for her that day, or any day in the coming week, the delivery guy lifted his chin to address the neighbor.

It was him.

The man she'd seen in the car. The man who had followed her to Mac's apartment.

Her heart slammed to a stop in her chest and she gasped. As if hearing her through the metal door, he looked straight at the spy hole she was looking through. Stumbling backward, she reached for the wall.

She should have let Mac do what he did best. Let him figure out if what she'd seen earlier had been a real issue or not. She should have stayed at his place. Her palms began to sweat, and her heart crashed to life again. She refused to be abducted again—or worse. What would Mac do?

"Hello. Miss, are you okay?" she heard the woman on the other end of the line say.

She was trapped in this tiny box of an apartment. *Think, Delaney, think.* With shaking fingers, she hung up the phone.

The handle on the door turned a half turn so slowly she wouldn't have noticed if she hadn't been staring at the door intently. He was trying to get inside.

The locks would hold him for a while. There were so many of them thanks to Mac.

Delaney quickly dialed three numbers.

"Nine one one. What's your emergency?"

Oh God. This was really happening.

"Police." Her voice broke as she said the word, and she forced herself to continue. "A man . . . he's trying to break into my apartment. He's been following me for a—"

"Can you confirm your address ma'am?"

Delaney attempted to stay calm despite feeling like she was going to vomit and rattled off the address and apartment number. She focused on the doorknob so hard that she no longer could determine if it was moving or not.

The sound of a gunshot ricocheted through the hallway and she screamed. She dropped to the floor and crawled toward the kitchen to hide behind the small counter. All she could do was pray it hadn't been aimed at her neighbor. It felt cowardly to hide but she didn't know how she'd be able to help. From her spot on the floor, she peered around the counter to look at the door.

The door handle turned again, and the knob on the inside fell to the floor. *Oh, God.* He was coming for her.

"Ma'am, are you okay? Was that a gunshot?"

"Yes. Yes. Please. Send someone quickly. Malachai MacCarrick has the details of the guy who was following me if anything happens to me. He runs Eagle Securities, he's . . ."

The door rattled as he shook it, and blood rushed to her head, making her vision spin. Keeping the police on the line, she looked around her room. All she could do was delay him getting to her. Give the police time to get to her. Hopefully her neighbors were calling too. The advice Mac had given her before he left about concealment and cover suddenly made sense. She needed to be out of the way of the door. She looked up at the knife block in the kitchen and stood, grabbing the one from there and another from the drawer. More bullets hit the door, leaving rounded dents in the metal. She ran to the bedroom and slammed the door shut before pressing her shoulder up against the dresser to slide it in front of the doorframe.

Quickly, she dropped to the floor on her belly, backing up into the space beneath the bed. She'd thought about hiding in the bathroom, but if the guy could find his way through a triple-locked metal door, the flimsy lock on the wooden bathroom door would offer no protection.

From the loud thuds coming from the corridor, it sounded like the stalker was throwing himself bodily at the door. From under the bed, she could stab at his hands if he reached for her to take her alive. If he wanted her dead, well, there wasn't a single spot in her apartment that would keep her safe from that.

Silence settled in for a few moments, and at first, she wondered if he was gone. Her heart beat loudly in the quiet. Was he through the door yet? Tears pricked the corners of her eyes as she watched for signs of the dresser moving and pressed herself bodily against the wall.

"Ma'am. Ma'am," the dispatcher called.

Clumsily, she pulled the phone back to her ear. "Yes, I'm here," she whispered.

"Police have been dispatched. I should have someone with you in three minutes. Is the intruder in the apartment?"

"I'm not sure. It's gone quiet. I just had a new frame and locks fitted this morning. The door is metal. He seems to have—" Gunfire resumed outside the door. Had he been simply reloading? "Shit. No. He's still trying to get in. He's dressed in a Lucy's Floral uniform."

"Stay calm. Are there weapons on the premises? Where are you?" The dispatcher was calm, and it helped her focus, catch her breath.

"He has a gun. I'm under the bed, no guns, but I did grab two cooking knives from the kitchen."

"If there is no other exit from your apartment, stay there. The police car is very close now."

Silence filled the hallway again, but Delaney put little

faith in it. Time passed slowly. The hammering on the door began again.

"The police are a minute away."

A minute away. Sixty, fifty-nine, fifty-eight.

The dispatcher kept asking questions, nonsensical ones that seemed repetitive. No, she couldn't see what he was doing. No, she didn't know how many weapons he had. No, she didn't know why he was trying to break in, other than the fact that she'd seen him following her a couple of times. Yes, she was alone. Yes, the front door was the only exit. Yes, those were more gunshots.

Time dragged by. The rest of her life hinged on the duration of that minute. She prayed for it to pass quickly.

"The officers are in the building. Stay where you are, ma'am, until I tell you otherwise."

The count of sixty passed. As did another sixty. Her reporting experience told her they were setting up to secure the building and then make their way up to her without getting shot themselves. But despite the pep talk she tried to give herself, she was about to fall apart.

There was a knock at her front door, and her entire body froze.

"Ma'am. It's okay to answer the door," the dispatcher said.

Delaney crawled out from under the bed, knives in hand. "What if it's not them?" she asked, her voice catching at the end. "Can you get them to say something to me, to identify themselves?"

"Ma'am," a voice came from outside. "We've been instructed to identify ourselves."

It was all the proof Delaney needed before she sprinted to the door. When she looked through the peephole and saw two men in police uniforms, she burst into tears.

Then she placed the knives down on the hallway table before opening the door.

Mac stretched his arms above his head, then leaned to the left and right feeling his neck crack in relief. His night shift was almost over, and within the hour, Ryder and Sherlock would be back for their handover debriefing in the hallway. With the doors closed to the suite and the door closed to the hotel corridor, there was no natural light, making it feel like a bit of a time warp. Mac was glad the job was nearly over. It had paid well, and the conditions were luxurious to say the least. But there was no adventure to it.

Overnight, he'd been reviewing their hiring plans and the performance so far of the guys already on board. He liked his team. Lazily, they'd avoided team names and just numbered them. Six led Team One with Buddha, Gaz, and newbie Jackson—a former SEAL who spoke both Arabic and Kurdish, perfect for what they were doing in Syria. Cabe led Team Three, with Lite, Bailey—a former DEVGRU intelligence specialist with balls of steel—and new member Harley, a former SEAL from one of Cabe's old teams. Which left him with Team Two, Sherlock, Ryder, and another newbie, Ghost.

The current job hadn't needed Ghost, so he was back in the office holding down the fort, for which Mac was hugely grateful. None of them liked paperwork, or inventories, or anything mundane, so he was quite happy to dump it all on the newbie. When he'd first joined the Navy, the older guys had hazed the shit out of him. Now that he was older, he thought death by paperwork was worse than any of the shit that had been pulled on him when he was younger.

He'd also texted Delaney who hadn't responded to a single message. The last one he'd gotten a reply to had been the image of the lilies. As soon as he'd seen them, he'd thought of her. Of his prom. He'd always thought of that night as their first night as an official couple. It was the first night Brock had relaxed about the whole thing, even though he'd threatened to beat the crap out of Mac if he so much as breathed a word about what he did with Delaney to the rest of the guys. Not that Mac had ever intended to disrespect Delaney that way. The things they did when they were together were private.

Like the way her hair had fallen in soft waves as he removed all the pins from the updo the hairdressers had taken an hour to do. He'd spent an age lying on her bed that night after he'd crept in through her window, just running his fingers through it. Delaney always joked she'd made him wait for sex, but the truth was he'd known she was worth waiting for. Because the way those lips of hers had felt against his that night was magic. And he hadn't been thinking about what would happen in the next hour or, or day, or week with her. He'd been thinking about forever at the tender age of eighteen.

Which got him to thinking. How on earth was he supposed to rebuild something with her if he wasn't around to spend time with her? A relationship by text would do for now, but not for the long term.

She could ignore his messages, but she couldn't ignore him solidly planted in her life in person. Would she turn him away if he showed up at her door with her favorite bagels and light cream cheese one morning for breakfast? Could she ignore him if he turned up one night with a copy of *The Thomas Crown Affair*—her favorite movie—popcorn, and a red Zinfandel? Hell, he wasn't beyond dragging his mom into it, asking Delaney to come over and spend time with his family.

No. Text messages were never going to cut it. He needed to be there in person.

The knock on the suite door jolted him from his thoughts, and he checked the cameras. Breakfast delivery by the looks of things. He opened the door, checked the food cart, checked the server, watched the delivery into the room . . . and then watched server leave.

He envied Cabe, who was in Colorado doing intel on a cult for a wealthy family from North Carolina who believed their daughter had been brainwashed. Way more interesting. Cabe had decided that if the job was over quickly, he was going to go ski for a couple of days. *Lucky bastard.*

Mac put in his earpiece and mic and connected with Cabe. "How goes it?" he asked when Cabe's face finally filled the screen.

Cabe was sitting in a large vehicle drinking a take-out cup of coffee, night vision goggles still perched on his head. He turned the phone to face out of the window of the moving truck. Mac could see nothing but darkness. "Going well. Although I am seriously fed up with this idiot's company," he said with a laugh, turning the camera toward Bailey, who was driving.

Bailey flipped the bird. "Asshole."

Mac laughed.

"We got the drones airborne so we could see what's going on inside their compound," Cabe said. "Spoke to local police who aren't being too helpful. They say these guys are nut jobs, but harmless. Our visual says they are armed, but amateur. I'm thinking of dropping a message in via drone tomorrow. Ask if she really wants to be there. If not, gonna ask her to send us something simple back with the drone. A pebble or something she can readily get her hands on. Something that will give us a clue as to whether we should go in and get her."

"Yeah, no point risking your neck if she doesn't want to leave," Mac said, although brainwashing in this kind of situation was real.

"I'm still trying to figure out how we fully determine that. Looks like a sweet young thing. Impressionable. I'm not sure that even if she says she doesn't want to be rescued, she means it. Depending on what she does, I'm tempted to go get her out of there anyway. She can always go back if she really wants to. Should be a straightforward in and out to retrieve her. Their attempt at security is three guys sitting together huddled around a tin can fire. We'd be on them in no time. We'll see.

"Listen, I got a call from Noah just before we connected." Normally a call from Noah, Cabe's brother and a detective in the major case squad, wouldn't have been a big deal, but there was something about Cabe's tone that told Mac he wasn't going to like what followed.

"And . . ." Mac wasn't in the mood for show-and-tell games.

"Someone tried to get into Delaney's apartment last night. Forensics just left," Cabe said, bluntly.

Mac stood, a cold chill slithering down his spine, and began to pace the entrance hall. "Describe *'tried.'* Is she okay?"

"Dude, stop pacing. You're making me dizzy with the video. Yes. She's fine. Should have started with that. And, yeah, *'tried'* as in seven bullet holes in her door."

What the fuck? Trouble had clearly followed her home. His chest tightened at the thought of how terrified she must have been. How close somebody had gotten to her. *How did they know where she lived?* They must have been following her. "I need to get home," he snapped.

"You know you can't, bro. You got a job and don't have enough backup to do that job right for another forty-eight hours. And did you hear the part where I said she's fine?"

"Then let's get Ghost out here. He can take the third spot on the team, Sherlock can take lead, and I'll—"

"Can it, Mac. I looked before you called. Even if Ghost got the first flight out to you in the morning, it's going to be late afternoon before he arrives. You might make it to the airport to catch a flight back that night, but you'll get in during the early hours. And Ghost can't go from a full day of travel straight onto a shift."

"We're SEALs. Of course he can." They'd survived on zero sleep during Hell Week, and on many occasions since.

"Fine. Well, he kinda could, but we all know security requires you to be alert. And. She's. Fine."

Mac looked around the stupid hallway for something to hit. He should have listened to his gut, should have followed up with his friend at the hotel sooner to get a picture on the guy who'd been following her. He'd screwed up, but he wasn't going to do it again. "I get it. This is the job, whether we like it or not. No matter how badly I want to, I can't leave. So, I'll call Ghost, get him over to her place and—"

"Already done. First call I made." Cabe looked at his watch. "He's probably there already."

"*Fuck*," he cursed. Even though he couldn't leave and go to her, there were still things he could do. "I gotta go."

"Figured as much. Let me know what I can do, man."
Cabe's face disappeared.

Mac grabbed the radio. "Sherlock, you awake?"

The radio crackled. "Yeah. What's up?"

"I need you to cover me for an hour."

CHAPTER SEVEN

"Pack a bag. Ghost is going to take you back to my place," Mac said. His voice was calm, his tone cool, yet Delaney could tell he was pissed. He'd held his tongue until she'd relayed the whole story.

Even she couldn't believe what had happened in the last twelve hours. And despite the way the dents in her door where bullets had hit but not penetrated, she didn't want to leave.

All her books, her research, her notes, were in this room. If she was going to figure out what was going on, who exactly had put her in their crosshairs, the information would be in there somewhere. It had to be. Somehow, someone she had spoken to somewhere along the way had gotten back to the people she'd been asking about, which was why trouble had followed her back home. There was no other explanation. She needed to follow the leads and see where she ended up.

"I can't go anywhere without all my research," she said, looking at the bankers boxes she hadn't even finished emptying yet. The shelves were full of the stuff she'd already unpacked.

"I don't give a shit about all that, seeing the guy is still out there," Mac said. "Step one is getting you safe. We can get the rest of your stuff later once you are secure."

She wanted to tell Mac she didn't need his help. That she wasn't his responsibility. Even though she'd said it a thousand times already. Even though he had ignored her at every turn. But what had happened to her the previous evening had shaken her. Her assailant had managed to evade capture by using the hallway emergency exit that led to the ground floor where he had forced his way into an apartment and escaped through a window on the side of the building. The police had secured her apartment and forced her to leave while the forensic team did its thing—collecting bullets, and a door handle that had been blown apart.

It had been the early hours of the morning when the police had finished their forensic work and roused her from where she'd dozed on her neighbor's couch. Mrs. Sandusky, an elderly lady, had taken pity on Delaney after seeing her sitting on the floor in the drafty hallway. When Delaney had finally closed and locked the door on all the visitors, she'd counted seven dimples in it where the shots had been fired.

While she wanted to put some distance back between her and Mac and didn't want him to think of her as the wounded heroine, she realized that until she knew what she was up against, she was better off with Mac than without him.

"I'll go, Mac. But promise my stuff will follow? I can't help but think that the answer to this is in my research."

Mac sighed. "Fine. I'll find some guys I can trust to meet you at my place, get your keys, and go get your stuff. Box up what you need up and leave it in the hall, but make it the essentials only. Then you are out!"

Urgency crept into his voice, and fear filled her. She was pretty certain that they didn't hand out a Silver Star complete with a vague, non-description as to how it was earned, to a SEAL who didn't stay composed under pressure.

"Thank you, Mac," she said, and meant it sincerely.

There was a slight pause on the other end. "You're welcome, Buttons," he said.

"No. I mean it. I'm . . ." Damn. She couldn't think of the right words.

"It's okay, Delaney. Let's just get you safe. I'll get the doorman to let you into my place. I'll give him a call to let him know you are on your way. Stay close to Ghost, sweetheart, please."

"I will. I promise."

She heard Mac curse under his breath. "Okay. Call me when you are locked in at my place. Let me speak to Ghost."

Delaney smiled. "That's not his real name, is it?" she asked as she tugged her suitcase from under her bed.

"No. It's Gjosta. Swedish, even though he's a third-generation American. But nobody can ever be bothered to pronounce it correctly."

"Well, I'm going to try," she said, stepping over the case and walking the phone to the tall athletic man with shaggy blond hair currently looking through her peephole. "Stay safe, Mac."

She handed the phone to Ghost. "He wants to speak to you," she said before heading back to the bedroom to pack.

Ghost's voice traveled only so far. She couldn't decipher his mumbled words. Not knowing how long she would be at Mac's, and having finally gotten her clothes from her mother's storage locker, she filled the suitcase and planned to leave it with the boxes she intended to pack in a moment. In a smaller overnight bag, she packed a couple of outfits, some underwear, pajamas, and toiletries.

Delaney dragged the suitcase and bag into the hall and began to grab the boxes with the files she was going to need.

"Confirmed . . . yeah. You too." Ghost ended the call and handed Delaney her phone. "You doing okay?" he asked, grabbing a bankers box and placing it in the hall.

Delaney nodded. Cold had seeped through her bones since the moment she'd realized just who had been standing outside her door, but suddenly she felt the sting of heat flowing through her veins. While she wanted to attribute it to doing something positive, moving somewhere safe, going through her files, taking positive steps, she'd be lying if she didn't admit that a large part of it was about Mac, and feeling . . . what? Being taken care of?

Staying focused on the task at hand was impossible while thoughts of Mac filled her head, and she shook it to clear them. Getting to the apartment was most important. When the last of the boxes were stacked, they prepared to leave.

"Keep close," Ghost instructed as he reached into the waistband of his pants and pulled out a gun. She had no idea what kind it was, being unfamiliar with how to operate the weapon, but he slid something back and looked the gun over.

"I thought concealed carry wasn't allowed in San

Diego," she said, more to lighten the mood than any-thing. Her stomach was clenched so tight she felt nause-ated.

"There's going to be nothing concealed about this carry, plus I'm friends with the sheriff. My truck's at the curb. I want you to stay in the lobby while I check out-side. Then I'll come get you. You're going to climb over to your seat, and I'm going to follow you in. Then you're going to stay down. Clear?"

"Like crystal," she said. Her palms were damp, and she wiped them on her jeans before lifting her bag onto her shoulder.

"Normally, I'd offer to get that for you, but . . ." He let the words trail off as he held the gun in the air.

"I'm fine. I got this," she blurted, more to calm her-self than to reassure him.

Ghost checked the peephole one last time and then si-lently opened the door to her apartment. He slipped into the hallway, gun in both hands as he looked over the stairwell.

Per his instructions, she closed and locked her door, then stayed on Ghost like he was her second skin. They made their way down the steps, Ghost with his gun raised, all the way to the lobby. Thankfully they didn't pass anyone. Ghost pressed his back against the glass doors to the building and looked over his shoulder onto the street.

"Wait," he reminded her. He pulled his keys from his pocket, and the lights flashed on a beat-up truck. Silently, he slipped out onto the street, looking left and right, and opened the driver's side door. Just as quickly, he stepped back inside for her. "Ready?"

She wasn't. Chances were that she never would be. It

was highly probable that she was going to puke any minute, but she nodded anyway.

"Throw the bag in, then climb over it fast. Let's go."

With the possibility of her life on the line, Delaney did exactly what he said. She wiggled over to the passenger side, fastened her seat belt, and placed her head in the brace position she often saw on in-flight safety cards. The truck roared to life, and Ghost navigated their way through the city. Familiar with the roads, she knew he wasn't taking the quickest route.

"Is somebody following?" she asked, glancing up at him from her tucked position.

His eyes flitted from the windshield to the rearview. "Not that I can see. I'm just being cautious."

She gasped when Ghost applied the brakes harshly, her nerves shot to hell. Relief flooded her when she saw that they were in front of Mac's apartment. A security guard hurried to the doors and unlocked them to let them in quickly. The doorman met them as Mac had promised and ushered them into an elevator that had been held for them.

It wasn't until the door to the apartment clicked shut, and she heard Ghost slide the locks into place that she allowed herself to breathe. It was dark, so she reached for the light switch.

"No lights," he said, placing his hand over hers. "And don't go anywhere near the windows," Ghost said. "Until we know who we are dealing with, it's best to assume the worst."

She watched Ghost stay in the shadows as he closed the drapes.

With the curtains closed, Ghost turned on a lamp and dimmed the setting.

The light gave her little comfort as she placed her bag on the floor and sat down on the sofa. She wished Mac was here. Hell, she wished Cabe and Six were with him. All these years she'd done just fine without them, but now their presence felt vital to her survival. It wasn't that she didn't trust Ghost. It was just that . . . well, she didn't know him, and right now, she didn't know who she could trust. Her breathing shallow, Delaney tried to force herself to relax as Ghost disappeared down the hallway—to close the curtains, she assumed.

Her phone rang, making her jump. *Mac.* "Hey," she said, answering it quickly. "We're at your place."

"Good. Any problem getting there?" He sounded calmer now, which helped. His tone was normal, like he was asking her what she'd like for dinner instead of whether the man who had tried to shoot down her door had reappeared.

"No. Ghost just closed everything up." She looked down the hall, keeping an eye out for Ghost. "What should I do, Mac? I can't just sit here and wait until you ride back into town on your white charger. And even when you do . . . then what?" For all she'd been trying to convince herself to be calm, she finally acknowledged the underlying feeling of sheer panic that had her standing up and stepping to the counter to pick up a sealed bottle. "And can I open this Jack on the counter?"

"Use whatever you need," Mac replied. "Just don't get any urges to go drunk skinny-dipping like you did that last year up at the lake."

The last summer they'd all gone camping, before Brock had died, was the first time she'd tried Jack Daniel's. The sting of the memory was there, but for once it didn't hurt quite as much. All the thinking she'd been forced to do about Brock recently was making things easier rather than harder. "I wasn't the only one. And I seem to recall you started it." Delaney was grateful he couldn't see the heat she could feel rising in her cheeks.

"I did. I just didn't expect you to follow me in, is all."

His comment hung between them as she remembered what had happened once she'd joined him. Out of sight of their friends, in the darkness, they'd pleasured each other while lamenting the lack of a condom.

"I'm sorry, Delaney. I didn't mean to—"

"It's okay, Mac. I guess we should focus on what happens next . . . now. Not then."

Mac coughed gruffly. "I have a friend of mine trying to run the face of the guy from the street, but there isn't a clean shot of him. I'll see if I can get any information from Noah about whether he was spotted on the street coming to your place. He's obviously experienced at evading cameras. The plate he was using came up as a fake. We need to assume that whoever is after you knows their shit. Sit tight until I get home, okay? Cabe might get there first. And I got a few of the guys lined up to get your stuff. Give Ghost the key. He'll make sure they get it. And he's gonna stay, so you need to move into my room and let him have the spare."

Delaney shook her head. His bed. It would be too much. "Mac, I can't. I—"

"Just being pragmatic, Delaney. It's farther down the hallway, so anybody would have to get past Ghost to get to you. And it has a bathroom that you could lock yourself in if you needed to."

Of course he was being sensible. And she was being difficult. "I'm sorry."

There was a pause at the end of the line. "We'll figure this out, Delaney. I promise you. I'll keep you safe."

Mac leaned back in the plush ivory leather seat of the private aircraft that had just stopped off in Colorado to pick up Cabe and his team. He rested his ankle on his knee and his elbow on the armrest next to the window, watching the miles pass beneath them.

It had been Lochlan's idea to hire the jet. When Mac's brother had heard what had happened to Delaney, he'd offered to get Mac out of Washington as soon as Mac's clients had left D.C. that evening on their private jet home to Riyadh. Rather than have Mac and his crew wait for the first available commercial flight in the morning, Lochlan had arranged for a private jet to be ready to get them back to the west coast. Lochlan had sounded amazed that Mac had let him pay, given that Mac had stood hard and firm about not taking money from his brother for any reason, including starting up Eagle Securities. He wanted to be a self-made man, or die trying. But this had been different. This was Delaney.

Cabe had just debriefed him on the rescue job, and while they'd committed to working through what they learned from every job they did so they'd keep improving, be better prepared, and figure out whether their cost estimations were any good, he really wasn't in the right frame of mind to do it.

Further down the aisle, Lite was reliving the rescue. The young woman had wanted to be saved, and it had been an easy matter to find a weakness in the cult's boundary to creep in under cover of darkness and extract her. No shots had been fired.

They'd reconfigured the flight plan to collect them en route. It was logical, cost effective. Everything about the decision made sense. Except it kept him away from Delaney for a little while longer than he'd hoped. Being away from her was something that had fermented in his gut since the moment he'd listened to her explain, with hitches in her voice, what had happened.

He looked down at his watch. She'd been shot at on Sunday, and he'd found out on Monday. Now it was the small hours of Tuesday heading into Wednesday. Even with Cabe's brother, Noah, ensuring that Delaney's case was getting the right kind of priority, they weren't getting any leads. The marking on the shells and bullets that had been recovered hadn't matched anything on file. The security cameras in Delaney's apartment building had turned out to be fakes, a ploy by the owner to convince tenants the place was safe. And there was no CCTV, traffic camera, or anything else of use aimed at the front of Delaney's apartment. Dead end after dead end.

He looked at Cabe, who was seated across from him in almost the identical position. Alert. Anxious. Thoughts already on what was to happen when they got home. Mac and his team were going to relieve Ghost, who had been Delaney's security guard for the last thirty-six hours, and he was going to try not to break his friend's face for his comments about how he'd never had a charge that was so easy on the eye.

If she'd walked around in that baseball shirt that she slept in, he was going to lose his mind.

"Relax, Mac. I can hear your teeth grinding all the way over here."

"Fuck off."

"She'll be fine," Cabe said.

Mac looked at his watch again. It would be four in the morning before they were home.

Six had called Mac earlier in the day to let him know how things were going in Syria and had asked him to check in on Lou when he got back. Knowing how important it was to not give Six anything else to worry about beyond what he was in Syria to do, he didn't mention what had happened to Delaney. Nor would he tell Louisa when he saw her. This was the kind of shit he could handle. He leaned his head back and closed his eyes. There was nothing he could do in the air, so he did what every good SEAL knew how to do. He stole a few minutes of sleep while he could.

Several hours later, after they'd landed and collected their weapons, Mac let himself into his apartment building. As promised, he texted Ghost as the elevator silently took them to his floor. After he knocked on the door, there was a moment during which he assumed Ghost was checking that it was them before he heard the locks slide.

"Welcome back," Ghost said as the door opened. "You sure you don't want me to stay?"

Mac shook his head. "No. You've done more than enough," he said, hugging his friend and slapping him on the back. "Thanks for taking care of her."

Ghost laughed. "Wasn't hard. Trust me."

Mac bit back a curse. "Yeah, well. Go home. Get some sleep."

He watched Ghost leave and then locked up all the doors. Finally, now that he was home, he could relax a little. All he needed was the reassuring feel of cold metal in his hand, and he'd feel better. Quietly, he placed one of the weapons cases he'd transported with him onto the kitchen counter and unlocked it. Once he had his SIG in his hand, he felt better. He carried the case down the hallway to his room and for a moment, until he remembered that Ghost had been using the guest room, was surprised to find Delaney in his bed.

She was still in the damn baseball shirt, but she'd thankfully added some light gray sweatpants. As always, she was splayed across the entire bed. One of her arms was under his pillow, and the other was angled strangely onto the bedside table. One leg was tucked under the covers, and the other was on top. Basically, she looked like a starfish, which made him smile. She'd always slept like this when she wasn't crawling all over him in sleep. Most guys might hate it, but he'd always thought there were a hell of a lot worse things a woman could do than crawl all over him while naked in bed. The thought of her doing just that had blood flowing to his dick.

He should go sleep in the spare room. Should be a gentleman, give her space, ask her permission. But she was his. Always had been. And somebody had tried to hurt her. He couldn't stay away from her a moment longer, and he prayed she wouldn't make him.

Silently, he slipped out of his clothes but grabbed a pair of basketball shorts from the dresser drawer.

Mac crept over to the bed, the side he'd always slept on, and now, seeing her lying there, thought of as *his* side. Carefully, he slid her hand from under his pillow and folded it across her chest. Delaney didn't stir. He pushed back the sheets and slid under the covers. His pillow smelled of her, as did his sheets. Of something soft and floral.

Not wanting to wake her, he turned onto his side and studied her profile. The cute rounded tip of her nose that she hated so much, the soft pillow of her lips. She'd gone from being an attractive girl to a spectacular woman.

And he'd nearly lost her.

Unable to resist, he laid his arm across her stomach, just needing to touch her. To know that she was alive. In the dark, he could admit he'd been terrified. Fear had never been a part of his vocabulary. It served no purpose. Dulled the brain. Took thinking time away from useful pursuits like planning and strategy and patience. But here, with her so close to him that he could hear her breathe and could see the way her chest rose gently with every breath, he could admit he'd been terrified that he might lose her.

"Nobody's going to hurt you again, Delaney," he whispered. "I promise."

Without opening her eyes, she rolled to face him and snuggled against him, her chest to his. "Mac," she mumbled, still very much asleep.

He slid his hand beneath her and pulled her close, her head tucking in under his—the missing piece in the jigsaw puzzle of his life. "Yeah, Buttons. I'm here. Go to sleep."

Her knee crept up his thigh as she wrapped herself around him. He'd once joked she was like a spider monkey, or one of those snakes that unhinged its own jaw to swallow a man whole. She'd slapped him at that one.

"Mac," she mumbled again as she got comfortable against him.

He did his best to ignore the way he could feel her warmth pressed against his thigh and the way her nipples pressed against his chest. "Yeah, Buttons."

"I missed you."

He knew it wouldn't count in the morning. He knew

she was just sleep-talking, like she used to. But as he fell asleep with her in his arms, he imagined she'd meant every word she'd said.

Half asleep, unwilling to fully waken and face the day, Delaney snuggled deep into the covers and allowed the dreams that danced on the edge of her consciousness to enter. In it, she was naked, in a large white bed, with a man behind her. A hand spanned her stomach, pulling her back against a firm, warm chest. Spooning. Her favorite thing.

Lazily, the hand moved upward until it cupped her breast, and Delaney secretly urged it to squeeze gently, but it didn't. Whoever the hand belonged to was definitely aroused. She could feel the heavy erection pressing against her back. Teasingly, she wiggled her butt against him in the hope he'd get the message, but nothing. No response.

Sun shone in through large open windows with white billowing curtains as she reveled in feelings of being turned on.

She turned in the man's arms, grateful when he pulled her closer to him. His chest was wide, with a light smattering of hair, and she pressed her forehead to it as she slid her hand between them to the waistband of his shorts.

A hand gripped her wrist.

"Don't," a voice said gruffly.

Hard to get? That was a new one. She moved closely and pressed a series of soft kisses to his chest. But she could be that girl. The one who was confident enough to initiate. She licked his nipple and heard him gasp.

"Delaney, please. *Fuck*. Wake up!"

Suddenly the bed shook. Covers were dragged off her body, and her skin was cold. Then the realization hit her.

Shit. Shit. Shit.

It wasn't a dream.

Delaney forced one eye open and confirmed her worst nightmare. Mac stood naked, apart from a pair of basketball shorts and a huge erection. And if the tenting was to be believed, his chest and bicep dimensions weren't the only muscles that had grown. His hair was ruffled, standing up every which way as it always used to, and his eyes told her that she'd woken him up. *By attempting to grab his dick.*

Dear God. She was going to die.

While she'd never tell him, Mac had featured in her dreams for as long as she could remember. When Brock had first died, she'd hated it. Hated the way the man she'd loved with every ounce of her heart still forced his way into her dreams, loving her, reminding her that they weren't done. She'd attempted to use imagery and tools from her therapist to redirect them. At her instruction, every time Mac popped into her head, she tried to say goodbye, to send him on his way. Hell, she'd even tried hypnosis, but nothing had worked.

So, by day, she'd gone about her business, hating the man for tearing her family apart, while at night . . . well, he'd quite literally filled her dreams.

And now, he was staring at her with a look that said if she would only say the word, he'd climb back into bed and take her in all the ways she'd dreamt about.

"Good morning, Delaney," he said gruffly, his eyes heated.

Torn between the embarrassment of trying to grab her ex-boyfriend's penis and the frustration that she was now aroused yet unable to do anything about it, she was uncertain what to do next. "You aren't supposed to be here."

He folded his arms across his chest, which only served to make his upper arms look even bigger. "Glad I was, because I would have hated to come home and find you in bed with somebody else."

"I'm sorry. I didn't mean to . . . you know." She gestured toward his shorts, and he laughed, the sound rich and full.

"Wouldn't be the first time you'd touched it." He sat down on the edge of the bed. "Should I put a pillow across my lap like I used to when we were making out in your bedroom and heard your mom coming up the stairs?"

"Urgh . . ." Delaney flopped back onto the bed. "Shut up and go away."

"It's my bed."

Delaney raised an eyebrow. "And you weren't supposed to be in it until today, by which time I would have laundered both sets of bedding and been back in the guest room."

"Your grabbing for my dick is *my* fault?" he asked, making no attempt to hide the humor he found in the situation.

"No, you grabbing my boob is your fault." The words fell out of her mouth before she could stop them, but she'd give anything to suck them back in.

"So, me touching your breast turned you on, which in turn made you grab my dick?"

She grabbed his pillow and tossed it at his head. "Shut. Up. Go make me coffee, and I might forgive you."

He leaned over her, placed a hand on either side of her shoulder. "I'd rather go back to talking about breast and dick grabbing." His tone had turned way too serious for her liking.

"Mac," she said, quietly. "That isn't us. Not anymore. I was half asleep, and you were . . . convenient. I was so asleep that you could have been anybody."

Mac huffed. "What a glowing recommendation." He snatched his hands from the bed. "I'll go make coffee."

She watched him walk through the door and instantly wanted to call him back. This wasn't fair to him. The thought stopped her in her tracks. It was the first time she'd considered his feelings. His wants and needs. He'd made no secret of his willingness to explore what they once had. And now, unable to satisfy the dream-induced arousal, she didn't know what to do.

The fair thing would be to leave. Like *really* leave. Fly to New York, stay with her friend, Maria, her former college roommate who worked for *The New Yorker*. Lose herself and the reminders of Mac in the big city. A different coast had been enough distance once before. It would be again.

But she wasn't stupid. Self-preservation needed to be her first concern. She was safer with Mac in the luxury, gated, and guarded apartment than in Maria's one-bedroom apartment in a less than salubrious part of Brooklyn. Momentarily, she considered calling Six to see if she could go to stay with him, but it didn't seem fair to take trouble to him and Louisa when they had already been through so much. And then she remembered he was in Syria. *Shit.* There was always Cabe.

Confusion sucks.

You still have feelings for him.

STOP!

Delaney climbed out of bed, threw her hair up into a messy bun, and wandered to the kitchen where Mac was watching the coffee splutter into the pot. "I'm sorry," she said. "That was spiteful of me. This isn't me. I'm not normally confused, and weak."

Mac turned to face her, his face not revealing a single emotion. Just flat.

"It's not fair to you to let you think anything can come of the two of us, Mac," she continued. "But I'll admit, I'm freaked out by what is going on and I know I'm safer with you. Which makes me selfish."

Mac turned back to the pot just as it finished hissing and reached to the cupboard above it where he kept his mugs. Silently, he poured coffee into each and added a generous helping of sugar to his own before handing her a mug.

"It *is* selfish, but you know what, Delaney? It's okay. I didn't want to lose you all those years ago. I let you down. I didn't just lose Brock that day. I lost the woman I saw forever with." Mac shrugged. "It is what it is. I've lived my entire life trying to make up for it. If this can help me make it up to you, I'm more than happy to do it."

Payment. He thought of it as some way to pay her back for taking Brock. Could she be that callous?

"Mac. I don't know if I can think about it like that. The idea that somehow things will be straight between us. I don't know."

He took her coffee out of her hand and placed it on the counter. "I can't expect you to forgive me for that day. *Fuck*, I can't even forgive myself. So even more than I owe it to you to take care of you when you need it, I owe it to Brock. Because it's my fault he isn't here to take care of you himself."

Tears stung the corners of her eyes. At his words. At Brock's memory. At the look of hope on Mac's face.

"Let me do this, Delaney. Don't run."

Could she do it? Could she stay here with him? Would she be strong enough to resist the man he'd become, the way he looked at her, the way he'd felt pressed up behind her even though it had only been a dream?

"We need lines, Mac. Hard ones. None of this sand shit. I want them drawn in concrete and reinforced with steel." The very same materials she'd be applying to her heart.

Mac shook his head, but she cut him off before he began to argue. "I don't want you to cross over to my side of the line."

"The invisible one. The one not drawn in sand, the one reinforced with steel and concrete?" His eyes sparkled the way they used to when he was about to pick her up, throw her over his shoulder, and toss her in the surf.

"Yes, that one. And stop looking at me like that."

Mac laughed. "Like what?"

"Like you used to," she blurted.

The words hung between them until he leaned forward and pressed his lips gently against hers. Something must be wrong with her body because no matter how much her brain instructed her to step back, to berate him, to tell him that this was exactly what she was talking about, she stayed exactly where she was, addicted to the feel of his lips against hers. Until it was over.

"I pulled away there. Did you notice that?" he asked. Mac ran his tongue over his lips, and she could have sworn he did it to tease her.

Unable to speak, feeling wholly vulnerable, she nodded. "It doesn't mean what you think it means, Mac."

"Maybe it does, maybe it doesn't. But you're staying, and we have work to do," he said, pointing toward the stack of boxes that hadn't been there when she'd gone to bed. "But first," he said, picking up his cup of coffee, "I should go put a shirt on so you don't get distracted." Then he winked.

She waited until he was out of the room before she smiled.

CHAPTER EIGHT

"Are you sure Lochlan won't mind me doing this?" Delaney asked as she used decorator's tape to stick papers to the walls of the dining room area. She peeled a corner of the tape back, checking that it didn't pull any paint off.

Mac grabbed another of her boxes from the hallway and carried it across to the dining room table. "Not at all. But if he complains, I'll beat the shit out of him, or redecorate . . . whichever I feel like." He stopped and watched her for a moment. A piece of paper fell from the bundle she was holding, and she bent forward to pick it up. *Fuck*. Inwardly he groaned. She was wearing tight gray leggings, white sneakers, and a fitted navy T-shirt. That ass of hers was driving him wild.

When she stood up again, a piece of wet hair fell out of the messy bun she'd pulled together after her shower. A shower that had tortured him as he'd stood in the kitchen and listened, trying not to think of wet water running over her curves. Soapy wet water that would run between the valley of those—

"Mac?"

He shook his head. "What? Um, sorry?" Jerking off in his shower to clear his mind had been a weak substitute for the real thing. Never in his life had he had a problem dealing with the fluctuations in his sex life. When he'd been deployed, he'd taken care of business when he'd needed to and he'd enjoyed his downtime with women immensely, but whether he was getting any or not had never bothered him. But now . . .

"I asked if you could hand me the tape."

Mac grabbed the blue tape and slid it across the table. The soft touch of her fingers brushing his was more than he could deal with.

"I wish you'd just sit down and let me do that. You're still favoring that ankle."

Delaney shook her head. "I'm *fine,* Mac. It's feeling better."

He didn't believe her. The wince when she put any weight on it gave her away. "Until you can hop on that foot while twirling a baton, I don't believe you."

They stared at each other across the table for a moment, and then her mouth twitched, the corner turning up. "I hate you," she said in jest, and he wondered if she realized exactly what she'd said. Those three words had accompanied the slap he'd received all those years ago.

"Fine. I'm going to go call the guys. Back in a sec."

The clock on the stove told him it was a little after ten in the morning. Despite the late arrival, anybody who was already up was probably already at Eagle. He called the main office, hoping somebody was there already. If not, he'd call Cabe directly.

"Hello, Eagle Securities."

The voice was grumpy, but Mac knew immediately

who it was. "Wow. We really need to get you some personality training, Cabe."

"Yeah, whatever, asshole. What's up?"

"Was talking with Delaney this morning. Wondered if you could get the rest of the guys convened here. Figured it wouldn't hurt to get everyone to hear what's been happening. See if we can't then break up into teams to divide and conquer to figure out what's going on."

There was a clatter in the background. It sounded like Cabe was opening the roller shutter doors of the warehouse. "Wouldn't it be better for the two of you to come here?"

"Yeah, it would." He looked over at Delaney, who was still pretending not to hobble and shook his head. "But Delaney is still hurting, and I'd rather not force her to walk on her ankle unless she needs to."

"I'm fine," she shouted. "Stop talking about me like I'm not here."

"Just stating facts, Buttons," he replied.

Cabe laughed. "Can't decide if this reunion between the two of you is the greatest thing to happen to you or a ginormous clusterfuck in the making."

"Would it help if I said I felt the same way?" Mac said.

"Probably not. Look, I'll gather up the guys once we've finished writing up our reports, probably noon, one-ish maybe. You'd better be prepared to feed everyone."

When Mac returned to the dining area, Delaney was crouched down taping things to the wall. Pictures of crates of weapons, a map of the Middle East, documents that looked like flight manifests. "Take-out it is, and I'm expensing it, asshole."

He looked over to Delaney, his concern for her growing with every new piece of information she stuck to the damn wall. And if his gut was correct, which it usually was, she was going to need him a lot more before it was all over. Which meant a point would soon come when he would be unavailable for work. As much as he loved his brothers—and cared about Eagle—Delaney was at the top of the priority list.

"Deal. I'm on it. Let me wrap up here. See you in a couple of hours." Cabe hung up the phone without waiting for Mac to respond.

As he placed his phone on the kitchen counter next to Delaney's, her phone rang. *Benjamin Streep.* He grabbed it and handed it to her as she hobbled toward him. "Wish you'd sit down," he said, sweeping her into his arms.

She squealed as he lifted her into the air, rolling her eyes as she answered the call. "Benjamin. Hey."

Mac couldn't decide which was worse. Holding her in his arms like he longed to, knowing she just wanted him to put her down, or the fact that some guy was calling her and she sounded happy about it. Instead of putting her down on a chair as he'd originally intended, he sat down on the sofa with her in his arms. He could hear the guy talking as Delaney wiggled around in his lap, trying to get out of Mac's grip.

Delaney glared at him, but he kept hold.

"I'm sorry. I didn't want you to worry. No, it was too late, I didn't want to wake you." Delaney pinched the bridge of her nose.

There was a pause while "Benjamin" said something. Mac watched Delaney, trying to figure out what the guy was to her.

"No. Honestly. I'm fine. It's a good thing, honestly."

A good thing? Being shot at was never a good thing.

Dude's voice escalated but he couldn't quite hear the words, just the tone and volume. Mac felt his pain.

"Look at it this way," Delaney said into the phone, seeming to momentarily forget she was in Mac's lap. "The fact that someone is so worried about what I might uncover that they want to abduct me, kill me, whatever, means I'm on to something. One of the chains I've rattled in pulling all this together has somebody so worried they'll take significant action. I've just got to figure out which chain and who."

Mac forgot about Benjamin. She was right. She was definitely on to something. And while he hated that Delaney was the one doing the uncovering, *what* she was uncovering had the capacity to save lives. Lots of them, by the sound of it. Theoretically, she could help his fellow military personnel on the battlefield by preventing munitions access to those who fought against them. Or could stop chemical-poisoning disasters.

"I know. I know I said I'd take some time off, but I can't. This forces my hand. Yes. . . . I will. . . . No, I'll protect myself, I promise." She looked Mac right in the eye. "I'm staying with a friend who knows his shit when it comes to that stuff."

Damn right he did. So, the douche canoe on the other end of the phone could fuck right off. But it did make him think. She needed to learn how to take care of herself. He looked down at her ankle, which was still strapped up in her sneakers. Still, she needed to be able to protect herself.

She'd stopped fighting him, and he tried to ignore how her leaning back against the armrest with her shoulders back presented her breasts in a way that made it hard to keep his hands to himself. *And speaking of hard*. God-damn.

"Look. This is all good, Benjamin. I'm set up. I'm healed. And, honestly, I love it that you care, but I need to do this. I'm close. I can feel it."

Mac didn't love it that the dude cared. In fact, he didn't know who or what Benjamin Streep was to her, but he needed to keep all his caring shit to himself. Unable to resist, Mac ran a hand up her thigh. It was a simple gesture to remind her of his presence, to remind her that it was *his* lap that she was sitting on. When he reached mid-thigh, she slapped her hand down on top of his to stop his progress. He should have been pissed, but the way her eyes were bright told him that she didn't altogether hate it.

He grinned and slipped his hand away.

"Okay, Benjamin, I will," she said, and hung up the phone. "We talked about lines, Mac."

"You talked lines but we didn't agree on where they should be placed exactly. Who was that?" he asked, knowing his tone sounded borderline accusatory.

Her eyes narrowed. "Now you are talking semantics. And that was my *editor*. My boss. My business partner. Pick one."

"Good. Listen. I've got a plan before the guys come over in a couple of hours. While I want you to rest that ankle, I think this is important." Mac played with her fingers, intertwining them, and she let him for a moment before pulling them away.

"We need to get on with this," she said, easing herself off him. "And we obviously need to have another conversation about boundaries."

He stood, perhaps a little too close to her. So close he could smell her shampoo, could feel the warmth of her on his arm as she brushed against him. "I know. But trust me, you're going to enjoy this."

Forty minutes later, Delaney looked as cute as a button wearing industrial-sized headphones and a pair of his safety goggles at the gun range owned by one of Mac's friends. They stood in lane number four, his favorite SIG lying on the shelf, muzzle facing down the lane, ejection port faceup, and slide lock back. He'd just walked her through the most basic elements of being in a gun range. Things like gun safety protocols, never passing the firing line, what to do when someone shouted "Cease fire."

Now for the fun part.

"Let's talk grip," he said, picking the gun up off the bench. "Your index finger should sit along the side, here." He tilted the gun so she could see his positioning. "And your other fingers should wrap around the handle firmly. Keep 'em flat and vertically stacked. You should have a nice line down the side of the gun and your arm."

Next, he explained where to put her left hand, the firmness of the grip, and how to make sure her left hand had contact with the gun. Delaney watched him with wide eyes, but if he wasn't imagining things, she was enjoying watching him. "Isometric tension." He forced the phrase out to stop thinking about the way she'd just bitten her lip. "You're going to push forward with your shooting hand and back with your support hand." As he explained tension to the left and right and how to manage recoil, he looked at her. She was staring straight back at him. He placed the unloaded gun back on the shelf. "Your turn."

Delaney grinned. "This is going to be fun."

Mac watched her pick up the gun and repeat what he'd done. She took the time to position her index finger and push her hand as high up the gun as she could. As she stood pointing the muzzle downrange, she grinned.

Shit, the silhouette of her fitted workout clothes, straight back, long neck, and extended arms holding his favorite SIG was the kind of thing that would fuel jerking off for the next ten years. To refocus, he walked her through the basics of muzzle, and sight, and trigger.

Delaney put the gun back down on the shelf and laughed. "I feel like a total badass holding that thing."

"All right, you're going to load it," he said, placing the magazine on the shelf. Delaney reached for the gun with her left hand, and he reached for her wrist to stop her. "No, never pick it up with your left. You always pick up your weapon with your dominant hand."

"Why's that?" she asked, doing as he told her.

Forcing himself to look at the target that was hanging a couple of feet away, he composed himself. "Because once it's loaded, you'll have to change hands, and there's a chance you could drop it or accidentally discharge it while doing so. You really want to minimize that kind of thing."

"It's heavier than I expected," she said, turning the unloaded gun over in her hand.

Mac watched what she was doing. Accidents could happen, even between friends. "Yeah. They can be. Okay, pick up the magazine, and using your index finger, seat that first round properly."

"It's kind of springy," she said.

"Kind of the point, Delaney. Now you're going to slam that magazine in that opening there."

The sound of things clicking into place assured him that

everything was properly seated, but he checked it anyway. The gun did look big in her hand, but he didn't have anything smaller. Their first stop had been to fill out permits to carry a weapon. Due to the very real threat against her life on two occasions and his personal guarantee to teach her how to fire the goddamn thing, nobody had thought her application would have an issue. Their final stop was going to be the gun store. He was going to buy her a weapon with his own documentation while they waited for her permits.

"Is there a particular way of standing?" she asked, holding the gun like in that stupid *Charlie's Angels* pose.

"Muzzle down the range!" he shouted, and she quickly did as he asked.

"Sorry, got a little carried away." Lines appeared between her brows.

"I want to say it's okay and be cool about it, but gun safety is paramount. That's a loaded gun. Literally. To answer your question, because this is about learning how to defend yourself—rather than becoming a sniper, for example—I'm less concerned about you achieving a perfect stance. Really, who knows where you'll be or what you'll be doing when you need to use your weapon. The key thing is comfort and stability. There's no point going to all that effort of aiming if a gust of wind is going to knock you off-balance."

Delaney stood, feet hip-width apart, and arched her back. Mac couldn't resist. He stood behind her, way closer than necessary, and placed his hands on her hips. The recoil might be a bit of a surprise on the first round, so he placed his hands over hers, bringing her right up against him.

"You're not going to squeeze the trigger hard, Buttons,"

he said against her ear. "I want you to work it slowly back toward you."

"Is it going to knock me backward?" she asked, her voice as low as his.

"I've got you, Delaney. Now work it. I want to see you fire your first shot."

He felt her sigh, then fix herself. When the bullet fired, he did exactly as he'd promised.

He caught her.

Who knew firing a gun could turn a girl on?

Shit.

It had been fun handling the gun, learning how to shoot straight, learning how to take care of a weapon. Watching Mac, with those strong forearms and large hands of his, pulling the slide back and forth like a boss. She couldn't remember the last time she'd done anything other than work. Stephen's idea of a good time had been binge-watching new shows and seeing every Oscar-nominated movie to learn what was successful. She couldn't blame him. As a screenwriter, it was a way to advance his career. Which matched her idea of a good time . . . work, work, and more work. So basically the opposite of firing bullets.

But the morning had been entertaining, and informative, and empowering. She'd finally toppled off the fence she'd sat on with regard to guns. Funny how being shot at could change an opinion. And Mac had been so darned competent. She could imagine him in uniform, in command on a battlefield somewhere, shouting orders to his team while gunfire went off around him. While she still struggled to get past the fact that Brock's death is what had spurred Mac to join the military, there was no question

Mac had performed a highly commendable service for his country.

What hadn't been fun? Well, Mac had stood so close behind her that she could feel the heat of his chest through her T-shirt. And not just the heat. She'd felt the curve of his pecs, the firmness of his abs. It had been chronically hard to focus when he'd wrapped his hands around her. Every single thing she'd loved about him came flooding back. The way he'd always handled her—like he couldn't keep his hands off her, though back then she'd been so new at the sex and intimacy thing, and he hadn't wanted to push her. And she loved the way he had so much freaking patience when he taught just about anybody anything.

He was a good man.

He'd helped her. Was continuing to help her even now, as he let them back into the apartment after having helped her find a gun that was a perfect fit in the palm of her hand. He'd taught her how to protect herself and given her a safe place to stay.

It was too easy to fall back into old habits and routines with him. She hadn't forgotten how to be with Mac. And her body had wanted to be, as he'd put his hand on her hips, holding her gently. He'd turned her on. Again.

She needed a moment to steel herself against him. The ease with which he was edging back under her skin frustrated her. He was slowly winning her over simply by breathing and being himself. He hadn't taken her to a fancy restaurant or tried to woo her. There were no flowers in fancy vases. Her housewarming present had been three new locks and a doorframe, hardly the stuff of romance novels.

Silently, she wandered into her room and walked to

the window with a view over the city. The apartment, despite looking half lived in, was starting to feel more like any home she'd ever had, though she'd only spent a handful of nights there. After what had happened back at her own place—on which she'd had to pay a full six months' rent—she'd probably never go back. She was terrified of exploring the thought further and concluding that the only reason it felt like home was Mac.

She heard Mac walk past her door as he ordered pizza, followed by the click of his own bedroom door. It felt desperately ungrateful to feel so conflicted when the morning had given her so much joy. Wondering if a cup of coffee and a few moments on the balcony might shift the ever-changing direction of her thoughts to something a little more positive, a little more solid, she headed to the kitchen.

"Okay," Mac said, joining her. "The guys will be here in thirty, pizza is ordered to come in an hour. We should get started." He walked to the table, *her* table, and picked up one of her reference books. A loose paper fluttered to the floor.

"Don't mess with my stuff," she said, marching as best she could on her ankle and collecting the paper from the floor. It was an old grocery receipt, but had been her placeholder. Where had it been? She flicked through the book until she came to the chapter heading she was certain she hadn't read yet.

"What do you think about breaking down the afternoon into three parts? We'll start with you going through all the pieces of your investigation. We'll make a list of all the possible leads you'd been chasing. Then we'll flip to the night the guy tried to grab you. Call up Noah at the police department, see what has progressed. Then, we'll take all those leads and assign a guy to each of them to shake the tree, deflect the attention away from you. What do you think?"

It sounded like her story was being taken away from her. "How about I tell you the pieces that I could use a little help on if you guys have better connections? I have a list of questions that are still unanswered, and the sooner we answer them, the sooner I can publish the story."

The coffeepot continued to hiss in the background. Mac narrowed his eyes and walked over to her. "We aren't on the same page as to what this mission is."

Delaney placed her arms across her chest. "I wasn't aware this had become a mission." Irritation laced her words, but she didn't care. "I'm a journalist writing a story, and I need to nail down some facts."

Mac stopped less than a foot away from her. "You nearly got killed. Twice."

"Says a man who got shot in the line of duty. I'd say you came closer to getting killed than I did." Mac's nostrils flared, but she didn't care. Frustration bubbled within her, and she was more than willing to let it out.

"Says the man who got shot trying to save four aid workers who were being held hostage. Not to write a story."

She shook her head. "You don't understand." Stepping away, she put the book back on the table and began to sort through a pile of flight manifests and cargo logs.

"I think I do. My job is to find the person who wants to hurt you." Mac hadn't moved, but she could hear that his irritation matched her own. "Right now, I couldn't give a shit about any other part of it. I just want to know that you are safe. I don't get why writing a newspaper article is more important to you than staying alive."

She spun, internally wincing as her ankle rejected the action. "I get that my job is unsafe. I know the risks. My job is to nail the men who insist on arming ill-prepared third-world countries that could end up decimating themselves and the rest of the world."

"There are professional organizations who deal with that. The CIA, the FBI," Mac countered.

She'd heard this so many times before. People who didn't recognize the value of investigative journalism. "Yes. And sometimes they're great and do a fine service for the country. Sometimes the bad guys lose. But sometimes those organizations have agendas. *Sometimes* they are happy to let it happen. There's a reason for the popular belief that Osama Bin Laden was trained by the CIA, even though they vehemently deny it.

"And anyway, it sometimes takes the CIA and the FBI years to do what they need to do because they have to dot every *i* and cross every *t*, do it all with visas, and official orders. Journalists can get through the cracks and into the inside of these organizations."

"Why is it so important to you, Delaney? This," he said, gesturing his hand over all the work spread around the room.

She wasn't sure he would understand, wasn't even sure she could say the words to him without breaking down. "Because I promised Brock. I promised him that if he couldn't be of service to his country, I'd do it in his place. And I promised my dad that I would always follow my dreams, and my heart, and my goals." She ran her tongue along her teeth and swallowed down the bubbling rising tide of emotions.

"They wouldn't want you dead, Delaney." Mac said it bluntly, which hurt more. He didn't understand.

"You know, you act like we can just pick up and carry on from where we left off. But this conversation shows you still think of me as I used to be—someone who was curious but not driven. The girl who wanted you to decide if we should go into the lake but who would never just jump in on my own. I'm not that girl anymore."

"And I'm sure as shit not the same fucking guy."

"So, you have evidence of a flight full of weapons leaving an airport in Arizona," Mac said, looking at the photographs they'd taped to the wall in awkward silence.

They'd worked in silence to set up the dining room as her study because the actual study was being used as a storage room for all the crap Mac had brought with him when he'd gotten out of the service. If Lochlan hadn't asked him to house-sit, he would have been screwed. At some point, he should probably nail down Lochlan on how long he was going to be out of town. If it was only for a few more weeks, he wouldn't bother unpacking, but if he'd be gone longer, maybe Mac could open an extra box or two.

The flash fire from their argument had disappeared. It was unresolved, but the energy around it had been quenched. Maybe that was something else that had changed between the two of them. They'd never really fought and it was clear they were going to have to learn how. But it appeared as though Delaney was willing to move on, and he would too.

For now, at least.

"But why Arizona?" Cabe asked as he helped himself to another mug of coffee. It was their third pot, with Ghost and Ryder doing the most damage as they studied the flight manifests.

Delaney stood and moved next to Mac, a move she probably didn't think twice about, but he knew it had to do with those stubborn-as-shit walls of hers coming down, whether she liked it or not. And, yeah, a small part of him hoped it was because she was beginning to realize that she could depend on him, even if their conversation earlier made it seem like they were just as far apart as ever.

"Why Arizona? Gun laws," she answered.

"You aren't some die-hard liberal who doesn't believe in the right to bear arms, are you, Delaney?" Ghost asked. He said it with a grin, in a teasing way.

"I'm a huge fan of the right to bear arms, especially after what happened the other night. Not sure my bread knife would have been much use if he'd managed to get in. And by the way, Mac took me to the range this morning, so please keep the rhetoric civil."

To the casual observer, her comments would have sounded like a glib off-the-cuff remark, but Mac could hear the slight hitch in her voice. Despite the morning spent at the range, and despite her big words earlier about the importance of her job and understanding the risks, he could hear the fear. Which meant they'd be spending more time at the range with him up in her space, pressed up against that cute ass of hers, teaching her how to aim straight. It wasn't a technique they'd ever used in sniper school, but for her, he'd make an exception. Plus, he was going to make plans to take her shooting outdoors, on the move, however she needed to. Should the day ever come when she needed to pull the trigger, he was going to make sure she was as good a markswoman as she could be.

"Arizona ranked forty-seventh on a survey of the hardest places to own weapons," Mac said. "Few states are as relaxed, except maybe Kansas, which ranked dead last. Heck, I bet students can even carry on college campuses there."

"We should have set up in Arizona," Cabe laughed. "Would have saved us a freaking fortune on all those damn licenses we applied for."

"Except we'd have been living in Arizona, which is about fourteen hundred miles from water. Not the best place for SEALs." Mac felt Delaney flinch, and he regretted bringing it up. "Okay, so let's assume lax gun laws making it easy to buy and transport without question is the answer to 'Why Arizona?'"

Cabe tapped his lips with his index finger. "Where gun running happens, drugs aren't usually too far behind, one funding the other."

"Exactly," Delaney said, pulling another photograph out of her pile and taping it next to the picture of the gun crate. "This was a picture from the inbound flight of a private jet from a small nonpublic runway in Sonora. That whole northwest coast is cartel territory, but this isn't from them."

"How do you know this shit, Delaney? You're a brainiac," Ghost said. Mac tried to swallow his jealousy at the easy way his team member spoke to her. He felt like doing something to mark his turf, like putting his arm around her or some shit. Anything to take the shiny-eyed look off Ghost's face. Nobody around the table knew about his and Delaney's past outside of Cabe and Six because, well, they were guys and didn't discuss that kind of shit. But he planned to drop a word in Ghost's ear before the day was out.

"I have a contact at the private airfield who gave me a heads-up. Tracking the flight manifests is a labor of love.

These kinds of exposés never happen quickly. Phoenix is technically under the Sinaloa Cartel's jurisdiction. It's the launchpad for their entire North American operation. Marijuana, heroin, meth, you name it—it comes into and disseminates out of Phoenix."

"This can't be news, though," Sherlock said, placing his forearms on the large table.

"Yes and no. Phoenix has always been a focal point, given that it's less than two hundred miles north of the border. But this has always been a predominantly U.S. supply route rather than a collection point for overseas deals. The United Nations is desperate to stop the flow of small arms and light weapons into conflict zones, but the people who trade weapons don't give a shit about arms embargoes. The Arms Trade Treaty was supposed to regulate the weapons trade by establishing a unilateral standard for the import and export of arms, but when it was adopted as a resolution in 2013, countries like North Korea, Syria, and Iran voted in opposition, and countries like China, Russia, and Nicaragua abstained."

Ryder shook his head. "There's a shocker, North Korea. And of course Russia is going to abstain. Since the Berlin Wall came down and the collapse of the USSR, they've been a major weapons source."

"National sovereignty is the big issue for most countries against it—they want to defend the right to create rules and regulations for their own country. For example, you can imagine the NRA was very outspoken about it in the past, thought it was some backdoor attempt to impose domestic gun regulations in breach of the second amendment. So even the U.S. balked at agreeing to it at one point. In 2006, when the resolution was first raised, the U.S. voted against it and even now have only signed but not ratified it."

"Fuck that," Ghost said. "I don't care what the law says. I'll always be armed."

There were mutters in support around the table. Every one of them had a weapon on him, Mac knew, gun laws be damned.

"We're getting off topic," Delaney said, bringing them back to the photos. "Suffice it to say that weapons only used to flow one way—out of the arms producers' countries into those that needed them. But now there's huge business in backflow and laundering of arms."

"And that's happening through Mexico and Arizona?" Cabe asked.

Mac pulled out a chair and listened to Delaney talk. While Ghost had pissed him off, he was right. Delaney was smart. She knew her way in and around the arms trade. As she talked about guns being brought to Mexico ports by water from Colombia, only to be cleaned up and moved on, she talked about crime families as if she knew them personally. When she connected the gun supply routes with drug routes, he began to see the enormity of what she'd been looking at.

"So, what you are saying," Mac said, leaning forward, "is that this transport network is being made to look like it is run by one of the existing known crime families, but in reality, somebody has layered on top of their infrastructure to set up their own enterprise."

"Yes. And I believe it's an underground Russian organization operating out of Los Angeles."

"*Lemtov?*" Mac stood and caught the looks that passed between some of the team members who remembered the name from Louisa's case the previous year.

"Yes and no," Delaney said, drawing a family tree of sorts on a sheet of paper she'd stuck to the wall. "Lemtov is here." She wrote his name on the middle of the sheet. She wrote another name above him. *Sokolov.* "Everyone from Sokolov on down is U.S.-based, but everyone from here up is based in Russia." She added a few more names along with details of the crime families they were involved with. "Lemtov is organizing weapons. It was one of his bosses who arranged the drop-off of this crate at the airport, along with others like it." Delaney went back to the photograph that had started their conversation. "They're transporting at night, when the roads are clear. Less chance of being held up. The manifests declare them as . . . hang on."

As she bent to fish through a pile of papers, her T-shirt slipped forward, revealing the soft curve of her breasts. Mac sat back in his chair and placed his ankle on his knee. Goddamn, she was beautiful.

"Agricultural supplies. They went straight through Russia, and ended up in Afghanistan. That's where I was supposed to meet them." Delaney's voice trailed off at the end. Amazing how she was filled with so much confidence and presence, and then showed just the slightest hint of vulnerability.

Mac stood and put his hand on her shoulder, guiding her to the chair. She'd been on her feet a while, and the color had left her face, probably at the thought of what she'd been through. "Delaney was supposed to meet the arms delivery north of Kunduz." He looked over at Cabe, remembering their own experiences in the volatile city. "Kunduz carries the nickname 'the hive of the country.' The province is the biggest producer of crops—wheat, rice, and others—in Afghanistan. It makes sense to label the weapons as agricultural supplies. But it's also the major link between provinces *and* a major drug trafficking route into southern Tajikistan, so it's critical it remain in government control."

"What makes you think this is all connected to what happened to you since you got back?" Sherlock asked.

"I'm not sure. But it seems too coincidental. It's clear that someone tried to get rid of me over there. Then I fly back here and I am suddenly under attack. I don't know what else to think, really. Is it possible that I just have a crazy stalker? Sure. It's possible. But there was something about the guy. . . . He was cold. Distant. Aren't stalkers generally obsessive? They want to be your friend? Lover, maybe?"

Ghost smiled and nodded. "You gotta admit, though . . . you're a good-looking girl. It's a possibility."

And Mac had to admit he was a millisecond away from punching Ghost in the teeth.

"I get what Delaney's saying," he said, forcing Ghost to look at him. "There was nothing remotely familiar about any of their interactions. Back to the point, regardless of whether this is all connected, I think we can help. Cabe, can we chat for a sec?" He nodded his head in the direction of the kitchen. "The rest of you, take five."

Cabe followed him and helped himself to yet more coffee. "What are you thinking?"

"Your team isn't due out for another ten days, but part of my team needs to start work on the Uruguay project for that new shipping company in Montevideo, helping with their security plans. Especially for those routes via the African coast. First thought is that we contact Andrew Aitken at the CIA again. This information might lead to something that will help them put Lemtov away, so it all feels connected. Then we apply everybody to this to help Delaney blow the doors off, get everything out in the open. By sticking around her, we can help Delaney—"

"Help me with what?" Delaney said as she approached him.

"Just talking resources," he said. "We want to help."

Delaney shook her head. "You're doing enough letting me stay here, helping me think through it, giving me a new set of eyes. I don't need anything else."

Cabe threw his arm casually over Delaney's shoulder. "Here's the deal, sweet cheeks. We're helping whether you like it or not."

A huff escaped her as she shook her head. "I don't need—"

"Shut up, Delaney," Cabe said softly, and Mac smiled. He'd been thinking the same thing, but would never have said it out loud.

"Fine, but I'm staying right here so I know what you guys are plotting."

Mac laughed. "We're not plotting. Just trying to work around our clients and see if we can reach out to our government agency contact to ensure what we do is aboveboard." He turned to Cabe. "I'm just wondering whether we could mix up the resources a little. Sherlock could probably do this without me anyway. Was thinking we could tag Sherlock as lead and send Ghost as planned, but borrow Harley and Bailey from your team. Leaving you, me, Ryder, and Lite as support here until your job kicks in. Then we could do a handover. Ryder and Sherlock can head down to Uruguay, and you can pick your guys up and head out. I'll decide where I need to be then."

Delaney nudged him with her shoulder. "I don't like that you're rearranging not just your lives but your work for me."

"Happy to help," Cabe said. "And agreed. We'll make it work. Now, should we sit down and figure out a plan?"

Delaney finally smiled. "That sounds like fun."

"It will be. But first I'm gonna call Aitken to get the wheels moving." Cabe headed to the living room to round up the troops who were currently out on the balcony.

"I'm sorry about earlier," she said, those sweet eyes of hers locked on his. "I hate to admit it, Mac, but you still mix me up just as much as you ever did. I mean it. Thank you."

Unable to resist, he slid a hand around the back of her neck and gently tugged her toward him to kiss the top of her head. "You're welcome, Delaney."

CHAPTER NINE

It was two in the morning, and Mac wasn't in his room. She hadn't heard his footsteps in the hallway, but he was like a freaking ninja that way. He'd scared her at least five times that day alone, creeping up on her when she least expected it. Like when she'd been pouring coffee and the shock of finding him standing directly behind her had caused her to spill it all over the counter. When he'd laughed, she'd suggested putting a cowbell around his neck.

Mac had suddenly appeared at her side, too, when Ghost had approached her on the balcony, beginning a conversation she was sure was going to turn into an invitation for a date she was in no mood for. His brow furrowed in a frown.

"You want to go check those policies we walked through in your first week of training?" Mac said.

Ghost said nothing, but nodded before he walked back inside.

Cabe watched until the door slid closed. "Because

you and Six set such a great example," he said gruffly
before he took a bite of an apple.

*Mac raised his middle finger at Cabe who put his
hands up in surrender. "Fine. But you can't break rules
and expect everybody else to honor them."*

Now, even more than at the time, she knew they were
talking about her and Louisa. Dating clients.

Mac wasn't the man she'd remembered. She'd demon-
ized him, and no matter which way she thought about
it, her mom was right. Perhaps it was time to find the courage to ask Mac what exactly had happened on that cliff
that day and find a way through it, past it. It might mean
letting go of Mac once she knew, which was almost as difficult as letting go of what happened to Brock.

He was smarter than she remembered. When they
were younger, lying around the campfire, she'd tell him
about all the books she'd read, and he'd say very little.
She'd always assumed he'd found them a little boring and
had assumed that the fighting man she'd heard had gone
off to war was just an adrenaline junkie looking for his
next fix. But he wasn't. He was more measured than he
had been. More thoughtful. More . . . commanding. Seeing him lead the group into a plan of action for the next
few days was nothing short of remarkable. She appreci-
ated that it included equipping her to defend herself. And
learning to fire a gun had excited her way more than it
probably should have.

And then the kisses . . . and the touches . . . and the
constant, *gah* . . . just *being* there. Breathing. Placing a
cup of coffee in front of her when she hadn't even mentioned how badly she needed one. Or his putting a plate
of her favorite Oreos on the table without saying a word
about how she'd once binge-eaten a whole box of them

while crying about the *C* she'd gotten on her English Language paper.

He was too much. He was . . . she couldn't let him be everything.

The click of the lights in the living room told her he was on the move. She heard no footsteps, but wasn't surprised when there was a gentle tap on her bedroom door and then it opened. Mac stood there, a slash of moonlight coming in through the blinds and cutting across his face. He looked dangerous, and for a moment she could imagine what it would be like to come up against him, soldier to soldier.

"I want to talk to you about those lines," he said, pulling his T-shirt over his head in one swift move.

His abs rippled, and while she knew it was wrong to stare, her mouth went dry. He looked like a man about to pounce. Her body betrayed her as her thighs tightened. She watched him slide the belt through the loops of his jeans, folding it in half and holding it between his hands. She should tell him to stop.

"I don't like them, Delaney. And I don't like that you drew them based on something you think you know but won't talk to me about."

Large fingers undid the button on his jeans, revealing more of the trail of hair that led down from his navel. He'd had a fine body when they were dating, broad shouldered from swimming and strong thighs. But now he was breathtaking.

Words failed her as she realized that despite wanting to tell him she couldn't do this, having Mac back in her bed was exactly what she wanted, what she needed. It made no sense, but as sure as he was standing there, she wanted to watch him slide the dark blue denim down his legs.

"So, here's the deal. I just got you back, and I couldn't bear it if anything happens to you. I'm a patient man, Delaney," he said, finally allowing his jeans to fall to the floor. Navy blue boxer briefs with a white waistband gripped his hips, every inch of his body defined muscle. "I can even wait for you to find it in your heart to forgive me." He stepped closer to the bed until he placed a knee on it and crawled toward her. "But don't make me wait to hold you. To comfort you. To show you physically I'm here for you. Please, Delaney."

Mac came to a stop several inches away from her. Using his finger, he drew an invisible line along the top of the comforter that she was snuggled beneath.

"What are you doing?" she asked, her voice husky from want of him.

"There's your line, Delaney. It's as real as the concrete and steel reinforced one you wanted, because I won't cross it. You need to come to me," he said, his voice rich with emotion. It moved her to her very core. "I'm going to be right here. All night. Every night. But I won't move an inch closer to you. You're going to have to close the gap, Delaney."

True to his word, he lay down on top of the covers. The air-conditioning quietly whirred, and she knew it was cool above the blankets. Thoughts raced around her head as the bed dipped ever so slightly in his direction. She braced herself from rolling up against him. What she believed, what she wanted, and what she needed no longer seemed clear. Closing her eyes, she tried to pretend he wasn't there, but the scent of him and the warmth she could feel through the thin sheets were a constant reminder of the impossibly handsome man lying next to her. No other man had ever lived up to him, even when she'd hated him.

They'd been good together. They'd *be* good together, it was undeniable.

The past—feelings of guilt and of this being wrong—tried to intrude, but she shook her head to clear them. Those memories had no place in a darkened room in bed with Mac.

"I'm confused, Mac," she confessed as she studied the ceiling. It was wrong to leave him hanging when he'd just said all those beautiful words to her.

Mac turned onto his side, she could feel it, and out of the corner of her eye, she could see he placed his head on his bicep. "I know you are, Buttons."

"Why do you still call me that?"

"Thirty-two of them. Did you know that?" he asked.

"Thirty-two what?" She turned on her side to face him. His dark blue eyes, the same color as his denim jeans, looked almost black in the half light.

"Buttons. I counted each one as I undid them. It seemed like an important detail to remember from the first night I ever got to sleep with you. It was the last thing I ever did without knowing what it felt like to be deep inside you. Each one of those buttons was pretty damn epic to me."

Her heart melted a little at his words. She'd forgotten how easily they came to him. To them. When had she lost the ability to share what was on her mind with another person? To trust someone she was with? The tips of her fingers drifted over the line on the sheet, and Mac placed his fingertips on top of hers, respecting the line.

"Fifty-three," she said.

"Fifty-three what?" Mac asked.

"Seconds. That's how long it took you to open them. I never knew how many buttons there were, but I remembered that it took you just under a minute to open them all." She slid her hand a little further across the line, and Mac took hold of it in his.

Memories of that night flooded her mind. How her heart had raced as they'd pulled into the parking lot of the motel where Mac had arranged for them to stay. How she had waited in the car as Mac had gone to pick up the keys. And how, while he'd been gone, she'd quickly eaten a Tic Tac and run a brush through her hair. But nothing could replace the memory of how his fingers had felt when they'd gently slid the thin straps of her dress off her shoulders to let it slip to the floor.

She wasn't that young girl anymore. She wasn't naive enough to think that what they had could last forever. But maybe there was a way for them to do this that would hold her heart safe, and even bring her closure.

Taking a deep breath, she lifted the covers and crossed the line.

Mac opened his arms wide. "You're safe, Delaney. Every part of you is safe with me, I promise."

"You can't make those kinds of promises," she said as she pressed up close against him. "Nobody can. Let's just try taking one night at a time, and see where we end up come morning."

"You can tell yourself that if it makes you feel better, but we both know that you and me, that this . . . it's unfinished business. I'm not going anywhere until it's finished, no matter how long that takes." Mac placed a finger under her chin and gently tipped her head backward until she was looking straight at him, his lips millimeters away.

Delaney's heart beat furiously in her chest at the thought of what might happen next. His eyes told her that he wasn't going to stop until they were both naked and spent in each other's arms. But she also knew that none of that would even begin unless she kissed him first, unless she fully crossed the line with not just her body, but also her heart and her mind.

Unable to wait a second longer, she pressed her lips to his, savoring their firmness. When his mouth opened she brushed her tongue against his. She knew her advantage would only last for a moment, but it had to be enough to hold her through what would follow.

"Delaney," Mac moaned as he threaded his fingers into her hair, pinning her in place with his strong hand.

He surrounded her with his scent, with his warmth, with his strength as he rolled them, blankets and all, so that she was lying on top of him.

She pressed her weight into her hands on either side of his head while he cupped her face gently. "You just ruined the line," she said, softly.

"I think that was all you," he replied, pulling her down until their lips met again.

He'd dreamt about this moment. The thought of her, the memory of her . . . it had kept him going, kept him alive through the toughest days of his service. When he thought he was beaten. When he was hurt. When he wondered what the hell he was boarding another plane to another country for. Instead of allowing those thoughts to take over, he'd thought about the two of them. She'd become his reason for battling on and through, until he was rescued or returned home. When he weighed up his life objectively in the darkest moments, she was his only piece of unfinished business.

And now, here she was, back on top of him, bundled up in his stupid comforter that he wanted to strip from between them. Along with the baseball shirt she slept in that had driven him crazy, and his own boxer briefs, which were doing him a solid favor by holding his dick in check.

Her hair hung softly around her face and was long enough to tickle the skin on his chest. He wouldn't have moved for a million bucks.

When her lips had been on his, he'd felt all the puzzle pieces fall into place. Her eyes were wide open and focused on him, and if he wasn't mistaken, there was the shimmer of tears, which hurt as much as healed him. Because he felt it too. It should have been a simple kiss. But it was everything.

Taking her in his arms, he rolled them again so she was back on the bed and he was above. He rose onto his knees. "You okay, Buttons?"

Delaney smiled softly. "I am. It just feels . . . big."

Mac grinned and looked down at his dick. "That's because it *is* big."

She laughed, exactly as he intended. "I meant *this*," she said, gesturing between the two of them. "You and me."

He cut her off from saying any more by assuming a push-up position above her and kissing her sweet mouth again. He'd never get enough of her, and he wanted to spend the night reacquainting himself with every part of her. "No thinking," he whispered against her lips. "You can think all those thoughts of yours in the morning, but for now, let me love you."

"Okay," she said quietly.

Mac climbed off her and went to his jeans, grabbing a condom out of the back pocket and throwing it onto the bedside table.

"Was I such a sure thing?" she asked.

"No. I was just extremely hopeful," he said, sliding his boxer briefs down his legs. Her eyes followed his actions, and like any hot-blooded guy, the look of appreciation and hunger in her eyes once she caught sight of his dick was enough to have him hard as iron. But he had things to do first that involved his lips and her skin. As much as he couldn't wait to slide deep inside her, he'd missed all the other fun stuff too.

He tugged the comforter off the bed as Delaney laughed. God, he'd missed that sound. So much about her had changed. Her legs seemed longer as he gripped her ankles and pulled her a little closer to the bottom of the bed. The baseball shirt rode up her tanned thighs, giving him a glimpse of white lace panties. Her dark hair spread out on the pillow, she looked like a siren ready to lure the sailor in him to the rocks. She certainly had the capacity to do him serious harm, yet all he could do was show her how much she meant to him in the hope that she wouldn't.

Slowly, he bent forward and brought one of her feet to his lips, placing a series of kisses along the tips of her toes, the arch of her foot, the dip of her ankle. When she propped herself up on her elbows to watch, he continued to press kisses along her calf, stopping to nibble the back of her knee, a place he remembered she was ticklish.

Automatically, she yanked her leg away from him in

a fit of laughter. "No. Not there. You know better," she scolded.

"Sorry. Now gimme that leg back," he said, holding out his hand as he crawled onto the bed, grateful when she did exactly as he instructed.

He brushed his lips against the smooth skin of her thigh, stopping just shy of the crease at the top which, should he go there now, there would be no coming back from. Instead, he returned to the foot of the bed. "You're one gorgeous woman, Delaney. You grew up real good."

Painfully slowly, he made his way up her other leg until she was squirming beneath him. He'd never been the guy who needed his woman to stay still. He didn't get the whole kink and control thing. Movement was such a natural expression of feeling, and watching the way she tried to press her thighs together, to get some relief in that heat of hers . . . well, his dick twitched in appreciation. Knowing he was the reason she was unable to keep still, knowing he was doing that to her, fed his ego in a way no medal ever could.

"Sit up, Buttons," he said, offering her his hands.

Delaney took them, and he pulled her until she was seated. Gently, he trailed his finger along her shoulder, between the valley of her breasts which stood high, her peaked nipples visible through the material of her baseball jersey. Anticipation surged through him at the thought of the fun he was about to have with them. Take them in his mouth, suck on them, tease them to see if she was as sensitive as he remembered, find out the ways her sexual tastes had changed and developed. He continued down the shirt until he reached the hem. He slid his fingers beneath it, gripping it, pulling it over her head.

Mac crumpled it into a ball and threw it into the corner of the room. It could stay there for all he cared because from now on, she was going to spend every night the same as him—naked and aroused.

Delaney fell back onto the bed, naked apart from a pair of white lace panties that he'd bet dust to diamonds hugged her ass like those shorts she'd worn to attempt yoga. But that suddenly made him remember everything she'd been through. Her ribs, her ankle. "Are you okay, Delaney? I mean your body? With everything that happened?"

Without answering his question, she slid her thumbs into the waistband of her underwear, slowly wigging it down over hips that were curvier and sexier than ever. Unable to take his eyes away, half disbelieving he was actually there, he watched as Delaney revealed herself to him one more time. His breath caught in his chest as she lay naked before him. Vulnerable.

Finally, he moved forward and lowered himself over her. His heart stopped beating in his chest as their bodies came together as if they'd never been apart. His leg slipped between hers, her breasts pressed against his chest, and her arms came around him as he held some of his weight off her.

"Kiss me, Mac," she whispered softly.

Not needing to be asked twice, he did as he'd been instructed, only this time there was no holding back on the way he kissed her or the emotion he let flow with it. She was his everything, and if tonight was the only night she'd let him prove that to her, then he was going all out. His lips collided with hers, his tongue probing hers, savoring the taste of her.

"God, Delaney. I missed this," he groaned, sliding one of his hands down her side and skimming her waist before sliding beneath her to cup that fine ass he'd seen in those yoga shorts. She lifted her leg around his back, giving him better access to all that smooth skin.

His dick pressed against her heat. It was already wet, and if he moved just a fraction of an inch, he could slide inside her. But, fuck, condom. And he wanted to taste her. Wanted to see if he could still drive her wild with just his tongue.

He slid out of her hold and kissed a trail along her jaw and neck, pausing to kiss her in that sweet spot behind her ear that she'd always loved so much. The faint scent of flowers and spring accompanied his slow journey to her breast. He cupped one firmly in his hand and licked her nipple before blowing on it, watching it pucker. She'd always been so sensitive, yet back then, she'd been shy, their actions limited to under the covers. Now, as he finally sucked her nipple into his mouth, she arched her back and gripped his hair.

"God, yes, Mac," she cried out.

Her throaty cry of need had him slipping a hand down over her stomach to dip between her legs. *Damn.* She was drenched. Mac continued to suck her nipple into his mouth before letting it go with a pop to blow across it, as he slid a finger deep inside her.

"Please," Delaney cried out. "Mac, you have no idea . . ."

But he did. His own cock was leaking, ready to go off so badly that he was worried that he'd last all of a minute once he slid inside her. She was twitching and tightening around him, right on the edge of coming.

"I think I do, Buttons," he said gruffly.

He added a second finger and slowly edged further down the bed, pressing kisses along her stomach, across her hip bone, and down the crease at the top of her thigh, where he pressed his nose to smell her. He wanted to remember everything about this night. Mac pressed kisses across her pubic bone. She was shaved, much more than she'd ever been, but it was a fleeting thought. Nothing could detract from the fact he was about to make Delaney come.

With a flat tongue, he licked her from top to bottom without removing his fingers, finishing on her clit with a flick. Then he sucked her into his mouth as Delaney attempted to lift her hips from the bed. Let her buck, let her move. He'd move with her, ride her until she came.

And she tasted so good that it didn't matter to him if she could hold out all night.

"Mac. Oh . . . Mac, I'm . . ."

He felt it. Felt the way she clamped down on his fingers, felt the surge of wetness, felt the groan that escaped her vibrate through his chest.

But most of all, he felt it in his heart. Felt it as the million pieces it had been left in for over a decade began to painfully weld themselves back together.

Holy shit.

Delaney couldn't remember anything so . . . *damn*, she was a writer. She should have words to describe what had just happened, but she didn't.

Her heart beat way faster than could possibly be healthy, and that orgasm had taken the top off her head. But it was way more than that. It was Mac. And her body had known it. Had come alive for him. Had recognized him. It had brought tears to her eyes faster than she could stop them.

Mac reached for the condom from the bedside table,

but dropped it as soon as he saw her. "Hey, Delaney, sweetheart. What's wrong?" he asked, stroking her hair off her forehead. "I didn't hurt you, did I?"

Of course his first thought would be about her, that he'd done something wrong. "I'm fine," she said, suddenly conscious of the emotion in her voice. She coughed to try and clear it. "It was perfect . . . and too . . . I don't know," she said with a sigh. "Too . . ."

"Close. Much. Everything," Mac said, filling in the gaps with words that matched her thoughts.

She nodded and slid her hand around the back of his neck to pull him close enough to kiss him gently. She didn't want it to stop. Didn't want it to end there. Didn't want to allow the thoughts to begin to slip in. Because she wasn't certain she could keep herself together to be with him like this if they did.

His lips were soft against hers.

"Please. Mac. Make love to me," she whispered.

Swiftly, he kissed her one more time, then put on the condom before lying back down with her.

"I missed you, Delaney. More than you can imagine," he said, watching her as he reached between them and guided himself slowly into her.

"Oh, Mac," she gasped, as he stretched her.

He stopped, pulled out a little, and then slid in a little deeper, groaning as he repeated the action until he was buried inside her. "Fuck, Delaney. You feel so good."

When Mac kissed her, he looked at her like she was a freaking goddess. Like he used to. Before everything had . . .

Mac pulled out of her in one long, slow movement, then pushed himself home with a grunt of satisfaction. His hands gripped her ass, positioning her in such a way that he slid against her clit, and ground against her just the way she did when she was home alone. He was bigger, filled her more fully, and had already done what no other man she'd slept with had been able to do, make her come without being inside her.

His pace began to increase, as did the tightening in her stomach. She hadn't thought she'd be able to orgasm so quickly again, but as everything tightened, she knew she was going to.

"Damn, Delaney, I thought I'd remembered," he said breathlessly. "I thought I remembered how incredible it felt . . . making love . . . with you." His hips thrust again, faster and faster. "But those memories . . . they were nothing compared to this."

He was right. Nothing could match the two of them together. She wrapped her arms around him as he placed his head on the pillow next to hers. She held him as tight as she could, wrapped her legs around his waist as he pounded into her way faster and harder than anything they used to do, but she wanted it. Needed it. And it would make it easier to recover from something as heavy as the moment they'd shared earlier.

An orgasm was sitting just out of reach. "Please, Mac," she begged. "Make it happen. Make me come again," she cried out.

Without needing any further instruction, he removed one of the hands from her ass and slid it between the two of them, stimulating her clit just like she needed him to. "Like this?" he asked gruffly.

"God. Just like that," she gasped. "Mac, I'm going to—"

"I'm right there with you, Buttons," he said. "I want this too, Delaney."

She could feel it. Feel the way his cock pulsed inside her, and it pushed her over the edge into her own second orgasm. Mac drove deeper and further into her, riding out his own release as she let go.

The room was silent apart from the hum of the air-conditioning and the frantic gasps of their breathing as they both attempted to calm down after what was the most incredible orgasm she'd ever had. Ever. There had been nothing youthful or naive about their lovemaking. Even back then, he'd been a generous lover, one who had taken her virginity with calm and patience, and had never pushed her beyond what she'd wanted to explore. Hell, she'd never given him a blow job back then because she had been too scared to try it. But there was nothing calm and patient about what had just happened. It had been hard, and fast, and greedy. Everything she had needed to come through it in one piece.

Mac pressed a kiss to her neck and loosened the grip on her ass. He slid his hand from between them, and used it to move her hair from her face. There was sweat on his brow and between the valley of her breasts.

"I missed you, Delaney," Mac said, quietly.

She ran her fingers up and down his spine, familiarizing herself with the strong muscles, the dips and the valleys. Uncertainty filled her. How did she answer that? Had she missed him? She'd spent so much time hating him for the day on the cliff, for those bad decisions. But underneath it all . . . she'd regretted slapping him at the chapel the day of the funeral and had always struggled with the hatred she felt for him over what happened.

She'd missed him. But how could she tell him without talking about that day?

"Don't read more into this," she said, though it cut her in two.

Mac rolled off her. "Don't say that, Delaney," he said as he removed the condom and placed it in a tissue on the bedside table. He walked to the bottom of the bed, picked up the sheets and comforter, and placed them back carefully. The bed dipped as he lay back down, and she didn't fight it when he tugged her into his arms. "You and I both know that there was plenty to read into that. Don't ruin it."

Delaney sighed. "There's so much unresolved, Mac."

"So in the morning we'll talk." He pressed a kiss to her hair. "But for tonight, can we just admit that making love as grown-ups blew the shit out of making love as kids?"

"It did," she admitted. "I guess we've both had a bit more practice since then." It was a cold thing to say, to bring up their pasts, and it choked her to say it. But she was defenseless against him, and he was going to wiggle his way back under her skin. Something she wasn't sure that she wanted.

"Maybe," he replied, not rising to her comment. "But none of them were you, Delaney. And it made all the difference in the world."

She should tell him that she'd had a great sex life. That all the lovers she'd had in the last decade had been at least as good as he had been. But she couldn't. She couldn't lie. And she couldn't hurt him with a cheap shot.

"What I said earlier . . . about being confused. None of that has changed," she whispered.

"I know." He ran his hand along her hair, the gesture reassuring. "But what we did, it changes everything. Go to sleep, Delaney, and we'll talk in the morning."

Nine hours later, Delaney woke to an empty bed and a soreness between her legs that reminded her of all the delicious things they'd done the previous night. Thanks to falling asleep in Mac's arms, she'd slept solidly, without the nightmares that occasionally filled her brain in the early hours of the morning. Slowly, she sat up in bed and pulled the covers with her, tucking them under her arms. She didn't need Mac returning from wherever he was to find her with her boobs out. He might just get ideas, and she was confused enough to let him do whatever he wanted.

Delaney scanned the room and found her underwear on the floor next to the bed and her sleep shirt thrown across the room in the corner. Leaning forward, she grabbed her underwear and stepped into it quickly before dashing over to pull the baseball jersey over her head. With a quick glance in the mirror, she headed into the hallway to find Mac.

He was in the kitchen making coffee, back in a pair of basketball shorts and nothing else. There were three scratch marks on his back. *Damn.* Had she done that?

"Morning, Buttons," he said without turning to look at her.

"Hey," she said, hitching herself up onto the bar stool on the opposite side of the counter. They had a full day ahead, one that was packed with research and phone calls. "I guess I should grab a shower and then we can make a start on hitting up some of the names I've still got to reach out to."

"Delaney," Mac said, placing the cup down in front of her. He pressed his lips to hers sweetly and sat down next to her. "I think we should have that talk first."

Her heart dropped in her chest. She wasn't ready.

Wasn't strong enough. "There'll be time for that later," she said as brightly as she could. "Because of the time zone difference, it's better if I get started."

"Delaney," Mac repeated. "It can all wait. I want to talk to you about Brock. About what happened that day. It's the only thing between us, and you need to know—"

"No!" Delaney stood and stepped away from the stool. "I can't. I can just about see my way through the fact that last night happened. Let me get my head around this first. Please don't push me, Mac."

Mac reached out for her wrist, and reluctantly she let him tug her back to him. "It's not what you think, Delaney. It'll help to understand."

Panic filled her, which surprised her. Just hearing Mac say Brock's name filled her with anxiety. "I'm sorry, Mac. Maybe us, last night . . . maybe it was a mistake. I can't . . . I don't even know where to start this." A wave of nausea started to roll in her stomach.

Mac tugged her against him and drew her close. "Okay, Buttons. I get that you're overwhelmed, so I'll wait for now. But we're going to have this conversation, you and me. Because until we do, you and me, we don't stand a chance. For now, I'll deal with the pieces of us, the pieces that still fit, the pieces that don't, the secrets." He pulled back and looked her in the eye as he spoke. "But we're going to resolve this, Delaney Shapiro. I promise you."

CHAPTER TEN

She'd pushed him away. Again. And he was getting sick of it.

He needed to tell her what had happened that day, meaning he needed to betray the promise he'd made to Brock. The one that would break Brock's family's hearts if they knew *they* were the real reason he was on that damn cliff. But breaking promises, especially ones he'd made to dead men, went against his grain.

It didn't sit well any more than it sat well that he was in Eagle Securities' large building trying to come up with a plan of attack for their shipping company client instead of helping Delaney. All he wanted was to sit her down on the damn sofa and force her to listen to what he had to say.

But he'd always promised himself that he wouldn't force any kind of resolution between them and that it would be up to her to decide if she ever wanted to reconcile their differences.

He'd thought they'd made progress the previous night. The way she'd crossed the line in the bed had made him hopeful that she'd crossed with every part of her. To find she'd only crossed the damn line physically was a kick in his balls.

"That should work, right, Mac?" Cabe asked.

Mac looked up to the image that was projected onto the wall, a giant map of the expanse of water between the coasts of South America and Africa marked up with every piracy attack made on major shipping vessels in the last decade. Then he realized that the rest of the guys sitting around the table were all looking at him.

"Sorry, what?" he said, attempting to clear Delaney's naked body and her cries as she clamored for release from his thoughts. *Shit.* He'd never had an issue with focus before.

"They could save funds by having outbound and inbound ships hand off security teams before they enter the hot zone here." Cabe pointed to the arc they'd drawn around the African coast. It was one of their cost-saving ideas. If security was only needed once they entered the zone where all the piracy incidents had taken place, why waste money having them sit on every ship from the South American coast out to the hot spot?

"Agreed," he said, forcing himself back into the game. "Cost overrun for security traded off against insurance premiums is a huge deal for them. And we're still waiting for a list of their policies of what they will and won't ship across borders."

Shipping. It made him think about the extent of the weapons trade that Delaney had filled them in on. He'd known it existed and that it was lucrative, and he'd even found himself staring down the barrel of one of those illegally moved weapons a time or two, but he'd been unaware of just how many Western governments were complicit in the trade when it suited them.

"Mac!"

He looked up again and found Cabe looking at him. "What?"

"I asked when we can expect to see it."

"See what?"

"The shipping list," Cabe huffed. "You know what? Take a break everyone."

Sherlock slapped Mac on the back as he went over to the coffeepot.

"Mac, a word." Cabe marched toward the medical bay at the back of Eagle Securities' large training center. Mac followed him inside, and Cabe slammed the door shut.

"What's up, bro?" he said. "Where the hell are you today?"

Mac rubbed his hands on either side of his face. "I know. I'm sorry. I don't know what's going on with my head right now."

"Or who?" Cabe added and sat down on the side of one of the beds that doubled as a dorm and infirmary. "This is like Six and Lou all over again."

Mac shook his head and sat down on the bed opposite. "It's not. Delaney isn't our client."

"Like hell she isn't." Cabe leaned forward, rested his elbows on his knees. "We're putting a lot of resources into someone who isn't our client."

"It's *Delaney*." Mac jumped to his feet. "We owe it to Brock to protect her."

"I know we do," Cabe said. "Just sit back down and let me finish."

Mac did, though not because Cabe was in any position of power over him or could take him in a fight. He sat because he just wanted the whole conversation over and Cabe wouldn't relent until he had said everything he needed to say. Compliance was the quickest route to getting back out there, finishing their strategy session, and then getting home to finish his own conversation with Delaney.

"I know shit between you, and her, and Brock is . . ."

"A fucking mess?" Mac offered, filling in what his friend was too thoughtful to say.

"Yeah. That," Cabe said with a sad smile. "She's back, she's in trouble, and I know you. I know you see this as some holy path of redemption or some shit, and I'm not asking you to not help her."

Mac let out a deep sigh. "So what are you saying?"

"Why don't you take some time out? Figure out how real and permanent this threat is. Aitken gave us his approval this morning, so anything we do is aboveboard. And if you need Eagle's help to fix it beyond the intel we're already doing, let us know because we'll be there for you in a heartbeat. . . . Well, at least as quickly as we can get from wherever we are to wherever you need us to be. Anyone who is beached can help when they aren't planning for their next engagement. But you . . . I think you should check out of here for a little while."

Mac looked down at his boots. He'd always been the one to give the orders. The de facto leader, just because he'd ranked higher than the other two, thanks to that military-ingrained respect of authority. But Cabe's tone suggested he wasn't asking Mac to take time out. He was *telling* him.

"Now's a shit time for me to do that," he said, looking his old friend in the eye. "With Six away, and two big jobs coming up . . ."

Cabe shrugged. "I've got big shoulders. And it's not like you aren't around if any of the jobs go to shit. Plus, if it makes you feel better, you can deal with all the admin around this place. Hire us an office manager so I don't have to go to Staples every time someone needs a goddamn pen."

"I'm going to be there for all comms with Six. He needs to see me, to hear from me. I don't want him to know what's going on back here. He'll only worry, and it sounds like the job is enough of a handful as it is. Heck, we might need to send more people out."

"Which is why you can also add resume screening and interviewing to your to-do list if it helps you sleep at night. Look, why don't you and Delaney set up office here?" he said, pointing in the direction of one of the conference rooms. That way, you can help her *and* get some shit done here."

Mac shook his head. "My head is split. I'm half here working on this but thinking of her. When I'm helping Delaney, I'm thinking about here. What if I can't get my head in the game for Delaney?"

Cabe stood and slapped him on the shoulder. "*That* I can't answer for you. But I think you owe it to Delaney, and Brock, to try."

A couple of hours later, after finalizing the handoff as lead of the shipping company portfolio to Sherlock, positioning it as helping Delaney, and reminding the rest of the men that this was not for discussion with the guys in Syria, Mac headed into his office.

He sat down in his chair and folded his arms across his chest. Never had he felt so torn about his responsibilities. It sucked that Six, who had gone through this with Louisa, was away. He was the one person who might have understood what he was thinking.

But now he had to commit. Sherlock was leading up

the team in South America, and he'd do a kick-ass job of it. The guy was a natural in the field, and the rest of the team going with him respected him. He needed to get his brain in gear now and focus on what was happening with Delaney.

Which reminded him . . . Quickly he flipped open his laptop and looked through their client folders.

Louisa North

He opened Louisa's files. They'd amassed significant information about Lemtov and his associates during their intel collection, and what might have seemed trivial or irrelevant back then might mean more now in light of the information Delaney had provided.

It was time to go back to doing what he did best: collecting intel for the mission he'd been given, securing his target, and building a plan.

A fucking watertight plan.

Because his ability to return to his duties at Eagle depended on knowing that Delaney was safe. It was impossible to separate the need he had to do both.

His duty and his love, two sides of the same coin.

What would a fourteen-year-old girl need that she could throw together in under four minutes?

Delaney's heart raced from the call she'd just taken. She needed to help, even though it landed her smack-dab on the line between right and wrong.

Delaney ran around the apartment, a CVS bag in one hand, picking up things that might be useful. One of her old hoodies, a change of underwear, an unopened bar of soap. Towels? She threw a couple in anyway and made a mental note to give Mac some money for them. Frantically, she ran into the kitchen and threw snack bars, water, and the contents of Mac's pristinely stacked fruit bowl into a second bag from the drawer.

Yes, she'd promised Mac that she would stay home all day, safe in the ivory tower of his apartment, to enable all of his team to carry on with their day jobs without having to worry about protecting her. And she knew he'd found it hard to leave that morning, even though he'd not said a word. His jaw twitched as he grabbed his keys and walked to the door. She knew he wanted to stay with her, to help her, to talk about things that were best left alone, but she was relieved that he'd gone. She didn't usually crave time to think, but today she'd needed some space. Not least because when he was around her, she couldn't stop thinking about how he'd looked, every perfect naked inch of him, standing before her.

So when he'd pleaded with her to stay inside, to stay in a building with security cameras on every floor, a security guard and doorman, and a triple-thickness metal door that apparently even an antitank missile couldn't get through (which she hadn't totally believed), she'd agreed because she was grateful to be left alone and felt she owed him something after the way she'd behaved.

Until the call.

It had come from an unlisted number with a hint of information that she couldn't resist and a story so horrific that she knew she needed to act. Not just to save *her* story, but to see if she couldn't convince her contact to leave his sister in her care.

Now, as she jammed the elevator button with her finger over and over, she prayed that Mac wouldn't be in it. That he hadn't popped back to check on her. Because she knew he wouldn't let her go.

She'd have no choice then but to face him. Before the

call, sex had been on her mind all day. The kind of sex she apparently could have only with Mac. The kind of sex that came with orgasms, and connection, and a feeling of . . . damn. She couldn't bring herself to say *"love."* It was too . . . *gah.* Nor did she want to consider how he'd gotten so freaking skilled in the bedroom department.

Years of practice.

Apparently, she didn't want to think about a lot of things.

All she wanted to focus on now was saving at least one life. To help her escape with her brother from the life he'd dragged her into. The information her informant had promised her was just gravy. Proof of a new weapon, he'd said. Could she meet him at the Amtrak station? If she didn't get there in time, he was boarding the train.

The elevator opened, thankfully empty, and she stepped inside. Her contact had said he only had a half hour before he and his sister had to go. "Go" as in disappear into the ether if they wanted to stand a chance of staying alive. She'd used him before, a guy with limited funds, a sly tongue, and a Russian surname who'd finagled his way into useful service as a runner for the mob. He was the guy who faded into the background. The person people forgot was in the room. The kind of guy who knew how to be helpful to the right people. Until one of those people had started to make lewd suggestions about the guy's sister, how young girls had the tightest . . . *God*, Delaney shuddered at the thought.

That was the reason behind his helping Delaney the first time he'd contacted her. She'd known it was a small spiteful act to cause problems for the man who'd been too interested in the anatomy of a young girl. But this time was different. She could hear it in his voice, in his inflection. He'd called her in a panic, saying the guy had moved on his sister and they were fleeing town in the clothes they were wearing. The least she could do was give them some supplies for the journey.

Delaney hurried out of the apartment out to the street and flagged a cab. It wasn't a long walk to the station, but it would take more minutes than she had. Quickly, she jumped inside. "Santa Fe station," she said. "As fast as you can, please."

"Late for your train?" the driver asked, thankfully stepping on the gas.

"Something like that," she replied, looking down at the time on her phone. Three p.m. Too early for rush hour, but the city was never clear of traffic. Relief hit her when she spotted the large hotel at Sixth and Broadway. It meant she was halfway there. Weaving in and out of traffic, beating lights—perhaps a little too closely to truly be legal—her driver sheared the ten-minute trip she'd been expecting down to eight. When she saw the large white Spanish Colonial–style architecture of the train station, her heart skipped a beat.

Now she needed to stay calm. Be cool.

She threw the driver a twenty, told him to keep the change, then got out and hurried across the street as best she could. Everybody had to pass through the white building to get to the tracks.

Tucked into one of the archways, exactly where he'd said he'd be, was her contact, Grigory. He'd asked her to call him Greg.

"What happened?" she asked.

His sister stepped out from his shadow. Her face was bruised and there was a bloody cut by her lip.

"Dear God, Greg. What did they do?"

The tall, lanky man dropped his head. "What they said they'd do."

"You need to take her to the ER. You need—"

"No." Greg put his hand on hers. "Don't make me tell you what I had to do to rescue her. We are both dead if they find us. We must go. Here. Take this." He shoved an envelope into her hand.

"What is it?" Delaney asked.

"It's a weapon. A chemical weapon. It is what they are about to start shipping. I stole it from the man who did this." He glanced back at his sister who was gray and in shock.

"Let me run to the drugstore," she said. "Here. Take this. It was all I could grab."

Greg shook his head. "Our train leaves in"—he looked down at his phone—"eleven minutes."

"I'll be quick," she said. "But if for some reason I'm not, be safe, Greg."

Delaney ran as fast as her ankle would carry her to the drugstore a block over. She grabbed a basket and began throwing things in: antiseptic cream, Band-Aids, painkillers, toothbrushes, toothpaste. Even a pregnancy test kit, a box of tampons, and some pads. Quickly, she scanned them through self-checkout, paid, and ran back to the train station.

When she arrived at the arch, Greg was no longer there. Neither was his sister. Maybe she'd been longer than she thought. She hurried into the tiled atrium and raced through the building to the outdoor platforms, then found them in line waiting for the station employee to allow them to cross the tracks for the train.

"Here," she said, handing the bag to Greg's sister just as the guard removed the chain and allowed them to go.

"Thank you," Greg said as they passed her. "Take care of that." He tipped his chin in the direction of the envelope.

What had happened to her of late was an anomaly, not the kind of thing that normally happened to a woman who had grown up in Encinitas. But for Greg, this kind of hustle for survival had been his whole life. And now, because of his actions, his sister's life would be the same way. She deliberately didn't look where the train was headed. She didn't want to know. It was safer for everyone that way. But she hoped somewhere along the line Greg would find some help for his sister. She was too young—too fragile—to go through what she'd gone through and then have to deal with it on her own.

She looked down at the large white envelope Greg had handed her but decided the best thing to do would be to get back to the apartment, back to safety, and then read it. As the train pulled away with Greg and his sister safely on it, she headed back through the atrium, favoring her ankle. It had been a little over three weeks since she'd been taken, and her ankle had been showing progress, but now she was certain she'd busted it again. She bent down to press either side of her Achilles to see if she could massage some blood into the damn thing to get some range of motion back.

Loud voices shouting things she couldn't quite catch hurried through the station, followed by a woman cursing in Spanish.

From her crouched position, she saw two pairs of feet hurry by. A chill crept along her spine, what her mother used to describe as someone walking over her grave.

Slowly, she stood but kept low enough to be concealed by the people sitting around her. A group of women stood by the door complaining to what looked like a station employee. They were pointing in the direction the feet had sped, and she looked toward the tracks.

It was *him*. The man who had tried to break into her apartment. There was another man with him that she didn't recognize. They ran outside to the track side of the station at a pace that matched the pounding of her heart. While a part of her wanted to sit tight and stay exactly where she was, she also knew that when they didn't find Greg on the platform, they would search the station to make sure he wasn't there. And in doing so, they'd find her.

A group of young women passed by, obviously having just disembarked one of the many trains, and she quickly jumped up and joined them, crouching low so as not to draw attention to herself. She followed them outside the station and then looked around for a cab or a place to hide. Plaza station was right across the street. She could run in there and grab a trolley. It didn't matter where it was headed—just away from the train station. As she ran across the road, a cab appeared, heading north on Kettner. Frantically, she jumped up and down in the middle of the street. She didn't care if she looked idiotic. She just wanted the cabbie to see her and stop.

As the reassuring indicator begin to flash that the driver was pulling over, the two men ran out scanning up and down the street, and the man she'd been trying to avoid suddenly looked straight at her.

The taxi was pulling to a stop, but the man was already running across the road. A car coming in the opposite direction screeched to a halt as he recklessly ran straight toward her.

Finally, the taxi stopped, and she sprinted to the door,

yanking it open. She dove into the cab and shouted at the driver, "Just go, please. Now. Head north while I find an address."

As she spun in the seat, she could see the man running up the street toward the cab. He was within reach of the trunk as the taxi pulled out onto the road. A wave of nausea hit her. *Not now, Delaney. Not now.* Thankfully, the road ahead was clear. "Get onto Pacific as soon as you can," she told him. There were fewer cross streets there, fewer reasons to stop.

She knew Mac was going to be pissed, but she pulled out her phone and dialed him. *Come on. Come on!* The phone rang four times before he picked up.

"Hey, Buttons, what's up?"

"Where are you?" she said, her voice rough with tears that threatened to spill.

"I'm at the office. What's wrong? Are you outside?" His pitch escalated with each question.

"I'm in a cab. What's Eagle's address?"

Mac told her and she relayed it to the driver.

"Delaney. You're worrying me. Is everything okay?"

She heard slamming in the background. "No. But I'm fine for now. I think I'm being followed. Is it safe for me to—"

"It's the only place that's safe for you to come," he said, his voice cool and in control, just like she needed him to be. "And trust me, I'm ready to deal with whoever comes after you."

CHAPTER ELEVEN

"You're about three minutes out," Mac said, shoving his hands into his bulletproof vest as a precaution.

He pressed the button to open the huge warehouse-style door and dashed outside, unlocking the truck as he ran. He started the engine and reversed it into the large training area.

"What are you doing? Are you driving to meet me?" Delaney asked, her voice wavering.

"No," he replied. "Just bringing the truck inside the shop so that when we're ready to leave, we don't need to worry about you having to step outside."

As Delaney relayed to him every street as she passed by, he pressed the buttons that brought down all the metal shutters on the exterior of the building. If any fuckers thought they were getting hold of Delaney once she was inside this building, they had another think coming.

She was close. Very close.

And he was the kind of dead calm that he knew made him lethal.

"Should I look out the window to see if I'm being followed?"

Mac raced to the front of the building so he could open the front-door shutter manually to get her inside. "Keep that pretty head of yours down," he said, sliding his SIG out of its holster. "I see you. Take a right, then a quick right again onto the lot." There weren't any cars behind her, no sign of anyone on her tail. Hopefully the cabbie had lost whomever was after her.

"Which building are you?" she asked.

"Come all the way to the end. We're the nondescript gray box with all the black shutters down. Stay in the cab until I come get you. I've got the fare."

When the cab came to a halt outside Eagle Securities, Mac stepped outside and looked around before handing the driver a fifty through the window. "Thanks for getting her to me safely."

"No worries, boss," the man said.

Mac clicked the door open and tried to ignore the track marks of mascara that stained Delaney's cheeks. Beneath the calm, he was pissed. At the situation, and at her for defying the most basic order he'd given for her own security. But now was not the time to discuss that. They'd talk later, when she wasn't terrified or in danger.

"Straight over to the doorway over there, Delaney," he said, tipping his chin in that direction. "I'm going to crowd the shit out of you. So hustle."

Pleased that she did as he said, Mac trailed her until they were both safely inside. He couldn't speak to her. Not yet. Not when the building needed securing. And most definitely not while she was still sobbing softly behind him.

He secured the door and lowered the metal shutter. If

somebody wanted to get to them, they'd need torches and something to blast through bulletproof glass. But he still wanted her away from the doors and windows. "Come on," he said quietly. "Only a few more steps, Buttons. Then you can lose it."

On the way to the blacked-out conference room, he hit all the light switches to give the illusion that the warehouse was empty. Only the lights in the room itself remained on, and once he shut the door, nobody would be able to tell from the outside. With four interior walls, no windows, and one metal door, it was as secure as he could get. Plus, it had screens that would show images from all the building's external cameras.

"Mac," she said, his name coming out as a sob. "It was him. The guy who came to the apartment and tried to shoot the door down. But he wasn't looking for me. He was looking for Grigor—Greg. And probably this."

With one eye on the screens to confirm that she hadn't been followed, he saw her put an envelope down on the table. "I don't give a shit about Greg and that envelope right now. Come here."

She fell into his arms, her fist gripping his T-shirt, and cried against him. "I'm sorry," she hiccuped. "I should have stayed home, but I got a call and—"

"Stop it, Delaney. Just for a minute. And yes, I'm going to yell at you when that moment's up, but just for a minute hold on to me." Mac wrapped his arms tighter around her and kissed the top of her head. Torn between wanting to offer her comfort and doing his job—confirming she was safe and not being followed—he positioned himself so he could do both.

He'd been taught in basic training not to give in to negative thoughts. That's what Hell Week had been all about. Your mind will give out before your body will. From the moment he'd picked up his phone and heard her terrified voice, he'd refused to believe that it would end badly. He'd ignored his macho ego that said he should just get in his truck and drive straight to her because his mind had told him that by the time he'd gotten into the car and hit the downtown traffic, he'd never find her. He'd ignored the need to go out and hunt down the asshole who'd dared to look at her again. Instead, he'd gone into business mode. Concealment, arms, security, and supplies. But now that he had her in his arms, he allowed his own heart to race for a moment.

In the warm light of the quiet room, Delaney settled, and he got his racing heart back under control. Nobody had entered the business park. Mac placed his hands on her arms and stepped back a little. She looked up at him with an expression that said she already knew she'd screwed up. Maybe it was his military training, but he needed to make sure she'd understood the lesson. It would be impossible to protect her if she didn't.

"Why were you out of the apartment, Delaney?"

She bit her lip and shook her head. "I know it was stupid, but it didn't feel that way at the time. It was an emergency."

"You didn't think to pick up the phone at any point in this emergency and say, 'Hey, Mac, something's come up and I need to leave the apartment'?"

Delaney flinched at his words and shrugged out of his hands. "Okay, I get it. I don't know what else to say, Mac. Can I at least tell you why I left?" Her cheeks looked a little pinker and her tone sounded a little irritated, both of which were better than the ghostly pale skin and sobbing he'd been met with when she first arrived.

"No. Not yet." He crouched in front of the chair she'd just dropped herself into. "Do you know why the military works?"

On a sigh, she leaned her head back against the chair and closed her eyes. "Discipline? Chain of command? The opposite of what I did today?" She opened one eye and looked at him.

"Pretty much," Mac said. "I didn't tell you to stay home today because I like bossing you around, Delaney, or because I wanted to take control or limit you in some way. I told you to stay home because given that your assailants are unknown, given that we aren't a hundred percent sure what they think you have, and given that all of our crew have other jobs coming up and we had nobody to leave with you, it was the safest place for you to be."

Delaney opened both eyes. "I should have called or texted."

Mac nodded. "You should've."

"Can I explain what happened?"

He stood and grabbed a water from the table, cracking the lid before he handed it to her. Then he pulled out a chair so he could see both her and the screens behind her. "Start at the beginning. What kind of emergency?"

Mac sat back and listened as Delaney relived what had happened over the course of the afternoon. Externally, he remained seated, calm and collected. But internally, he wondered if it was possible to ground a woman for being so stupid while simultaneously wanting to hug the shit out of her for being so freaking brave. He did neither. Instead he began to clarify what she was saying, to see if he couldn't draw out details she might have forgotten, no matter how small. Mac picked up one of the markers and started to write out the details on the huge whiteboard.

"So, you don't know where Grigor . . . Greg . . . has gone?"

Delaney shook her head. "I figured it was safer for both of us if I didn't know."

Fuck. He wished she did know because while he had a shit ton of sympathy for the sister, he had none for the low-grade rat and the mess he'd caused. If they'd known where the two of them went, Mac would have had them hunted down so he could pump Greg for more information. But at the same time, he loved that his investigative journalist still had just as much heart as he remembered. He wondered how hard it would be to tap into the security footage of the Amtrak, then track the train and follow the route to see where Greg and his sister had gotten off. They might lose them out of the station, but at least they'd have a place to start.

"Do you know who Grigor's boss is? Who it was that he was talking about?"

She stood up and began to pace. "Lemtov."

Motherfucker.

"So, what's in the envelope?" he asked, looking at the packet that lay flat on the middle of the table.

Delaney reached for it. "I have no idea," she said and looked like she was about to rip it open. "He mentioned something about a chemical weapon when he handed it to me but I don't know what's in here."

"Leave it," he said. "Let's go open it in the warehouse, where we can use some different tools and preserve any evidence, fingerprints and shit."

"Fingerprints and *shit*? Is that the technical term for

it?" For the first time since she'd arrived, she had the makings of a smile.

"Yeah," he said, taking one last look at the screens. He stood and offered her his hand, grateful when she took it. "I think it's time we ripped apart what happened to you and looked at it under a microscope. Don't you?"

Mac led Delaney into the space behind the offices in the warehouse, switching on nothing more than a small table lamp. "It's probably overkill, but honestly, given that it's just you and me, I'd rather not have to fight tonight if we don't need to. Not when you don't know one end of a weapon from another," he teased.

She raised an eyebrow in his direction. "I might not be a crack shot like you are, but I know my way around a firearm now, thanks to this guy I know."

"Just some guy you know? Should I be jealous?"

Delaney knew that he was teasing, trying to take her mind off what happened and get her refocused, but the way her stomach kept tightening, she wasn't a hundred percent certain that she wasn't going to puke. Plus, she wasn't entirely sure of the ground between them. They'd left their conversation that morning on less than stellar terms, but he'd been the only person she wanted to run to. And despite their argument, despite everything that had happened between them, she knew that counted for something. She shook her head and acknowledged what she'd been trying to bury . . . it counted for *everything*. Still, if he could fake them being okay for a little while just to get through it, so could she.

"Possibly. The guy has medals and shit," Delaney replied, and put the envelope down on the table.

"We're going to take a look at this, make copies even," he said, looking down at the envelope, "but we will need to update the police and *feebs* too. Courtesy call."

"And say what?" Delaney said, placing the item in question down onto the work surface. "I've been speaking with a known criminal who stole some information to make up for the fact that an alleged crime boss raped his underage sister, who I just allowed to escape on an Amtrak train to somewhere I don't know?"

In the half-light of the lamp, he studied her and then shrugged. "Fair point. But we *will* tell them the truth. Perhaps a bit differently than you laid it out. He called you, and out of compassion and panic you went to help a source. He gave you that information, and now you are calling the police to update them. You aren't going to prison for that. Plus, this is Eagle's case now."

"That's reassuring, Mac." She slapped his arm.

"Yeah. Well. Couldn't you have grown up to be a librarian, Buttons? Life would be a lot simpler."

Delaney shook her head. "And what? Die of boredom before I turn thirty?"

Mac studied her, his expression suddenly thoughtful. "Guess librarians don't generally end up in hospitals in Germany . . ."

And they wouldn't have been reunited. Her contrarian heart flipped in protest, so she changed the topic to something safer. "Whatever is in that envelope could be the answer to what I'm trying to uncover. Handing it over to the police could blow things wide open before we've had time to follow all the leads to see where it ends."

"That's the journalist in you thinking. Think with the part of you that wants to stay alive, Delaney. Let's get some supplies from the infirmary."

Delaney followed Mac through the cavernous space until they reached a series of rooms at the back of the building. One looked like the kind of showers you saw in a locker room, the other, a dorm with medical supplies.

"We're set up for basic triage," Mac said, pointing to a series of shelves containing sterile packages, bandages, needles, and the like. "I've got medic training, and so do a couple of the other guys. It's here in part because we're tight-assed when it comes to spending money on health care, but it's also convenient. Nobody has to wait an hour to get stitched up. And, no questions. We don't have to explain what happened to anybody nosy enough to care."

"Does that happen to you often?" she asked. The realities of his job were becoming more clear. Never had the word "sacrifice" meant so much to her as when she saw the lengths Mac and the team were willing to go to for their country or simply another person.

"Not as often as you'd think, more often than we'd like." Mac grabbed a scalpel, some tweezers, a sterile pad, and a pair of blue surgical gloves. "If there is any chance this is going to become evidence at some point, I don't think I should add my prints into the mix."

"Damn, I already held it." She hadn't thought about prints. Heck, she hadn't thought of it as evidence. Which showed how out of it she was.

Mac guided her back across the warehouse until they reached the table and lamp. "It was given to you, so that wouldn't be unexpected. But let's not add them to what's inside."

"This is quite the place you have here, Mac." Delaney trailed behind him, making out what she could in the dim light. "I mean, I can't see the half of it. But blackout conference rooms, warehouse training centers, medical rooms . . . This is a big operation, Mac."

Mac placed the supplies down on the table and pulled on the sterile gloves. With a snap of the wrist, he opened the sterile sheet and placed the envelope on top of it, then looked up and around the building. Pride etched his features. "It was Cabe's idea, you know, all this. A plan for when we retired from service. Hell, we just started saving for this five years ago. And Cabe . . . well, he's good with the money market. Didn't turn us into millionaires or anything like that, but gave us seed funding to at least get a place, equipment, that kind of thing. If we didn't have the volume of work we did, it would be hard to keep the doors open—but we do, and we are. Every dollar we saved is in this place."

"Shit, Mac, I'm sorry. Let me pay you back for Germany, see if there isn't something my boss can do to pay for the security, or help or—"

Suddenly, Mac faced her. "I wasn't telling you because I want anything from you, Delaney. We're holding our own, even beginning to make some of it back."

Delaney tucked her long hair behind her ear but it immediately fell forward again. "But I'm draining that."

"Listen." He turned and faced her straight on. "You didn't want to talk this morning. And I'm doing my best to be patient. But I would make the same decision to get on the plane a thousand times over. And a thousand times over again, I wouldn't take a penny from you for the privilege of doing that. Of helping you. So, stop talking about it like my helping you is some goddamn hardship."

"It's not right, Mac. I dragged you into this, and it's gone way beyond what you probably thought you were signing up for."

He shook his head. "No. What's not right is that you were kidnapped and that someone is trying to kill you. Let's focus on that. Let's start there. It needs resolving before we can think about anything else."

Delaney gripped his biceps and stood up on her toes to kiss him on the cheek. He sighed as she lingered there. It was too tempting to turn her face to the side and catch his lips with hers. "Thank you," she whispered, and as suddenly as she'd gripped him, she dropped back to her feet.

Mac swallowed hard. "Steady, Delaney, or I might just think you like me."

Not knowing what else to say, she looked down and stubbed the toe of her sneaker on the concrete floor.

"Okay," he said gruffly. "Let's get this envelope open." Carefully, he used the scalpel to break the seal at the top of the envelope. "I'm not a forensics guy, but I'd guess DNA could be taken from the licked seal, so let's leave that intact." Using the tweezers, he slid its contents out onto the desk—a mix of neatly printed reports and hand-written pages that had been ripped out of a ruled note-book, their edges all tattered as if they'd been removed hastily. "Thought we'd left the pen and paper era behind."

"Apparently not," she replied.

One of the hand-drawn pieces of paper contained what looked like chemical formulas, not that she understood what they meant. Hexagons butted up with other hexagons, the letters N, H, and O dotted across them.

"Louisa would be able to tell us what this all means if you don't mind bringing her in," Mac said, continuing to use the tweezers to separate the pages. There was an address. "Man, this handwriting is worse than mine."

Delaney went to grab one of the sheets.

"Stop," he said quickly, pulling her wrist out of the way and snapping the gloves off his wrists. "It's bad enough that your prints are on the envelope, but you don't need to get them on this."

The sound of car tires on gravel filtered through the warehouse, and a thin sliver of light filtered under the roller shutter door. Mac quickly hit the light on the desk, casting them into darkness.

"Shh," he breathed quietly against Delaney's ear.

"Okay," she whispered.

He took her hand, and, obviously familiar enough with the building to navigate it in the dark, led them back to the office. Once they were inside it, he flicked the lights on again and hurried to the bank of monitors.

For a moment, nobody got out of the car. It sat, engine running, lights off.

"What are they going to—"

"Shh." Mac focused on the screen, his eyes on the car.

She'd been around the block enough to not take offense to being shushed. Instead, she tried to make out the occupants. The car door opened. "Will they be able to get in here?"

Mac shook his head. "I doubt it. But if they do, they'll get a surprise." He pulled his SIG, the one he'd let her practice with earlier in the week, from its holster. "Don't panic," he said. "It will take them an age to get through all the security measures we have on this place."

The three men on the monitor separated. One went down the side of the building, and the other two went around the back. No one approached the front, which made sense as it faced out onto the road. Dressed in black, they blended into the night. Suddenly, lights flooded the area.

"How d'you like that, asshole?" Mac said, and then laughed. He must have installed automatic floodlights over the entrances.

The lights blinded the two around the back, and they scuttled back into the darkness of the shrubbery that edged their property.

He pulled out his phone. "Cabe," he said quietly. "I've got Delaney here and she was followed. There's company outside. Floodlights scared them for now, but . . . Shit."

On the screen, the lights went dark as one of the men fired shots at the lights.

"Yeah. Just shot the bulbs out."

Delaney listened as Mac railed off details about the three men and then hung up. "We'll have reinforcements soon. Faster than the cops would get here, and they'll be way better armed."

The guy from the front came running from the side of the building and gesticulated between the three of them. He was angry about something. And also twitchy, constantly looking over his shoulder.

A light from a car on the side road glanced over their faces, and all three men jumped. It only took one man to break from the group and head for the car before the other two followed.

And as they drove away, Delaney slumped against Mac's shoulder in relief.

CHAPTER TWELVE

Two hours later, after Cabe and Ryder had arrived at Eagle Securities and spent time freeze-framing images of the perps' faces to send to Noah to see if they could get a hit off SDPD's database and after they'd spoken to all the relevant authorities involved, Mac had finally gotten Delaney into his truck and home.

He reached for the corkscrew and opened a bottle of wine.

Delaney was taking a bath. She'd said she'd needed a moment, and he'd given it to her. But in return, he'd made her promise that when she came out, he was going to tell her about Brock. Yeah, the timing might be rough, but one thing he'd learned was that stepping out on the battlefield with any kind of bad blood between you and a brother was a recipe for disaster. He and Delaney needed to be on the same side—*fully* on the same side—for him to do his job, and they'd never get there with Brock between them.

He poured himself a large glass and walked out onto the balcony with a second one and the rest of the bottle.

"So, Brock," he said to the night sky as he sloshed his wine around in the bottom of the glass as if he knew what the fuck he was doing and placed the rest of the stuff he was carrying down on the table. "I'm sorry, brother." He didn't know why he felt compelled to talk out loud. It wasn't something he usually did. Usually he just spoke to his friend in his head, shared the experiences he was having with him. At first he'd thought it was foolish, but it had become a habit. Before Brock had died, they'd spoken all day, every day. Lab partners, swim team buds, wingmen. The first few weeks after Brock had died, he'd pull out his Nokia to call him over some stupid shit he'd seen, put it down and stare at it, pick it up again to call Delaney to tell her what he'd just tried to do, and put it down again.

"I'm gonna tell her what happened that day. I know I said I wouldn't ever talk about it. But that was before you died on me. Not telling Delaney what happened that day is killing me. And worse, it's killing her. I hope you can see how torn up she is. And yeah, if she forgives me, I get to keep her for the rest of my life, which seems so fucking unfair when you don't get a girl of your own, and married, and kids and shit . . ." His voice wavered. Tears stung the corners of his eyes like they always did on the rare occasion he let his real emotions bubble to the surface. "But, man . . . knowing will let us all breathe."

"Knowing what?" Delaney asked as she walked out. There was a chill to the air, so over her leggings she was wearing an oversize cream sweater that slid off her shoulder. She pulled out a chair at the patio table and sat, tucking her knees under her sweater.

Mac coughed gruffly to clear his throat and poured

her a glass of wine. "You were right. Brock didn't want to jump off that cliff."

Delaney pushing the wineglass away. "I knew it." The metal feet of the patio chair scraped across the patio and she jumped to her feet. "He looked up to you. Everybody did. He would have done it just because you said so."

Mac shook his head. "Yes, I goaded him, but it wasn't like you think, Delaney. He didn't want to jump, but he asked me to help him do it anyway."

Eyes wet with unshed tears, she glared back at him. "That doesn't make sense," she said. "People who were there said they saw you taunting him to jump."

"I did." Mac felt sick thinking about the way he'd at first encouraged Brock and then had pushed and cajoled. "And I regret every word I uttered that day. I regret not talking him out of it. I wish I'd never let him talk *me* into it. But he was convinced that he'd never make it as a SEAL."

"What do you mean, *you* wish he'd never talked *you* into it?"

Mac pulled a chair from the table and swung it so it directly faced hers. He reached for her wrist, which she attempted to tug away. "Just come and sit and listen. When I'm done, if you're still mad at me, I'll drive you to Cabe's myself.

"I've carried this around for too long, letting you suffer when I could have put it right. When you walked out, I was apologizing to your brother for giving up his secret."

Reluctantly, Delaney did as he asked, and took a long sip of wine. "I'm listening," she said, her tone terse.

"Your brother knew that you and your parents didn't think he would make it as a SEAL."

Delaney sank back into the chair. "That's not true. I thought . . . well . . . I didn't think it was a good fit for him, sure, but I didn't think it was because he couldn't do it."

Mac shook his head. "Well, that wasn't how he saw it. It put second thoughts into his head. And he knew, from everything he'd read, that SEAL training is eighty percent mental. He was doubting his abilities, which was the worst thing he could do. But he didn't want to go back on his word to enlist and prove that you guys were right all along. Once he saw the Twin Towers fall, he wanted to enlist so badly, but your parents made him finish college. As time went on, some of what you and your parents said made him begin to think he wouldn't be able to do all the things expected of him."

His thoughts drifted to that afternoon.

"Dude, it's not working," Brock said as he walked into Mac's room.

Mac closed his poly sci book. It wasn't like what he was reading was sticking in his brain anyway. It was a glorious day outside, but he needed to study, no matter how badly he'd rather be on the beach with Delaney. "What's up?"

"The fucking height thing . . ."

This again. Goddamn, he didn't know why Brock didn't just give it up. He'd tried everything to help Brock get over it. They'd started small on an indoor climbing wall, then Mac had tried to build him up from there. But nothing had worked. They'd gone to San Francisco for a state swim meet and Mac had arranged for the two of them to walk across the Golden Gate Bridge, which had turned Brock greener than their swim uniform.

"Dude. Have you considered you might just need to

move on? I mean, I get it, wanting to achieve this, but if you can't—"

"You know I can't."

Mac shrugged his shoulders. "So, kill or cure, right. Go big or go home. All that motivational crap."

Brock nodded.

It was a bad idea but Mac said it anyway. "What about cliff jumping? We could go jump off the Arch . . . you know, that bluff at Sunset Cliffs."

"Or take a ride up to Laguna Beach. You said it took ninety minutes to get up there. What was the name of that cliff you said was like a hundred feet tall? El Morro?"

Shit. That had been a fucking thrill jump . . . a once in a lifetime even for him.

"I mean," Brock continued. "I know you and Six have done it before and got a kick out of it. Maybe I just need to do something akin to the worst it's ever going to be. Experience that and know I got through it."

Brock was right, cliff jumping was way more exciting than poly sci, but if he was going to blow off studying, he'd rather it be because Delaney was going to blow him. Since they'd had sex—her for the first time—it was constantly on his mind. But he couldn't say that to his friend, who had only just gotten his head around the fact that Mac had broken the bro code and banged his little sister. Not that "bang" was how Mac saw it. Just being around Delaney brightened his whole world.

Then he noticed Brock, like really noticed him. He was bouncing on his toes like he did before the first swim of a meet. And he looked a little gray and was speaking a little too fast.

"I'm game, but are you sure you want to do that?" Mac asked, putting his textbooks in a pile.

"Not really, but how can I be a fucking SEAL when the idea of dropping any height into water makes me want to puke?"

"Fine," Mac said, grabbing his beach towel and keys. "But if we're driving all the way up there, I'm making sure you go over. Deal?"

Brock nodded his head. "Deal."

Mac shook his head to clear the memory and took a sip of his wine. "He was worried about jumping into the ocean and told me he wanted to get over it. I told him it was a stupid way to try to fix it. That he should start jumping from small cliffs first, build up confidence. But you know Brock . . . *knew* Brock. He did everything *big* and didn't want to wait."

"And you couldn't talk him out of it?" Delaney asked.

"I was twenty, Delaney. With balls of steel and shit for brains. That's why Brock asked me to help him. He told me that he didn't want to give you guys ammunition to talk him out of his decision. He said he needed to get out of his own head and stop doubting what he was capable of. He made me promise that I wouldn't tell anyone that he was terrified. It was an easy thing for me to do, so I was all in to help him. I mean, I'd jumped before. Six and I had been goofing around the summer before, thinking we were cool because we were too clueless to know better. So, we called up Cabe and Six, who happened to already be up there surfing, told them we were on our way."

"You should have talked him out of it, Mac. He was scared. If I'd known, I would have stopped him. You shouldn't—"

"Don't you think I know that now, with the benefit of hindsight, and maturity, and over a decade of nightmares about dragging my best friend's dead body back to shore? Fuck, Delaney. I know I should have."

Delaney tucked her knees back underneath her sweater and wrapped her arms around them, the wine-glass hanging loosely in her fingers. Pain—and worse, disappointment—etched her features.

"Anyway, on the drive up there, he talked about how he wanted your dad to be proud of him, how he wanted you to see your brother amount to something, how he wanted to get your mom to stop worrying about him by showing he was capable. And he wanted to have something to say when he joined the Navy. He wanted to be ready to sign up and get straight into BUD/s, the SEAL training program, as soon as the process would let him. He didn't want to show up on day one with doubt already planted in his mind that he was never going to make it."

Mac sighed as he recalled the way his friend's dark hair had flapped around violently as they drove with the windows wide open. "He made me promise to not let him back out. Told me to say *anything* up there to make him do it. And if I had to, I should pick him up and throw him off. I told him it would be easy, seeing he was such a lightweight. And he laughed."

"Mac . . ." A tear rolled down her cheek. He wanted to reach for her, but he didn't feel worthy of her right now, and she'd need to be the one to close the gap between them once his story was over.

"I joked that if I did that, I might . . ."—he swallowed hard—"I might kill him. And he joked that he was ready to kill me for fucking his sister, so it made us even."

He placed his wine on the table and rested his elbows on his knees. He could see Brock's face as clear as day in his mind. "He asked me to promise to make him jump, to use any means necessary to get his ass off that cliff. I tried to talk him out of his decision to enlist, or at least enlist for a different group. If he hated the idea of heights, and the combination of height and water so badly, go sign up for a hard-core unit in one of the other military branches. But he wouldn't have it. His mind was set. So, I did. I started light at first. We walked to the edge together, talked about timing it right with the waves. It's a hundred foot drop. Another guy went ahead of us, screamed all the way to the bottom, and then panicked when he hit the surf. It took him an age to get his head back above water."

Brock had begun to shake his head and step away from the edge, mumbling "I can't do this" over and over.

"He said there was no way he could become a SEAL. I asked him if he was sure because if he was, he should just back out now. I tried everything to persuade him. Positive shit, like Muhammad Ali quotes and that kind of thing, but he just kept going on about how your dad had been poking at him, asking him why he was wasting his life and education to go be a glorified sailor and saying that he didn't have the backbone it took to do such a job." Mac leaned back in the chair. "*Shit.*"

"So what happened? Witnesses said you were arguing on the way up to the cliff."

Mac nodded. "We weren't . . . I was just . . . I don't know. I was trying to motivate him. Getting all Bob Knight on his ass without the chair throwing," he said, referring to the controversial NCAA coach. "It probably looked like we were fighting. I thought I could get inside his head. Stop the cycle of doubt in himself by giving him something else to think about."

"They also said they saw you bump him."

"I told him I was going to say something that was going to make him mad enough to follow me over the edge. That I was going to make him kick my ass, but he'd have to come get me." Mac covered his eyes with his hand. He didn't want to see her when she heard the rest. "I bumped him before I walked back to take my run up, not on my way past him to the edge. I told him your dad was right, that he was a coward, that I was a bigger man than he was because I was jumping off that cliff with or without him. . . . And on the way past, I told him you were the best lay I ever had."

Silence hung in the air. Delaney didn't move or say anything. In his mind, he heard Brock's yell as he followed him over the edge. It had been too soon. Brock should have given him time to get clear. When Mac had hit the water, having timed the height of the wave, he knew there would be enough water to break his fall. Quickly, he'd swum clear and turned to watch his friend jump. But he was already halfway down, sheer panic on his face. He'd mistimed, hadn't waited long enough. Before Brock had caught the rocks at the base of the cliff and been thrown forward into the churning water, Mac was already swimming toward him.

Mac's breath caught in his throat as he remembered the burn in his lungs as he'd powered back toward the cliff and had begun to dive into the swirling salt water. He remembered the six dives it had taken to locate Brock. He remembered the way his eyes burned as he swam around the bluff and pulled his best friend's limp body onto the beach, shouting so loudly that his voice had given out. He remembered the blood covering the side of Brock's head, and the passerby who he later learned was a doctor vacationing from Salem knocking him out of the way to perform CPR.

And he sure as fuck remembered the paramedic declaring Brock dead on the scene.

Delaney watched as Mac leaned forward and made a sound somewhere between a sob and a cry of anguish, and her heart cracked open at the pain he'd been carrying all those years. Never in all the years she'd known him had she ever seen him lose control and cry. Not after he'd shown up at their home to try to explain what had happened, or at the visitation when Mac had quietly slipped in at the very end to say goodbye to his friend, or at the funeral when she'd slapped him.

She wanted to get up, go wrap her arms around him, hold him and tell them that one way or another, they'd be okay. But she still had questions.

"Why didn't you say any of this to the police when they were investigating his death, or the coroner, or anyone else?" she asked. *Would it have made any difference if he had?* Delaney wasn't sure. It probably would have made it worse. And she most definitely would have spent the time in between hating herself.

Mac took a moment to compose himself, wiped his eyes, and let out a whoosh of breath. He sat back in the chair and took a sip of wine.

The silence between them was deafening. And neither of them spoke for a while.

"Being in the SEALs reinforced something I always inherently knew back then," Mac said eventually, his voice hoarse. "It sounds easy when you say it, but never speak ill of the dead. I once worked with a guy who

was killed on a mission. The military has protocol for
that shit. Emergency next of kin and that kind of thing.
But this guy had a serious relationship on the side. And
she was four months' pregnant with his kid when we
deployed. He was killed two days before the end of the
tour. I knew the girlfriend worked at the Marriott by
the convention center, so I figured I should go tell her
but decided to wait until the funeral was over. Because
his wife, his three kids, his mom and dad . . . they
didn't need a scene. I couldn't let his infidelity ruin his
legacy."

"I don't understand what you are trying to say,"
Delaney said.

"There was nothing to gain by smearing Brock. Telling the police that he was shit scared and wanted me to
force him because he didn't want your dad to think he
was weak or less of a man would have torn your dad
apart. And having to explain to you that he thought you
didn't think he was good enough to be a SEAL. And telling you my final taunt was about something so . . . *Shit*,
it was perfect, Delaney, what we had. What we could
have had. It was destroyed, but at least you still had
Brock's memory in one piece."

She felt like a rough tide. Churned up, with all the dirt
being lifted off the bottom of the ocean and thrown about
as waves crashed over her.

"When I asked . . . when you came over and I asked
you if you goaded him into jumping . . ." Tears took over
and ran down her face, but she was determined to get the
words out. "You said yes. Why didn't you explain?"

Mac got up from his chair and walked over to the balcony, looking tormented. "Because you'd already decided.
Because you needed someone to blame. Because I'd

already let Brock down. I'd killed him with my good intentions and I owed it to Brock to keep him whole in your memory. Because it was already destroying your mom. Because your dad was a decent man who just didn't understand his son. Because I was a shit best friend who should have said no. Because I was young and thought I was being fucking noble. I don't know. *FUCK!*" He stepped back and kicked the wall of the apartment hard before placing his two hands flat against it and looking down at the floor. "Making sure the three of you got through it just seemed more important. And I loved you so much, Delaney, that I couldn't live with the idea of making you hurt more. A few months later, when I thought of coming to you, to explain, your dad died. And mom told me it was from heart complications brought on by stress from Brock's death. I knew you wouldn't want me back after that."

The logic of what'd he'd done made sense. It killed her now to know that Brock had died thinking she somehow doubted him. Maybe she should go to his grave. Tell him how much she loved him, and that her words had been carelessly spoken. It was the unfinished business that would hover between them until she addressed it.

And Mac . . . all those years, he'd carried this, and the weight of her hatred. He could have saved himself by telling them the truth.

She couldn't ignore the nobility in that. The sacrifice. Which made her wonder.

"Why did you all become SEALs?"

Mac pushed away from the wall. "I felt like I needed to take his place, and Cabe and Six decided they weren't going to let me do it alone. They've had my back since we were old enough to understand the concept. Plus, sticking it to Osama Bin Laden felt like a good use of time."

So he'd spent all that time pursuing Brock's dream instead of his own. "He wouldn't have expected you to do that for all those years."

Returning to his chair, he sat down and studied her. "You know the crazy thing, Delaney? Without what happened, I would never have enlisted. It wasn't my thing. But then for Brock, I felt like enlisting was the right thing to do. I've had an incredible career, but any thoughts about my future were impossible, because I couldn't think of it without you in it."

"Mac, I'm sorry I—"

"No. Don't ever apologize. At first, I signed up because I thought it would kill a few years and then I'd rethink what I wanted to do. But I was good, Delaney. I worked so hard on my fitness ahead of my first day that I nailed everything physical they threw at me. Everything I did, I did because my best friend would never get to accomplish it. And so, for him, I was going to be the best SEAL there'd ever been. So, I was good. No, I was *great* at being a SEAL. Leading came easily, but it was something I always took seriously, even from our days on the swim team. When it came time to decide whether to stay or go, I stayed."

Delaney took a sip of wine and placed her glass down on the table. "I guess sometimes we end up where we're meant to."

Mac reached forward and took her hand, his chilled fingers against hers. "I don't know about that, Delaney."

She knew what he meant. The two of them. He didn't believe their relationship had ended where it was supposed to.

Knowing the next step had to be hers, she placed her other hand on top of his. This good, strong man, who'd given up everything for her family, still wanted her.

"Mac. Do you think Brock will . . . do you think he knows that I didn't doubt him? Will he forgive me?"

He fell to the hard concrete on his knees in front of her, pulling her against him in a rib-crushing hug. "Oh, Delaney, don't think about that. I'm not sure I believe in the whole life-after-death, spirit shit. But I know he loved you more than life itself. He wouldn't hold this against you."

She wrapped her arms tightly around him, as much because she needed to hold on to him as she knew he needed to be comforted.

They stayed like that, silent in their thoughts, for several minutes until Mac found his feet, standing with her still wrapped around him. Without saying a word, she crossed her ankles around his back and laid her head on his shoulder. He lowered them to the sofa, he upright and her sitting astraddle.

Lovingly, he cupped her face. "I'm sorry I kept this from you for so long."

She leaned into his hand. "I wish you'd told me, but I get why you didn't. I think we should tell Mom. She already thinks she failed as a mother, and this might confirm it in her mind . . . but she deserves the truth."

Mac ran his hand along her shoulder, down her arm, taking hold of her hand. "I'll go with you whenever you want to go. Let me tell her, though. She deserves to hear it from me."

"I should have known." Delaney looked down at their joined hands. "I don't know why in all these years I didn't push you for the rest of the story."

Mac pulled her hand to his lips and kissed the back of it, then looked at her, his eyes searching hers. "Why would you? I'd never lied to you, Delaney. Outside of this. And everything people were saying was true. There were witnesses. I did goad him into it. He didn't want to do it. It killed him. I killed him as surely as I pushed him off that bluff."

Exhausted, she allowed herself to fall forward into his arms, allowed herself to feel and savor every moment of placing her head on strong shoulders that had carried so much to look out for her.

"We all know how persuasive Brock could be. He'd needle you over and over, like a pebble in your shoe, until you gave in."

Mac ran his hand up and down her back. It was soothing. A peaceful quiet fell between them. Their breaths slowed.

"I'm sorry for hating you all these years, Mac," she said quietly.

"I'm sorry I gave you reason, Delaney. Losing you was harder than losing him. At least with Brock I could rationalize why I'd never see him again. But you. I've lived knowing you had this whole other life I wasn't a part of."

She brushed her nose against the skin of his neck and buried her head against him. "But you're back in it now . . ."

When his arms tightened around her, she settled closer, trying to ignore how aware she'd suddenly become of his body. Of the planes of his chest, of the firmness of his thighs, of the way her core pressed deliciously up against him.

"Am I?" he asked gruffly.

How could he not be? After everything they'd gone

through, were going through? After everything he'd done to protect her? "Yes, Mac." She pressed her lips to the skin behind his ear, loving the way he shivered as she kissed one of the areas she knew firsthand to be his most sensitive.

"Be clear, Delaney. Because I was expecting you to leave after I told you what I did. How far back into your life am I?"

Was she ready to look him in the eye, admit that this man still moved her more than anyone she'd ever met? Slowly, she sat up, and this time placed *her* hands on *his* face.

"Every way that matters."

Then she did what she should have done a long time ago. She leaned forward and kissed him.

When Delaney's lips finally touched his, Mac could barely keep his shit together. There were too many emotions swirling around inside. He'd just confessed his most difficult secret, and she hadn't left him. Instead, she was pressing those sweet breasts of hers up against him, and kissing him with more . . . fuck, he didn't know . . . everything. And he couldn't get enough.

Maybe they should stop, go to bed, sleep on it. But the truth was, he was beyond waiting. And he was determined to never give her a reason to regret putting that wonderful mouth of hers on his.

She tasted of Pinot Noir and a shared history that was comfortable, reassuring. And yet it was all new and deliciously hot.

He licked the seam of her lips and she opened to him, and he wondered if she was aware of how she'd begun to gently rock back and forth against him. His hands were everywhere. Running a trail down her spine, holding her hips tightly, gripping her ass and positioning her so she was tucked up close against his cock, which had sprung into action faster than he could load his SIG.

Fucking and loving Delaney were the only things he could think about right now, but he needed to confirm the one thing that would ensure that what they were about to do wasn't hollow. "Delaney," he mumbled against her lips.

Her hands were in his hair, pulling her lips to his.

"Delaney." He gripped her wrists and tugged her away. Those lips of hers were ruby ready, her eyes wide, pupils dilated, and she had the look about her that he used to love. The one that told him she was in the mood for nothing but him when she'd suddenly drop her clothes in his dorm room. But he needed to know. "Are you really still here with me?"

"I'm right where you are," she said with a shy smile. "It just took me a while to get there."

"Thank you, Lord, for that."

It was time to build something new. As they were right in this moment. As the man he'd become. As the woman he'd still give his life for. He reached beneath the hem of her cute sweater and grinned when she lifted her arms into the air so he could remove it.

"Goddamn, woman." She wasn't wearing a bra, and those sweet nipples of hers were tight and pointing in his direction. Unable to resist, he leaned forward and sucked gently on one of them, loving the way the action of arching her back just pressed her more firmly up against his cock. Damn, he needed to take his jeans off soon before they cut off his circulation. Delaney tasted sweet, and the moan she gave was even sweeter.

"Oh, yes. Harder," she cried out, gripping the back of his head pressing him closer.

Giving in to her clear direction, he sucked more firmly, bit a little, immersed in the moment. Fully turned on by the way she clawed against him, he gave in to his more basic urges. Running his hand up her side, he gripped her other breast, alternately sucking and squeezing until she was frantically moving against him.

Slightly lifting her off his lap, he laid her down on the sofa. "I'm going to eat you like a starving man," he said, as she stared up at him with hooded eyes, her tongue sneaking out to wet her lips.

Delaney grinned. "And I'm going to let you."

After placing her next to him on the sofa, he tugged his T-shirt over his head and then grabbed the waistbands of her leggings and underwear, removing both in one clean sweep. "You have no idea just how much I have been thinking about your ass this week."

Without prompting, Delaney rolled onto her stomach, then got onto all fours, her forearms resting on the arm of the sofa, ass round and high in the air. His vision blurred as blood raced from his brain to his cock and back again. "Like this?" she asked, looking at him over her shoulder.

"Goddamn, woman. Yeah. Just like that." He rubbed his hands over her smooth skin, spreading her cheeks so he could get his tongue right where he wanted it. *Damn.* She was already wet for him. Unable to wait, he buried his face, and licked her firmly, back and forth, until she was wiggling beneath him. How badly she wanted him made him grin, made him feel like a hero.

"Oh, Mac. You're so good at this," she said, lowering

her forehead to her arms, which only served to open her up to him more.

When he'd finished eating his fill, he was going to take her just where she was.

Until she moved.

"Where do you think you're going?" he asked. "I was a long way from being done."

Delaney came to her knees and met him in the middle of the sofa. She ran her index finger over her lips. "Perhaps I'm hungry, too."

He wanted to be a gentleman, wanted to get her off over and over before he took anything from her. But then she gripped him through the denim of his jeans.

"Let me taste *you*, Mac."

Quickly, he jumped to his feet, and shucked his jeans and boxer briefs. His cock throbbed with relief at no longer being constrained as he sat back down on the sofa.

Delaney crawled forward, her hair tucked behind her ear. Taking him firmly in her hand, she licked the very tip.

Every part of Mac tightened as she tasted him, and he couldn't contain the groan that escaped as she opened her mouth into the most perfect O and took him deep into her wet warmth. It wasn't just the way she gripped him that he loved, or the way she kept her mouth so tight around him that it was a wonder he hadn't come already, but the way she did both things with those glorious eyes of her pinned to his. Never had he felt so *connected*.

"Fuck, Delaney. Just like that."

She let him slip out of her mouth and kissed along his length, her hands slipping lower to take hold of his balls, tugging on them gently as she made her way back to the tip.

No amount of warning prepared him for the way it felt as she covered him with her mouth a second time, teasing him, sucking him. Yeah. Sex with grown-up Delaney was going to be a whole bunch more adventurous. Delaney was on her knees on the couch next to him, that cute ass of hers jiggling as she worked him out, up and down, and he lazily trailed his fingers along her spine and over those sweet curves until he found the growing wetness between her legs.

Her eyes flared wide as he slid first one and then a second finger deep inside her, moving in time to the way she sucked him off so perfectly. When he felt the telltale tightening in his balls, he gently withdrew his fingers and lifted her to his mouth so he could kiss her. "I want to be in you when I come, Buttons," he mumbled against her lips, using those few moments to talk himself off the edge of coming. "Now get your ass back in the air."

Delaney grinned. "I never realized you were such an ass man."

Mac grinned as he walked to the bedroom to get a condom. When he returned, she was exactly where he wanted her. He crouched down, level with her face. "When it comes to you, I'm an everything man." Gently, he pressed his lips to hers. "Now hold on tight because this could get a little frantic."

"Do your worst," she teased.

Climbing back onto the sofa, he settled himself on his knees between her legs. She was wet, and open, and spectacular. Gripping his cock, he guided it to her opening and allowed himself to slide in a little. "You're perfect, Delaney," he groaned as she tightened around him and pushed back against him. He looked down and watched where he slid inside her, watched as his cock glistened with her juices. Unable to resist, he grabbed hold of her ass, squeezing it and kneading it, as Delaney's eyes fluttered shut on a groan.

"Mac," she muttered. "Oh, harder, please."

Never one to refuse a direct order, he did as she requested, pushing in faster, harder, until he was banging up against her ass. The noises their bodies were making as they collided were as much of a turn-on as the sounds she was making.

He leaned over her body, placing his hands on either side of her shoulders as he pressed up inside her, sweat forming on his brow. Delaney opened her eyes, and, head resting on the sofa arm, looked up at him with so much love in her eyes that even though she hadn't yet said that word, he could tell those old feelings were there. She began to move furiously, pressing back into him, bucking as he changed position, but he held her down because as much as he wanted to feel her steal what she wanted from him, he was close to coming and wanted her to get off first.

"Mac, I'm close," she whispered, her eyes filling with tears. Despite the almost animalistic way they were racing each other to the edge, he felt a calm recognition between them. Actions weren't going to get her there. Words were.

So, in the silence beneath the chaos he said them.

"I love you, Delaney."

She came before he finished the sentence, and he followed her right over the edge.

CHAPTER THIRTEEN

"I have something for you."

The words filtered through Delaney's brain, but it was the smell of coffee that got her attention.

"Hey, Buttons. Wake up sleepyhead."

Delaney opened one eye and groaned. "What time is it?" she mumbled, moving the hair that was temporarily blocking her vision to one side.

"Doesn't matter what time it is," Mac said, pressing a kiss to her forehead. "You need to get up, and I brought you coffee."

She'd barely slept. Mac had been insatiable, and it had all been so incredible. She had been more than happy to go along with his plans to make love over and over until the early hours of the morning. They'd moved from the sofa, to the floor, to the shower, and finally into bed. Each time had been perfect, and a revelation. When they'd finally fallen asleep, wrapped in each other's arms, she'd never felt more like she was home.

Yet she hadn't been able to tell him she loved him. The words had gotten stuck in her throat when she'd thought about saying them. Lingering feelings of disloyalty to Brock, with whom she was both furious at and distraught over, needed resolving, and the man who was currently looking at her as if she hung the moon and stars was never going to be able to fix it. Only she could put what had happened to rest.

"What are you doing up so early on a Saturday morning?" she asked, lifting herself into a seated position. When she could finally take him in, she noted that he was showered, the damp ends of his hair a giveaway, and dressed. Her thoughts returned to their shower the previous evening, the one where he had backed her up against the cool tiles, lifted her into his arms, and taken her where he stood. It had been fast, and hard. "Don't we have better things we could be doing?" She raised an eyebrow, and grinned.

"As deliciously tempting as that sounds, seeing you sitting there in my bed, naked, I think you are going to like this better." Mac handed her a cup of coffee from the side table. It smelled heavenly, and, as she took her first sip, decided it tasted the same way. "Plus, it's not early. It's ten a.m."

Six hours sleep. That wasn't enough for her to function properly. "Maybe by your inner military clock that's not early, but ten a.m. is just plain cruel after keeping me up all night."

Mac laughed. "Pretty sure you were the one who kept *me* up. Although, for the record, I loved every minute of it."

Suddenly, she realized that her still being naked while he was fully dressed was, while kind of hot, also distracting for Mac, who obviously had something on his mind.

"I loved it, too, but unless you want an action replay right now, I suggest you tell me why I need to get up."

His eyes worked their way down her body, coming to land on her breasts before working their way back to her eyes. "As incredible an offer as that is, there is somewhere we need to be. Before everything went down at the lab last night, we were trying to figure out what the chemical formulas were."

They'd brought the documents home with them, though she wasn't sure where Mac had put them. "Yeah. I suppose we do need to get started. I'm assuming you have some ideas. And did you hear back from Noah about the men?"

Mac shook his head. "No, Noah didn't get back to me yet. But these things take time, and he's going to have to be discreet in getting that done for us. And yes, I do have an idea about where to start with the formula. I just called Louisa and asked if she would be okay doing a consult with us. It's Saturday, and she's home, but I know being in Encinitas was difficult for you when we were there last, so I didn't want to put you under any pressure to have to go with me."

What Mac had told her the previous evening had begun to sink in, but there was still one thing she needed to do. "Can we go visit Brock on the way?" she asked.

"Of course. Whatever you need to do. I probably need to have a word with him myself."

Ninety minutes later, after a hot shower, a long debate with herself over what clothes were appropriate to wear, and a short drive, Delaney found herself walking toward the corner of the cemetery. The drive over had been stressful, but only because Mac had been concerned that they might be followed. Despite her need to talk and burn off nervous energy, Mac had been too busy repeatedly looking in his review mirror and out the side window to be of any conversational value. So Delaney had sat quietly, dangerously alone with her thoughts, until Mac pulled his truck over in front of the cemetery.

Mac squeezed her hand. "Why don't you go ahead and have a few minutes with him first. I'll just sit over there until you're done." He nodded in the direction of a wooden bench not too far away.

"I'm not sure I know what to say," she confessed. "I've never liked the idea of him being buried here, it doesn't feel right. And to be honest, I don't really know where to start."

Mac stopped and drew her into his arms. "So just start with sitting by him and go from there. I think you might be surprised with what you finally end up saying. I know I usually am."

Mac's words surprised her. "Do you come here and talk to him often?"

"Not as often as I used to, but if I'm in town I try to come on his birthday, the day it happened, New Year's Eve, and when I have a big decision to make, like when I was deciding when to leave the military. Those kinds of things."

Delaney sighed. "I should have been here for those things too. For both of you." Words stuck in her throat, but she hoped Mac understood. The way his arms tightened around her told her he did.

"Go make up for it now. Take as long as you need." Mac let go of her and turned toward the bench. She waited for him to sit before she closed the last few feet to Brock's headstone. As Mac had suggested, she took a seat on the ground and studied the writing on the cool gray marble.

IN LOVING MEMORY OF BROCK ETHAN SHAPIRO
APRIL 29, 1984–JULY 7, 2004
LOVING SON AND BROTHER
LOVED BY ALL

It made her stomach tighten to think of him lying in the damp earth beneath her. "I'm sorry they buried you here," she blurted. It was all so impersonal, so cold and uninviting. "I told them you wouldn't want this." Delaney tugged the light denim jacket she was wearing tighter around her. It was a mild day, the sun shining gently down on the plot, but she felt chilled to the bone. "I'm sorry, Brock. It's crazy that it's taken me fourteen years to get here. But it's also crazy to me that you've been gone for almost as long as I knew you." She took a deep breath, and looked around at some of the other gravestones close by before returning her eyes to Brock's.

"I'm also sorry that I made you think for even a millisecond that I didn't have faith in you." She picked a blade of grass, and ran it between her fingers. "You were my big brother. I thought you were infallible. I had no doubt that you would become a successful SEAL. I guess I just wondered a little too loudly *why* you wanted to do it. I'm sorry, Brock. But I hope that wherever you are you can hear me. Because I loved you, still love you. I just want you to know that I always believed in you and I can't begin to count the days that I have doubted myself and wished you'd been around to tell me how to make it all better."

Tears began to choke her, and she ran her fingers under

her eyes to swipe them away. "I'm mad at Mac for keeping this from me for all these years. But you need to know he did that to keep your memory sacred. He lied to us all about what really went on up there to spare us the additional pain of knowing we were part of the reason why, so that we wouldn't blame ourselves. He's the most loyal of all of us, and despite wishing he'd been able to get through to you that jumping off the cliff was not a good idea, he's never let you down. Not once."

She looked over her shoulder toward Mac, who appeared to be studying her through his dark sunglasses. His arms were outstretched, reaching along the back of the bench. His legs were stretched out in front of him, ankles crossed. Looks were deceiving, though, because while he looked like a man relaxing in the sunshine, she knew that he was not only armed but would be highly dangerous if anybody approached. And he was also in love with her.

"He loves me, Brock. And unless I'm seriously mistaken, I think I'm in love with him too. So please, don't haunt him for still wanting me." She smiled through her tears, remembering the way Brock used to mercilessly tease her when she first began dating Mac.

Delaney stood and wiped the grass from her jeans. "I love you, and I promise it won't be this long before I come to see you again." She kissed her fingertips and pressed them to the top of the gravestone.

Mac stood as she walked toward him.

"You okay, Buttons?"

With a nod, she stopped in front of him. "I think I am. I guess the first time was going to be the hardest. But we'll figure it out. We always did, and we always will."

Mac tucked a flyaway strand of hair behind her ear.

"Do you mind if I just go have a word?" He looked around the graveyard, then back at her. "I haven't seen anybody come or go." He took her gun out of his jacket pocket and handed it to her. "You see anything suspicious, you just shout, okay?"

"Don't worry, I'll cover you," she said as she smiled at him.

"I'll settle for you not shooting me," Mac said over his shoulder as he walked toward Brock's grave.

He didn't sit down like she had. Instead, he crouched right by the side of the headstone and rested his forearm on it. She could see him talking out loud, but she was too far away to hear what he said. She was certain it was about her, though, given the way he would periodically look up and over at her. To give him his privacy, she continued to look around the perimeter, paying close attention to the main path they'd taken there.

She suddenly started to feel weird, watched. She couldn't say exactly figure out why, but something was giving her chills. Relief flooded her when Mac finally stood, and she hurried to his side. "I suddenly got a bad feeling," she said, relieved when Mac immediately put his hand on the waistband of his jeans where she knew his SIG was holstered.

His eyes scanned the area. "I don't see anything, Buttons, but I trust you. Let's get out of here."

Mac pressed the buzzer to Louisa and Six's home, and playful barking erupted from inside, followed by cries about giving a shoe back.

Louisa opened the door. "Did you know anything about this?" she said, eyes narrowed and looking slightly flustered, as a spectacularly cute Labrador retriever pup bounced around her leg before making a dead run for the door, and Mac, and freedom.

"Not so fast, mister," he said, scooping the pup up and foiling its bid for the open road. "And no," he answered, hugging the pup to his chest, relishing the comfort the little squirmer was providing after his conversation with Brock. "I have no idea. Am I to guess that this is a surprise from Six?"

Louisa sighed, then smiled. "Yeah. Come in, please." She opened the door wide, and he let Delaney walk ahead of him.

As they'd left the graveyard, they'd both been on edge, looking around them for any signs of danger. But once they had been safely locked in the car, they'd been quiet, not in a strange and awkward way, but more of a reflective and peaceful one. One that was healthy. Delaney had linked her arm through his and rested her head on his shoulder as he'd driven the short distance to Louisa's.

Mac put the puppy down on the floor and laughed as it bounced around chasing its tail. "Do we have a name yet?"

Louisa gestured toward the sofa, and they took a seat as she sat in the chair facing them. She reached for an envelope that was sitting on a side table and pulled out the piece of paper. "There is some sweet stuff, which in the interest of avoiding making you vomit, I'll keep to myself. But there is a P.S.: 'Oh, and Lou, remember a dog's for life, not just Christmas, so while I trust you to name him, please don't give him a shit name that I'm going to hate shouting out loud at the dog park.'"

"Oh my God," Delaney said. "You need to give him the girliest of girl's names. He'll hate that. Something like

Cupcake, or something that makes no sense, like . . . Mouse."

Mac looked over at her. "*Mouse*? Is that really the best you can come up with?"

Louisa laughed. "I did think about doing something like that, but I think I'm settling on Rollo. You know, the Viking who became the first Duke of Normandy. That feels like a good dog's name, although I'm not sure Six really considered the logistics of the two us having a dog."

"Rollo. I think it suits him," Mac said, watching the way Rollo had flopped onto the floor by Louisa's feet, where she was mindlessly tickling his stomach.

"You said on the phone that you have a chemical formula you wanted me to look at. Can I ask why this formula is so important and where it came from?" She slid the letter that had come with the pup back into its envelope.

Mac turned to Delaney. They'd had this conversation in the truck. There was no way that somebody as smart as Louisa was not going to ask questions, but Mac had assured Delaney that Louisa would never compromise him, and by association, her. "I explained to Delaney some of what you went through last year, and the easiest way to sum it up is that Delaney is going through something remarkably similar. What we told you that night before Six left was the tip of the iceberg. We have good reason to believe that the things Delaney was looking into have put her on the radar of the people involved."

Louisa looked over to Delaney. "That must be terrifying for you," she said, her voice filled with sympathy. "Literally, I don't know how I would have survived if it hadn't been for Six, Mac, and the rest of the guys. I commend you for doing the kind of work you do, even if it puts you in the line of fire."

Delaney relaxed and leaned back against the sofa. "Says the woman who just single-handedly opened a not-for-profit medical research center. Coming from you, I'll take that compliment."

The normally nervous Louisa smiled at Delaney, and Mac was filled with a sense, as he'd been on their day at the beach, that the two women held each other in high regard and were building a foundation to be friends. It was great to see Louisa and Delaney finding their own rhythm, and he wondered what kind of woman Cabe would end up with to round out the group.

"Any time you'd like to come and visit the lab, or perhaps get behind my push to make medicine a not-for-profit industry, I'd be more than happy to show you around. But I want to know more about this formula."

"Why don't I email it to you, and then we can look on your laptop?" Mac watched as Delaney sent the images from her phone. They'd decided that the fewer people who saw and handled the originals, the better, so before they'd left Eagle the night before, they'd painstakingly photographed each sheet, both sides, which Delaney had then compiled into one document.

"Mac, why don't you serve some coffee while I get us set up at the kitchen table?"

He complied while the girls got set up. For a moment, he felt like the male assistant to two very smart women. It was kind of cool. He was used to being the alpha guy in the room, but he was confident enough in himself to admit that these two had the bigger brains.

"I don't know if Mac told you already," Delaney said

as Louisa opened the files, "but it looks like we have some crossover between what happened to you and what happened to me. The files you are about to see came to me via a man who worked for an organization headed up by a guy named Lemtov."

Louisa looked up at Mac. "You are sure these are the same people?"

Mac nodded. "It certainly looks that way. Lemtov is becoming a major player on the West Coast. Do you know what that is?" he asked, tipping his chin in the direction of the code that had appeared on her screen.

"Give me a little bit of time to look through this. Why don't you guys take your coffee and Rollo out into the garden?"

Louisa didn't look up as she spoke, and by the time she'd finished, Mac was pretty certain that it wasn't as much a question as a statement. "Come on, Rollo," he commanded, but Rollo just lay on the floor looking up at him.

"Wow. You're a regular dog whisperer." Delaney laughed. She grabbed her coffee from the table where he had put it. "Come on, Rollo."

The puppy leapt to its feet and trotted across the wooden floor. *Traitorous little shit.* But still, Rollo was a boy, and he was following Delaney's ass, which looked perfect in ink-blue denim.

"You can come too," she said to him over her shoulder.

"I'm on it."

He followed Delaney into the garden and sat down on the patio sofa. Rollo ran off and began to dig in the soil. He should probably stop him, but he'd save the dog training for Six.

"I think it's amazing how she just keeps going as usual

while Six is away," Delaney said before taking a sip of her coffee.

"Yeah. I always used to think it was easier to be the one deployed than the one left behind at home. Not that being in the military is a cakewalk, but I always knew where I was, I always knew whether I was okay or not, and I always knew what precautions were or weren't being taken on my behalf. The people left behind have to pick up all the slack on top of their own responsibilities. For the most part, my mom was lucky if she even knew which theatre I was in."

"Theatre?" Delaney asked.

"Region of the world we were operating in, like the Middle East Theatre. Sometimes, my mom didn't even know *that*. But your family has had to go through some similar experiences with you doing what you do, right?"

Delaney pursed her lips as she often did when she was thinking, and he couldn't resist stealing a kiss, a sweet soft one designed to reassure rather than seduce. "Sort of. I mean Brock died before I was in college, my dad shortly after. Dad knew that I was set on being a journalism major, even though I think he secretly hoped that I would follow him into screenwriting. And by the time I graduated, my mom's drinking had gotten worse. It would be hard to say whether she really worried about me. It's like when he died, my mom's capacity to be a parent died with him." She shrugged her shoulders and sighed, a casual gesture that belied the hurt he could see etched in the lines between her eyes.

Mac put his arm around her shoulder and pulled her close. "I'm about to scare the crap out of you. Are you ready?"

Delaney tilted her head to look at him. "I'm not sure."

"Well, here goes nothing. I'm going to lose my shit when you go off to do this in the future. I'll lose it if it's somewhat dangerous, if it's somewhere I can't go, if it's somewhere I can't look after you, and most of all if it's somewhere I've been and the idea of you there alone gives me fucking nightmares. But I need you to know that even when I'm questioning every single element of what you're doing, I'll support you doing it. Even if it doesn't look like it or feel like it."

Her eyes went wide as she took in everything he'd just said. And maybe he should be worried. She'd had plenty of opportunity to tell him that she loved him, but she hadn't. Yet he could tell how she felt from the way she looked at him, from the way she'd looped her hand through his arm, from the way she pressed her forehead to his bicep.

"Shouldn't we start with dating?" she asked playfully.

"Hey. I took you to the gun range. And we've been dating on and off for fifteen years."

Now she did laugh. "So you're saying we've just been on a really long freaking break?"

Mac pressed his lips to hers, longer this time. Hotter. Stirring up feelings that told him he should just bundle her up and get her back to his apartment as quickly as he could. They had a lot of reconnecting to do, and he always did his best connecting naked.

"Hey, guys, sorry to interrupt your lovefest." Louisa stepped out onto the patio. "Mac, I think we have a problem. That formula you sent me. It's the same one that was stolen from me. And there's only one other person who would know what that formula is."

In the thirty-six hours since Louisa had informed them that the sample she had created, the one that Russian mobsters had stolen from her, was the weapon being sold on the black market, Eagle Securities had become a hive of intelligence and surveillance.

With Delaney's investigative skills, Louisa's knowledge of chemistry, and a group of armed and capable SEALs with foreign language skills and intelligence networks, they were closing in on the perpetrators. Leftover pastries from breakfast were slowly going stale on a plate in the middle of the conference table; a large map of California was pinned to the wall, covered in pins of information; and that unmistakable, slightly gross smell that always came about when too many were trapped in too small a space for too long had settled into the room.

Plus, the garbage can was close to overflowing, but nobody had a moment to deal with it.

Delaney walked to the door and kicked the wedge to prop the door open in the hope that this time it would work and give them a little fresh airflow.

Louisa, sitting at a desk tucked away in the corner, was on the phone to yet another supplier of equipment that would be required to manufacture the drug she'd created. At Delaney's suggestion, they'd researched the equipment required to create an airborne chemical weapon. With Louisa's industry clout and incredible brain that could look up, interpret, and understand the manufacturing methods of toxic chemical weapons of everything from Sarin and Tabun in World War II to more modern drugs like Novichok agents and Ricin, she'd come up with some interesting hypotheses. For instance, developing countries would probably only have access to cheap dispersion methods, like spray tanks attached to low-flying planes, which had Delaney pulling out the orders she'd seen shipped for "agricultural" helicopters. Everything was being cross-referenced to ensure that every feasible avenue was covered.

Delaney, with Bailey's help, was creating a list of vendors who sold the types of equipment necessary to both manufacture and disperse the chemical aerially. With the help of Miller, the sniper and tech expert from Cabe's team, who was hacking company files to retrieve orders and delivery addresses, she was also able to find out which companies and individuals were *buying* that kind of equipment.

Cabe and Ryder were taking the names of all the companies doing the buying, and were researching them for legitimacy so that they could come up with a short list of companies that looked to be shells, companies that had been open only a short period of time or ones that had any flags to suggest they were anything other than regular businesses.

Ghost and Harley were plowing through property rentals and sales, cross-referencing them to licenses to produce hazardous materials. It was a long shot that these chemicals were being produced legitimately, but in the same way Al Capone was sent away for tax evasion instead of all the crazy shit he'd done, it was always possible that they'd be tripped up over leases, licenses, and permissions. The names on the leases were being checked against the list that Cabe and Ryder were compiling.

Which left Mac and Sherlock to find the whereabouts of all the key players in the puzzle. They were standing in front of a whiteboard filled with a giant hierarchy of individuals, both ones above and around Lemtov. Mac was staring at Ivan Popov.

"You want to tell me why this guy has you concerned?" Delaney asked.

Sherlock cast a look toward Mac and then turned back to his laptop. There was clearly something she didn't know. Louisa and Mac had been whispering about Popov earlier, and if Delaney wasn't mistaken, they'd looked at her while they were speaking. So, she'd made her excuses to go to the washroom then googled "Ivan Popov." His grandfather had been arrested the previous year—right around the time Six had met Louisa. Some distant family member had been brought in to manage the lab where Louisa had formerly worked. But Ivan Popov appeared to have disappeared into the ether.

"He should be a dead man, that's all I know," Mac said, rubbing his hand across his day-old stubble.

Delaney had a feeling there was more to it than that. "You want to tell me why you're so confident he should be a dead man? As opposed to a man who is missing? A man whose grandfather was arrested as part of the plot to abduct Louisa has been missing from their family business for roughly the same period Six and Louisa have been dating?"

Mac looked over at her. "Shit. Okay, go to my office. I'll be there in a second."

Delaney wandered across the hall to Mac's highly organized office, but stopped to cast a glance over her shoulder. Mac was leaning in close to Louisa. She nodded her head, and Mac placed a hand on her shoulder.

"You doing okay, Delaney?" Ghost said, suddenly appearing in the doorframe.

She jumped. "Oh my gosh. You're as bad as Mac. Stealth should be your middle names."

"Nah, whatever it is, I'm better than Mac," he said, his tone teasing. "So you and the boss, huh?"

"Me and the boss, what?"

"Never mind," he said, a shy smile on his face. "I was kind of hoping that maybe you'd consider going out to dinner with me if you guys aren't serious. I kinda enjoyed hanging out with you while Mac was away. Are you? Serious, I mean?"

"I think we might be," she said without malice.

"Might be what?" Mac asked stepping up behind Ghost.

Ghost's smile slipped a little, and Delaney realized she could make things right.

"Making progress . . . on where all the players are," she offered, holding her hand out toward Mac, who took it without thinking. It was an easy situation to clean up. Ghost needed to know she wasn't interested, but she wasn't comfortable throwing him under the bus in front of his boss.

"Yeah. Hopefully we'll nail that down today." Mac turned to Ghost. "Did you get all those licenses worked through?"

Ghost looked down at where her hand was joined with Mac's. "Just about. I'll take you through them when you've finished in here." He left the room as quickly as he'd appeared.

Mac closed the door behind him and then pressed her up against it. "One second. Then I'll get serious," he said before kissing all the breath out of her lungs. It was instant, the connection between them. She felt as though someone had connected her to a live battery. When this was over, she was going to suggest to Mac that they take a vacation. Somewhere hot and sunny, where he could cover her in sunscreen with those large hands of his and they could laze on a lounge together as they got to know one another again.

"Sorry," Mac said, although the look in his eyes said more about taking her clothes off than apology. "Okay. Ivan Popov. Yes, he's the guy who stole the formula Louisa created. He was her lab partner. It was a drug she was working on to prevent the chorea movement of Huntington's, but it was a failure in that it was *too* successful in its trial. Instead of just stopping the shaking movements of the disease, it caused paralysis from a mobility standpoint but not from a pain and comprehension standpoint, making it a perfect airborne chemical weapon."

"I already gathered all that from the conversation we had yesterday. Oh, and the *discreet* looks you and your guys are throwing every time I mention the name are about as subtle as the Incredible Hulk ripping the roof off this building to let a little air in. I want to know what's going on." She could feel her temper rise, and a rush of heat hit her cheeks.

"To save Louisa, we had to work closely with the CIA to attempt to put some people away in prison for a while, and there was some collateral damage. And while none of us killed Ivan, we believed he was caught up in the fire because we never saw him leave the building before it all went down, though no body was ever recovered."

Collateral damage. He killed someone. A stupid thought. Of course he'd killed someone. He was a SEAL. Those guys racked up confirmed kills, not to mention ones that didn't hit official radars. But this . . . this had happened on U.S. soil. She wasn't sure how she felt about that.

"You want to know why I didn't tell you, Delaney? That look right there on your face. The one that says it shouldn't have happened. That you're horrified."

"No," she said, quickly. "It's just . . . I'm processing. Give me a minute to catch up."

"You shouldn't need a minute to catch up." Mac rubbed his hands along his stubble. "You either inherently believe I am a good man, with integrity, and honor, and courage. Or you believe I killed someone in cold blood for kicks."

"Mac. That wasn't what I said. I just . . . It's a lot to take in. I mean, I guess I knew what this was all about," she said, swirling her finger in the air to gesture around the building. "But this is U.S. soil, you can't just—"

"Can't just what? Save Louisa's life? Save her mom's life? Get rid of some low-grade scumbags who attempted to kidnap her so they couldn't come back and hurt her again?"

"I'm sorry . . . I should have realized what you do. I thought I did, but I guess it was only at a superficial level."

Mac shook his head. "Shouldn't make any difference, Delaney. You either know who I am or you don't."

She did know who he was. But she had questions, ones she had a feeling he wouldn't answer. Like where it happened, how many people were killed, what the circumstances were. She didn't recall it being reported and was concerned it had been swept under the carpet by the CIA, which flew in the face of her beliefs about freedom of the press and right to public disclosure. She needed the answers to those questions before she could decide whether what she had heard bothered her. It was her job. It was the way she had always dealt with things. Gather the facts, assess them, determine the headline, and scope out the meat of the story before deciding which side she fell into.

"Mac, I'm sorry. I didn't mean that I think less of you,

but . . . goddamn . . . I'm just trying to make sense of this."

"There shouldn't be any 'buts,' Delaney."

There was a ruckus in the hallway and the door burst open. "First," Six said, his usually stubbled chin now showing signs of a beard, "I'm going to find my woman and hug the shit out of her. Then I'm coming back here to kick your ass for dragging her into whatever shit you've dragged her into. Fair?"

Mac shrugged. "Fair."

Six marched across the hallway, and she heard Louisa's squeal as she noticed him. Mac made a move to follow him.

"Wait," she said, gripping his hand as he made a move to walk by. "We should talk."

"Not now," Mac said. "My friend just got back from a shithole, and I need to do for you what we did for Louisa. Unless it's too distasteful for you."

Delaney shook her head. "Now you're putting words in my mouth. I never said that." Her stomach sank. The happy, carefree Mac who'd pushed the door closed and kissed her like his life depended on it had been replaced by the SEAL Mac.

He crossed his arms in front of his chest. "Maybe. But I haven't heard a word of support."

"I want the people alive so they can be arrested and tried, so their organizations can be dismantled. I don't know that killing them is the right thing to do. That only takes down one person. Their testimonies could take down entire structures."

"And because you want the story?" Mac accused.

Delaney took a deep breath. "Yes, I do."

"Well, I want you fucking alive." Mac stepped out of

her reach but paused in the doorframe. "I'd prefer them alive, too, for all the reasons you said, but keeping you safe will always be my first objective, no matter how little you think of me for keeping you that way."

CHAPTER FOURTEEN

Two goddamn steps forward and one back. Maybe that was how he and Delaney were destined to be. Maybe it would take them a lifetime, or more time than either of them had, to get their relationship over the line, no matter how badly he wanted it.

He hadn't seen that coming. Well, maybe he'd always known that the story was at the top of her priority list, but he'd never imagined her looking down on him because of the lengths to which he'd had to go to protect his brothers and his country. To protect Louisa. Or the lengths to which he'd go to protect her.

When he entered the room, Louisa was in Six's arms, her legs around his waist, her head buried in the crook of his shoulder. Jealousy surged through him so fiercely that he could feel its searing heat. Not because he had any emotions for Louisa, or resented Six his luck at finding the perfect woman for him, but because they both had what he wanted.

Six kissed her one more time then lowered her to her

feet. "One sec, Lou," he said, before turning and sucker punching Mac in the stomach.

"Oomph!" Mac shouted. "What the fuck!" He grabbed his ribs, sucking in air, thankful that Six hadn't put his full weight behind the hit. "That was a low blow."

"Yeah, so was not telling me this shit was going down," Six said, pulling Lou back under his arm.

Cabe walked into the office. "Hey, man. You're back," he said to Six.

Six pulled the exact same move on Cabe that he'd pulled with Mac, and the two of them began to brawl, much to the cheering and chanting of the guys on the team.

Delaney entered the room and hurried over to Louisa. "What the hell? Mac, stop them," she said.

Mac shook his head, but it was Louisa who stopped Delaney. "Apparently, they've been fighting like this since they were five years old. You missed the punch Six laid on Mac, but he wasn't in the mood to fight back. Right, Mac?"

He looked over at Delaney. "One more sucker punch today wasn't going to hurt." It was bitter, but it was all he had right now.

She flinched—either under the weight of his stare or the truth hitting home.

Finally, Cabe and Six stopped long enough to hug it out. "Good to have you home, brother," Cabe said, gasping for breath.

Six was doubled over. "Didn't think *this* was the type of physical activity I was going to get to welcome me home." He winked at Louisa, who rolled her eyes.

Cabe blanched. "TMI. Those are things I don't want to know about."

"Assuming I can't just whisk Lou out of here, can the three of us catch up?" Six said, looking between Mac and Cabe. "My office?"

"Sure thing," Cabe said, and they filed behind him. "As long as you shower as soon as we're done. You stink."

Mac finally laughed. He could always rely on his brothers to break the tension.

Once the door to Six's office was closed, they relayed the story of everything that happened while they'd been apart. How Delaney had been smart enough to outwit the assailant, and how she'd come to have the chemical information in her hands.

"I wish I could say that if I'd known it would lead us back to what happened to Lou in the summer, I wouldn't have asked Lou for a consult," Mac said, as he perched on the edge of the low unit that doubled as Six's filing cabinet. "But the truth is, I'd do it again in a heartbeat."

Six rubbed his hand across his jaw and yawned. "I get it, Mac. But this," he said, pointing to the conference room. "This isn't Lou."

The guy was tired, but Mac knew he'd never complain, never let it interfere with what needed to be done. He wondered if he should illustrate that point to Delaney. "I think Lou might be coming out of her shell. When we first got her over here, she holed up in your office—which is why it looks so goddamn organized." Mac smiled as he remembered the first time Louisa had come to the Eagle offices and had rearranged the books on the shelves into alphabetical order.

"Yeah," added Cabe. "But then yesterday, she just appeared in the other room. Pulled a desk into the corner so she was out of the way, but she put herself in there."

"Did she really?" Six said with a grin. "Want to see

something totally crazy?" he asked, reaching into the rucksack he'd used as a carry-on. His hand appeared with a box in it. A ring box. "Used the time during the Dubai stopover to do a little shopping. Not going to propose just yet, but I do intend to do it." He grinned as he opened the box to reveal a simple solitaire on a narrow band.

"Holy shit," Cabe said as he jumped to his feet and hugged Six. "Best news, brother."

Mac stood too. "It's perfect for Lou. She's gonna love it." He slapped Six's shoulder.

"When are you going to do it?" Cabe asked quietly. "Because I'll tell you, it's the craziest feeling in the world."

Mac fell quiet. He'd been so excited by Six's news that he'd forgotten that it had been only eighteen months since Cabe's fiancée had been killed by an IED while deployed.

"Shit man," Six said. "I'm sorry. I should have thought about how this would—"

"Nah," Cabe said, brushing Six's comment aside as if it was nothing, although a little cough at the end gave him away. "It's good news. And it had to happen to the two of you eventually. It'll be Mac next up before we know it."

Mac shook his head. "I always said that if I ever found her, I'd put a ring on it before she had the chance to say no. But we just . . . shit. Never mind. Maybe our ship sailed no matter how badly I wish it hadn't."

A loud knock sounded on the door. Six shoved the ring box back in the backpack just before the door opened.

Delaney pushed it open. Her cheeks flushed as soon as her eyes landed on Mac. "I think we have something. Come see." The door closed behind her as she went back to the conference room.

"For what it's worth," Six said, making sure the diamond was hidden away, "I don't think that ship has sailed . . . I think it's well and truly docked."

"Yeah. We'll see."

They returned to the main room to see Louisa, Delaney, and a couple of the guys standing in front of the map. "What did you get?" Mac said.

Delaney stepped up. "Since we know that the formula was only available from September onward, we looked for leases of buildings and facilities that would be suitable to run this kind of op." Delaney gave a nod toward Ghost, and Mac had to bite down the urge to fire Ghost on the spot for being so fucking helpful. "We got us a ton of listings, *but* we then cross-referenced with the names on all the leases and pulled out those that were companies—which reduced the listings by half. We then went through and dismissed all legitimate companies, like grocery stores and manufacturers."

"I pulled together a list of companies that sold the kind of supplies needed for something like this," Louisa said. Her bangs still hung covering her eyes, and she stood ever so slightly on the outside of the group. "I pretended I was looking for supplies for the lab I was setting up. People were happy to talk when I told them which lab I was talking about. I told them I needed references and wanted to go see these items in action. We were able to cross-reference this with the locations Delaney's team had found." When she'd finished, she looked over at Six, who was staring at her as if she'd found the solution to world peace.

Mac couldn't help but smile at the way these women had aligned his men into two teams beneath them and at how the suckers had gone along willingly. "How many locations did that leave us with?" Mac said.

"Initially, twenty-two," Delaney answered. "But there are two other things. We took those companies and researched them to find out about their trading histories, their financial performances, who was on their board of directors, and whether those people on the board were real. Less than ten of those companies ended up looking suspicious."

Mac rubbed his hand along his jaw and took a long breath. As much as he was frustrated with Delaney, he had to admit that what they'd put in place was genius. Plus, she looked incredible while she stood up there presenting all this to them. The color in her cheeks was high, her eyes were bright, her body language was animated. It was contagious, and he found himself wanting to get to the answer. "So, how many places are left?"

"Eight," Louisa and Delaney said at the same time, and then, rather ridiculously, they high-fived each other.

Eight they could work with.

"We thought maybe we could fly a drone-thing or something into them," Delaney said.

Six laughed. "Drone-thing? You come up with all this shit, then call it a *drone-thing*?"

"You know what I mean." Delaney stuck out her tongue at him, and Six winked in return.

Mac looked at the map. It might take some time. Some of the facilities were much closer to L.A. than San Diego. "Why don't we start with the ones closest to us?" The clock told him that light was going to become an issue if they didn't move quickly. "Bailey, how quick can we get on that?"

Bailey looked at his watch. "Right away, I can always attach a night vision camera to the drone if necessary."

"Get on it. Take Sherlock with you. If I assume we're going in tomorrow to get a better look at whichever places pay off, I think the rest of us should go get some rest, come back fresh."

"I can get behind that plan," Six said, marching over to Louisa and reaching for her hand. "We're out."

Mac watched as his guys began to pack up, and he offered to help Buddha and Jackson get the gear they were going to need but they didn't need his help. So he waited until the room was empty except for him and Delaney. "We should go. You ready?" he asked. They'd driven in together after visiting the gun range that morning.

She reached for his hand. "Mac, can we talk?"

"Just wait until we get home, okay?" If he had to hear her say that his job bothered her, he didn't want to hear it in the very place he did it.

"I'm sorry," Delaney said as soon as the door clicked shut.

Mac didn't stop walking until he reached the living room. He turned on a couple of lamps, dropped his keys onto the kitchen counter, and slipped out of his jacket, which he threw over the back of one of the bar stools. Then he turned to face her. "Tell me what you're sorry for. Why?"

There was a right answer here. She could feel it. And the idea that she might get it wrong squeezed her stomach so badly, she thought she might throw up. She'd offended him deeply, but she wasn't a hundred percent okay with his choices and she needed to articulate why.

Mac wandered to the fridge and pulled out a bottle of

white wine. She watched as he removed the cork, grabbed two glasses from the cabinet, and poured them each a large glass.

"Cheers," she said, offering her glass toward him, but he simply raised his in silence and took a sip.

Delaney followed suit, allowing the dry wine to settle on her tongue for a moment before swallowing. "I'm sorry that I made you feel like I don't respect what you do. A thousand times over, I would always pick defending those around me, so I get why you need to look after Louisa and me that way."

"But . . ." Mac said. "I know that there is a 'but' on the end of that sentence."

Delaney shook her head. "Listen. I'm probably going to screw up articulating this, but hear me out and don't get mad."

"I'm not going to get mad," he said. She raised one eyebrow at him. "Fine," he agreed. "I'm already a little mad."

"I figured that." Then she had an idea. "Come with me."

"Where?"

"Bed. We're going to have this conversation in bed."

"Delaney, please. It's been a long day, can we just—"

"No." She grabbed his hand and took him into his room, to where his bed was made with a military precision. "You don't need to get naked or anything weird, but this is a conversation about us, and I think those kinds of conversations should be had somewhere important to us."

"We're adults, Delaney. We can have conversations without being in bed."

"Just shut up, Mac," she said, placing her wine on the

bedside table before she climbed on. "Lie down and face me."

Once they were in position, she was suddenly inspired to say what she needed to say. "We stand on the same side of right and wrong. I believe, like you do, that perpetrators of crime should be found and dealt with for what they do, whether that's Bin Laden in a cave, or Bout for trading arms, or the men who tried to hurt Louisa and her family. Where we differ is how they should be dealt with."

She slid her hand down Mac's arm and slid her fingers through his. He didn't shake her off, but he didn't close his fingers around hers either. Still, it was progress, and she'd take it. "I want to be the girl who *makes* the news. I want to be the girl who brings those people to justice. Sometimes death is too easy. I want these people to be forced to give up names. I want to tug at the loose threads of a criminal organization and unravel it, pick it apart, find all the evidence, give them nowhere to hide. I want them tried and found guilty."

Mac sighed. "And sometimes those people get off on technicalities because they have great lawyers, or they have a long reach—and when you are least expecting it, someone slips through the net and someone you love is gone. Sometimes those who are opposed to violence need to be protected by those who aren't. With Louisa, if we'd called the police when the Russians had her, they'd have brought in SWAT and negotiators, which can sometimes make those bad guys you're talking about do crazy stupid things to the hostages they have. Or just as bad, the hostages get shot in the crossfire. I could never, *never*, leave you at risk that way. The same way Six couldn't leave Lou."

She cupped Mac's face gently and kissed him. "I know you couldn't. And I am sorry if I made you feel like you needed to make that choice. In this case, I still want the story, Mac. Do you know who Nellie Bly was?"

Mac shook his head. "No idea."

"She was an American journalist who worked for Joseph Pulitzer."

He turned and kissed her palm. "The Pulitzer Prize is named after a real guy?"

"Yeah, based on money he left to Columbia University a hundred years or so ago, but I'm getting off topic. Nellie Bly did this incredible investigative reporting to reveal the horrors taking place in a lunatic asylum in 1887, by pretending she was 'crazy.' She was so convincing that a swath of doctors declared her insane and she was admitted to the Women's Lunatic Asylum on Blackwell's Island, now Roosevelt Island, in the East River in New York City. Her 'act' was so convincing that the administrators didn't believe her when she came clean and told them who she was. She was stuck in there for ten days, and it took her newspaper, the *New York World*, to get her out."

"This is a fascinating story, Delaney, but what does it have to do with you and me?" Mac slid his hand over her waist, skimming the line between her jeans and her T-shirt. Never had contact on that tiny sliver of skin felt so good.

"She could have just reported that she'd heard stories that the asylum was bad. Interviewed people who had been there. But I doubt she would have gotten anything to change. But by staying those ten days, being able to report firsthand about rats crawling over her skin, about how the only way to bathe was with freezing water poured over your head, and about being physically beaten and mentally tortured, she helped bring about changes to the way people cared for the insane. If she'd just gone after the current manager, gotten him removed, nothing would have really changed for the residents. And it certainly wouldn't have started the domino effect across the whole mental health sector."

Mac sighed. "I get it. You want the story."

"I do. And I won't be able to get the story if you kill them off—because I won't be able to report it without drawing attention to you, and I would never make you a target like that. I'd rather you had my back while I figured all this out, than have you kill them to keep me safe, but I never get to solve a part of the bigger arms trade issue."

She looked into his eyes, the ones that used to reveal his every emotion but which he'd somehow learned to control with poker-face accuracy. They showed he was beginning to come around. "Fine. We'll go about this from a reporter's perspective, but I swear, Delaney, any-one tries to hurt you, I won't have any problem pulling the trigger, whatever the implications are for the story or for me. Even if we didn't have CIA privileges, I'd serve time first."

Gently, she pressed her head to his shirt, almost too overwhelmed to speak. It would never cease to amaze her how far he would go for her and how lucky she was to have a man with such a strong moral compass. His hands rubbed up and down her spine, dipping lower until one rested on her butt, strong and warm. She was so lucky to be loved by this man and to get the chance to love him in return. She looked up suddenly. "I love you, Mac," she said, and meant it with every inch of her fragile heart. "I'm sorry I couldn't say it earlier. But I do."

"Thank fuck for that," Mac said as he pulled her against him, pressing his lips to hers. "Say it again, Buttons."

"I love you, Mac," she mumbled against his mouth.

"And I love you too, Delaney. Do we get to have make-up sex now?"

Delaney laughed. "Yeah. We can have make-up sex now."

Mac stripped them both in record time, put on a condom, and then settled back on the bed facing her. "Give me that leg," he said, gripping behind her knee and dragging her leg along his thigh, opening her to him fully. He slid a hand between her thighs and pressed his fingers against her clit. "God, you're already wet for me. Do you know how much that turns me on?"

"Getting turned on by each other has never been our problem, Mac," she said playfully, using the line she'd once used to hurt him in the hope he could see they'd moved beyond it.

"I know we have to deal with what's going on. But you and me . . . we don't have any problems now, right?" he asked, running himself against her opening.

She jerked in response. How could it be that time after time, he always made her feel this good? "No. We don't have any problems. Please, Mac, make love to me."

As he slid inside her slowly, he kissed her tenderly, so tenderly that she felt like her heart was going to explode. "I'll make love to you for the rest of your life if you want me to."

It was a statement she didn't need to think about twice.

"I'm still pissed at you." Six lay down next to Mac on the ground in the dark as they looked at a building they'd decided had all the factors necessary: a preexisting lab with new ventilation equipment; a facility that had changed hands in the last six months; a lease signed by a shell corporation with no trading history, no financial performance, and untraceable directors. It was at the top of the list in terms of being the most probable candidate.

Through night goggles, they watched the security team that surrounded the building. They were reasonably trained but not visibly armed, which he knew meant nothing.

"I know you are," Mac whispered. "But I'd make the same decision in a heartbeat, so either try to break my other ribs, or get over it." It was an exaggeration—his ribs weren't actually broken from Six's earlier punch—but it sure felt that way when he took a deep breath in his protective gear. In fact, he was praying tonight didn't involve running because he'd be screwed. "And again, in my defense, when I asked Lou for a consult on a chemical formula, I didn't know it would lead to this."

"Can you two shut up?" Cabe said quietly through their earpieces. He was on the other side of the building with Gaz. "You're like two old fucking women."

"I'm still pissed at you too," Six shot back.

"What are you? Twelve?" Cabe laughed. "You sound like a pouting kid. Plus, there was no shaking Louisa once she figured out the formula."

"Plus," Louisa joined in, "I'm actually kind of good at this stuff, Six." The women were back at base, but connected in via radio.

"Didn't say you weren't, Lou." Six rolled his eyes at Mac, and mouthed *This is your fucking fault.*

"Shouldn't you guys be quiet?" Delaney asked.

This time Mac rolled his eyes and for a moment questioned the logic of having the women patched in through cams on their foreheads. They were a distraction the team simply wasn't used to on a mission. But a very smart and necessary distraction. Only Louisa would be able to tell them what they were looking at once they got inside. Delaney wanted proof of what was going on inside— shipping documents, freight carriers, intended destinations. Anything that would link the facility to Afghanistan and to the Russians they'd been following. And Louisa wanted to stop production safely. Apparently, there was a way to destroy any chemicals in production, depending on where they were in the process and how they were being stored. All Mac wanted was to protect the women on the other end of the line.

For once, Mac was worried. His conversation with Delaney had him second-guessing whether drawing his weapon and killing someone was right—which was a surefire way to get himself killed. Right now, lying down in the dirt with Six, his ability to switch off and concentrate was nonexistent.

He needed that back, so he focused on the routine of the security guards. Yesterday, Buddha had sent a drone up around the facility, which was on the outskirts of Vista, about forty-five minutes north of San Diego. There was a cluster of industrial units on the premises, and from what the camera on the drone had recorded, it looked like only one of the buildings was in active use, or at least only one had a continuous rotation of security guards. A second building had a stationary security guard by the door, and it appeared to be where the chemicals were being stored.

Which reminded him. "Ryder? Got anything?"

The radio crackled. It wasn't the best connection.

"Truck is due in about ten. We'll get in it, see what we can find."

Louisa had contacted the vendor who had provided samples to the lab she'd worked at for and with the Popovs. When she'd asked about who was ordering the chemicals she was interested in, the vendor had started his answer with, "Well, besides your lab . . ." It was an innocuous enough sentence, except for the fact that that lab didn't need those chemicals in any significant quantity. So she'd called an old contact there in the spirit of catching up and inquired about what research was still going on there. He was someone she trusted, so she'd asked him about the chemicals specifically. He'd investigated and found out there had been a delivery that couldn't be accounted for in the lab inventory.

Which meant her old lab had been buying the required supplies. It made sense. The lab had the facilities and the permits to store them. It also supported Delaney's theory that Ivan Popov was alive and well.

The vendor had confirmed another delivery was due that evening, so Ryder and Lite had gone to catch the handover.

"From what I can tell, there's nobody permanently on the inside," Cabe said. "But I've seen one of the security guys go into the building to grab stuff for a smoke break. Leads me to think that the alarms aren't on."

Mac agreed. All they needed to do was get through the perimeter unnoticed. "I still think it pays to have Gaz check it out before we go in there and blow everything to shit." He looked down at his watch. "My patrol just went by. By my reckoning, it will be another three minutes before I see him again. I say we go."

Next to him, Six moved from a lying to a crouched position, and Mac did the same.

"On it," said Cabe.

Under the cover of darkness, Mac ran forward first. Never once did he doubt that Six had his back, even though the guy was still pissed at him for Louisa's involvement. Professionalism and years of friendship meant that nothing could ever come between the three men.

He pressed up hard against the fencing, pulled wire cutters from his vest, and snipped the wires down the post until he could create a hole big enough for the two of them to pass through. Once he was inside the perimeter, Six raced forward and joined him, passing through the hole with ease. Using a couple of cable ties, Mac pulled the fence back down into position and secured it at the bottom. In the dark, it would be difficult to tell that the fence had been interfered with, which was important, given the regular patrols.

Together, they hurried across the open yard until they could press up against the side of the building. Across the lot, Mac could see Cabe and Gaz make their way to a set of doors at the rear of the building. Several years ago, a developer had bought the site and had applied for permits to build the current buildings. Attached to the request were several drawings, which the team had studied in detail. The plan was for Cabe and Gaz to disable power to the building, including the alarm. In the meantime, Six and Mac were to head through the manufacturing area up to the offices on the mezzanine floor to retrieve documents. Once Cabe and Gaz were done with the power, they would go out into the production facility and, guided by Louisa, create video footage of what was inside. If there were any obvious places where they could cause some damage to keep the facility out of production for some time, Louisa would let them know.

At Delaney's request, they were not to cause any harm to people or property, at least not until they were certain that this was indeed the facility they were looking for. Mac hoped he could live up to the request, but even as the team had acknowledged it, they all knew deep down that it would be impossible if their mission went to shit.

Silently, Mac kept watch as Six picked the lock of the side door. They wouldn't open it until they got the all-clear that there was no alarm.

"What's taking you guys so long?" Mac whispered.

"Everything is shut down tight," Cabe replied. "Just taking a while to pick all the locks."

Matt looked down at his watch. "We have nineteen seconds until the guards are back."

"Flash, I love you, but we only have nineteen seconds to save the Earth." Gaz laughed. "Done."

"Fuck you," Mac replied. "And it was fourteen hours, asshole." He knew because he'd watched *Flash Gordon* a million times as a kid.

He grinned at the quiet chuckle from Gaz. "And Dale Arden was a lot hotter than you!"

They entered the building with their guns drawn, and immediately all of Mac's fears about being able to shoot disappeared into ether. Adrenaline coursed through his veins. He could feel its icy tingle working its way down his spine and along his arms. He loved the chill of it, the calm of it, the way it chased away anything else cluttering his brain. This is what he had trained for, this was what he was good at, and he inherently knew that he was going to do the right thing.

He and Six stayed close to the unlit walls, making their way past equipment until they reached the stairs to the mezzanine. Despite the stairs being made of expanded metal, they crept their way to the upper floor without a sound. The offices were locked, but it was easy for Six to slide a thin piece of plastic between the doorframe and the door. The click of the door unlocking seemed to reverberate around the building, causing both of them to freeze momentarily.

Once inside the office, they split up to search the room. "Okay, Delaney," he whispered. "Guide us if you see anything."

"I will. Be careful." Her voice wavered slightly at the end.

Inappropriate humor had saved them from the horrors of these situations a million times over. If Delaney was going to understand more about what he did, and who he was under those situations, she could start now. "Given the quality of Six's aim, I need to."

Six, a man with around a hundred recorded kills as a sniper, chuckled. "Fuck you."

Systematically, they began to open filing cabinets, looking through one hanging file folder at a time. "Who knew criminals took the time to alphabetize their files, and group shit together like this?"

"Fact. Psychopaths are one of the most methodical groups of people on the planet," Delaney said.

"Did you know Louisa tells me weird shit all the time too?" Six chuckled quietly.

"I heard that, Rapp," Louisa said, using Six's last name.

"There!" Delaney's voice made Mac jump. "Right there, the shipment folder. Take it out and flick through it. You know, this would have been quicker if you just let me come with you."

Mac pulled the folder out as instructed. Inside were hand-scribbled notes and manifests.

"That's the address of the airport in Arizona, the one where the delivery I was supposed to meet originated. It's too much of a coincidence. We should take the folder."

A loud clang sounded outside the room, and Mac hurried to the window, opening the white blinds a fraction so he could look out over the production area. "Everybody quiet until I say." On the other side of the building, a security guard, gun drawn, came running into the manufacturing area. A slash of light caught the guard's face, a reflection from the outside, as he looked around the room. "You hidden, Cabe?"

The sound of two taps came through Mac's earpiece, something they did when they couldn't talk. Two taps for yes, one for no. Mac scoured the darkness, one eye on the guard. It had fallen so silent that even through the glass of the window, he could hear the guard's footsteps on the concrete floor.

Six brushed by him, a pile of papers under his arms, and Mac assumed he was finishing off the cabinet Mac had started.

Two more guards entered the manufacturing area. "Do you see anything?" one of them shouted to the first guard, who was still walking around every piece of equipment, gun shakily pointed in front of him. He turned and silenced them with a shush. Smart move. He shook his head, but gestured in Mac and Six's direction, toward the stairs and offices.

Quickly Mac gestured to Six. If those guys started to walk up the stairs, they'd need a distraction in order to get out. Six collected everything they had found and stuffed it into his backpack. One option was to get Lite and Bailey, who were currently parked outside in separate vehicles, to create some kind of diversion. The other was to ask the same of Cabe and Gaz, depending on how close they were to the guards.

"There's nobody in here," one of them shouted. "Probably rats or some shit. Let's go."

The guard closest to them grabbed a handrail and placed one foot on the stairs, but then looked up to the office and paused. Finally, he stepped off and walked out of the manufacturing area. Mac let out a breath and then another when he saw Cabe and Gaz crawl from beneath the machine near where the two other guards had been standing.

It took them another twenty minutes to get the rest of what they needed and for Louisa to walk them through how to disable as much equipment as they could on their way out. Once they were back in the car and close to San Diego, the pressure valve came off.

"I think we might need to send Gaz back to lock-picking school," Six teased. "Longest break-and-enter ever."

Gaz laughed. "Maybe it's because you were just finished too soon as usual. I don't know how Louisa puts up with you."

"Oh my God. You guys are awful," Delaney said, and Mac couldn't help but laugh.

"It's always like this once a mission is over."

A loud bang filled the truck, accompanied by a scream from Delaney. Mac's heart went into overdrive. "Delaney, what the hell was that?" he shouted.

CHAPTER FIFTEEN

Delaney rushed to the monitors, where she could have a full visual on what was going on outside. "There are men outside, Mac. They're blowing the lights out." She looked at different views of the same scene, her heart pounding so violently that she felt spacey. "Oh my God, they have Ghost. He'd gone for pizza." Two men were beating him, but Ghost was putting up a good fight. Upturned pizza boxes lay on the floor by his feet.

"Bailey," she heard Mac shout. "Put your foot down. Buddha, Sherlock. Update?"

She looked over at the table where the two of them had been sitting as backup with aerial coverage and saw their headphones sitting on the table. They'd all thought it was over, that the mission had been completed. "Their headphones are in the conference room with me. Because you were out and on your way home, they went to the gym area to work out," Delaney said, her voice sounding as panicked as she felt.

"I'm starting the timer," she heard Mac say. "We're about nine minutes out, Delaney," he said. "All I need you to do is stay calm. Find cover. Can you and Louisa get to the showers?" he asked. "There are several lockable doors, plus there's a manual handle you can use just inside the second door that can lift the shutters to access the frosted glass window. We did that for emergencies in the event the shutters failed and someone was trapped in that end of the building in a fire."

Delaney looked at the monitors again. They'd been so busy making plans to attack that Delaney hadn't considered what it would take to defend.

"I'm there, already," Louisa said through the earpiece. "But Delaney is still in the office."

"Ryder, Lite, what's your ETA?" Mac shouted. Through her earpiece, she heard Ryder explain that they were a good ten minutes out because they'd left their vehicle and gone in on foot to spy on the incoming truck so as not to draw attention to themselves.

"Okay, Delaney. Stay in the conference room and lock the door," Mac instructed.

She looked at the screen again. The roller shutter door was open just enough for several men to attempt to crawl underneath, all of them armed, and fire shots toward where Sherlock and Buddha were. She couldn't just sit there twiddling her thumbs while two unarmed man faced off against a group of people who had come for her. Especially when she saw Buddha racing to close the double doors separating the warehouse from the offices, effectively giving them one more barrier to get through before they could get to her. He was unarmed, and, hell, he wasn't even wearing a shirt, but his first thought was to keep her safe.

Grabbing the headsets off the table, she opened the door to the conference room and ran to the secured doors, which required a key code to be entered before they could be opened. She pulled on the handle. They were both solidly locked, so she pressed the buttons in sequence.

Two of the men squeezing through the opening were making good progress. Sherlock, in workout shorts and sneakers, was slamming a chair down on one. The other fired his gun straight at Sherlock, and Delaney screamed. Fortunately, the bullet appeared to have only grazed his calf.

Despite her fear, she checked that the coast was clear and opened the door. "Here," she said, throwing Buddha a headset to where he was concealed. He couldn't quite make it through the doors safely without being shot at.

"Stay inside, Delaney," Sherlock yelled over his shoulder.

A bullet whizzed past the side of her face. It was so close she could feel the rush of air. Quickly, she jumped back into the hallway and slammed the door shut. Watching through the tiny sliver of a window, she saw Buddha attempt to make his way to the locker rooms. Maybe he was going there to help Louisa, but Delaney hoped it was because that was where his weapon was. He was making slow progress, though, because another assailant had spotted him and was firing at him occasionally while providing cover for the other men who were with him.

"We're three minutes out. Delaney, tell me what's happening," Mac said.

"The gun safe—give me the number of the gun safe." Delaney ran to where she knew the weapons were kept.

"Delaney, leave it to Sherlock and Buddha," he said in a voice that was so calm, he could have been offering her a cup of coffee. "They've got it covered."

"They *don't* have it covered," she replied, aware of the

rising hysteria in her own voice. "Two men are trying to crawl under the roller shutter doors, firing at Sherlock, who isn't armed because he was in the middle of a workout. And Buddha is trapped in gunfire behind the workout equipment. Now give me the safe number."

"Okay, Buttons, here you go." Mac recited the combination. Her finger shook as she attempted to hit numbers she immediately recognized as Brock's birthday. "Are you in?" Mac asked.

"Yeah, I just want to get something loaded that I can get to Sherlock. I didn't see Ryder, and last I saw, Ghost was being beaten up outside. So talk me through this."

She followed his instructions and grabbed a gun significantly larger than the ones she'd been using at the shooting range. Mac told her which ammo went with it, and to make sure it was fully loaded.

As she ran back toward the door, she heard Six tell Louisa how much he loved her. Delaney's throat tightened as it occurred to her that he might be doing it in case he never saw her again.

She keyed the number into the door. "I love you, Mac," she whispered before she pulled it open.

"*Shit*, I love you, too, Buttons." It was the first time he'd sounded anything but calm. His voice was thick with emotion.

The first guy trying to get in through the door managed to get to his feet. "Sherlock," she yelled, and, as he turned to head toward her, she slid the gun along the floor. In what seemed like slow motion, she watched Sherlock dive for the weapon as the other man's gun went off. The bullet nicked Sherlock's thigh, but he ignored it, grabbing the gun and returning fire on the man, who immediately fell to the floor.

Bullets started to come from the direction of the shower room. Buddha had obviously made it to wherever he had left his weapon. But there had to be more she could do—at a minimum she wanted to be able to protect herself if they got to her. She hurried back to the gun safe and repeated the steps Mac had explained on the phone. She saw from the way Sherlock had moved as he'd fired the gun that there was going to be a lot of kickback and it was going to be difficult to handle, but it was better than being a sitting duck.

"Delaney, we're less than a minute away. How many people are inside? Be our eyes to make sure it's safe."

Picking up a gun, she ran back to the doors. Sherlock had made his way to the other side of the warehouse leaving her alone at that end of the building. "Buddha and Ryder are down by the medical center, and I see three men." Suddenly, out of nowhere, a fourth appeared right in front of her, his face lining up with hers through the narrow pane of glass. It was him. The guy who had tried to break into her apartment. Delaney screamed as he pulled his gun level with her and pulled the trigger, but miraculously, the glass stopped the bullet and the doors remained locked.

Blood splattered the window, and the man fell to the floor, obviously shot from behind by Sherlock or Buddha. She didn't have the time to thank them, or to puke, which was what her stomach was telling her to do. She breathed deeply, trying to keep the waves of nausea at bay.

Turning on her heel, she ran back along the corridor to the conference room, noting the shadows of people outside the front entrance. Mac had asked her to be his eyes, and doing so would also give her something to focus on. "I think there are a couple of people trying to get in through the front," she said, her throat dry. She slammed the door shut and locked it. "I'm back in the conference room." She raced to the monitors. "Yes. There are definitely two people trying to get in through the front. There are four people already inside, there are two cars in the parking lot—the driver is still in one of them—and . . . oh my God. Ghost is down on the floor outside, but I can't see how badly he's hurt because the lights have been blown out."

"Good girl," Mac said. She heard car doors slam. "We're coming in."

They'd pulled over down the street a little, even though it would have been faster to pull up right to the front door. But this gave them the element of surprise, and allowed them to cast a wide net so that nobody could escape. Plus, it gave them the opportunity to scope things out a little before they were right in the middle of the action. The sound of gunfire, though, had them heading toward the building at a dead run.

"Same teams," Mac called as he hotfooted it across the parking lot. "How many still inside, Sherlock?" He needed the details that would help them once they were in. There'd been plenty of times in his career when he'd had no information at all, when they'd had to drop in blind to a situation and figure it all out on the fly, though, and either way, their training would kick in and make it work. But today, when it was Delaney on the line, he wanted as much information as possible.

"One down, three left," Sherlock replied. "I've got the door to the offices covered. Nobody is getting to Delaney right now. And we're by medical, so we have Lou covered."

He couldn't think about how Delaney was isolated in the offices without any kind of cover because if he did, his whole world would fall apart. But there was one detail that could help put his mind at rest.

"Buttons, are you armed?" He thought about the weapons they'd all taken with them, many of which would have been perfect for Delaney. Instead, all that was left were high-grade assault rifles and various pieces of heavy-duty equipment. Should they all make it through this, he was going to see what he could do to fast-track her license and gun ownership.

"I am," she said, her voice wavering. "I'm in the conference room. The doors are locked, and I've barricaded some of the tables up against it. But I don't think it will stop somebody if they really want to get in here."

"We're right outside," Mac reassured her. "But we aren't rushing in, unless shit goes tits up. You want your story, right?" He wanted her to remain focused, wanted her to stay calm and think of something other than her immediate life-or-death situation, because people did crazy shit in this type of environment and he wanted to make sure that she was under control.

"Just hurry, Mac, because as much as I hate to admit this, I'm freaking terrified right now."

"Medical status, Sherlock?" Mac asked, running down the side of the building, covering Six as they took turns providing cover, then leap-frogging ahead of each other. One covering while the other made ground.

"Nothing critical, but I'm hit," Sherlock replied. "And we're running out of ammo."

"Cabe," Mac said, grateful that they were still wearing their headsets. "You guys take the front. See who's knocking. Maim, disarm if possible. We need information. Don't take risks, though. Shoot to kill if you need to."

"On it." Cabe moved toward the right and began to give his team orders. With years of experience between them, nobody hogged the airwaves, and communication was reduced to the minimum.

"Bailey, the vehicles . . . take them out and disarm the driver. I don't want anybody having wheels to get out of here."

Mac watched as Bailey pulled a large knife and drove it into two of the tires of the unoccupied vehicle before disappearing around the back of it. The driver of the other vehicle was sitting at the wheel, engine running, window open. A rookie mistake. Even if he was supposed to be on guard, there was absolutely nothing he could do to avoid the handle of the knife that Bailey brought down against his skull through the open window. He slumped forward, and Bailey helped ease him down so he didn't hit the car horn.

"Sherlock, as I look into the building from the side lot, where are they?" Mac asked as they approached the opening.

"Two o'clock. Tucked in behind the metal cabinets at the front of the room."

Mac and Six crawled along the wall to the point where the shutters were raised. There were three men hidden by the bank of metal cabinets, just like Sherlock said, and a dead body on the ground by the door.

In the quiet, Mac yelled. "Guns down! Guns down!"

Nothing, but he wasn't expecting them to give up quite so easily.

"We have you surrounded. Put down your weapons and step out from behind the cabinets."

"Fuck you," one of the men responded, but the jerk jumped when he heard rapid gunfire from the front of the building.

"There are a lot more of us than there are of you. Your friends out front are down. Your driver is down, your vehicles are down."

There was a moment of silence and then a flurry of gunshot from within the room. Mac cursed. It didn't take a rocket scientist to figure out that they were trying to blow away the security panel where the code needed to be entered to get through to the office area.

The gap for the roller shutter doors was narrow, and he was going to need to lose his vest to stand a chance of being able to fit through. It was a risk he was willing to take, but there was no way that Six, who was bigger than Mac, would be able to follow him.

"Louisa, we're going to need you to open those rear window shutters so that Six and Lite can climb in." Mac stood up and began to shimmy out of his vest. He hated wearing the thing, but it had saved his life more times than he cared to remember. But for Delaney, he needed to take a risk.

"Don't take that off," Six said. "Come around the back with me. With all the ammo we have between us, we can push forward, provide cover."

"We don't have time, and you know it. Get in the back, make it fast, and guys, have my back." Mac looked at Six, who nodded and took off toward the back of the building at a dead run.

"Front of the building is clear," Cabe said. "All survivors, some casualties. Coming around the side to back you guys up."

As Mac began to crawl under the roller shutter door,

Ghost, who was lying by the exit, began to move and groan. "Cabe, get Ghost out of here."

"On it," Cabe replied.

Gunfire streamed across the warehouse as Mac finally pulled himself inside. Aware that both Sherlock and Buddha were about to run out of ammo. Mac knew he should be more cautious, just as he knew they could probably pick off each of the assholes as they tried to approach the door, but the thought of Delaney, sitting alone barricaded in a conference room ripped at his insides. His duty was probably to subdue the men trying to hurt her, but for love, he would fight his way through every single mother-fucking one of them.

Gun raised, knowing his men had his back, he crawled his way behind the low shelving that contained the binders of the protocols for security guard training. It was made of wood, not the best thing to hide behind but better than walking across the warehouse out in the open minus his vest. There was too much gunfire, too many shots . . . but then a thought struck him. Since every-body was already inside, what harm would it do to raise the roller shutters completely?

Jumping from his spot, he ran to the wall and hit the red button to begin that process. On a sprint, he dove back through the gap that was now increasing between the floor and the shutters and careened around to the front of the building, where Gaz and Lite had two of the sus-pects cable-tied on the ground.

"Lite, follow me in." Mac fumbled with the keys on his chain, found the one he wanted, and yanked it to the front door, opening it as quickly as he could. From his vantage point looking through the front door, he could see straight down the hallway to the men who were trying to beat him to the conference room. When the door finally opened, his heart lurched, his chest tightening as he powered his legs down the hall.

"Delaney, it's me. I'm about to hammer on the door three times. Let me in." After he did, he heard furniture being dragged across the floor. When the door finally opened, she flew into his arms, her eyes red-rimmed with tears. Never in his life had he been more relieved to see her face. "I'm with Delaney," he said into his communication unit. "Rain down hell."

As gunshots echoed through the building, his only thought was for her safety. "Let's secure this place back up again," he said, lowering her to the ground. There would be time to hold her later, time to tell her everything he wished he'd said to her already. But first, he needed to have confidence that his brothers would conclude the battle in the warehouse and simply protect Delaney.

He locked the door and piled the tables in front of it just as she had. Then he cleared another of the tables and turned it on its side, pressing its legs against the back wall. "Jump over," he said. "If for any reason they do get past my guys, they'll come in shooting high, so stay low. Nobody ever shoots toward the floor."

Once she was settled, he stepped over the table and joined her, kneeling, with his weapon pointing toward the door, staying that way until he received the all-clear from Six, at which point he threw his earpiece to the ground, lowered his gun to the other side of the table, and pulled Delaney into his lap.

"It's okay, Buttons," he said, holding her shaking body against his own. "I've got you. I promise you, I've got you a thousand times over."

Delaney looked up at him, those eyes of hers killing him more than the feel of her chilled skin or the way her chest was expanding and deflating rapidly as she sucked in air to deal with the shock of what she'd just gone through. "I've never been so scared," she said. "Even when I was in that damn room in Kunduz."

"I would never have let them get to you," he said, running his fingers through her hair. "Never in a million years would I have let them reach you."

Delaney brushed her lips against his. "No, I wasn't worried about me. I didn't want them to hurt you."

This time Mac pressed his lips to hers. After everything she'd gone through, *he* had been her biggest concern.

"I'm serious, Mac. I get it. I get what you do. But promise me you'll always come home to me."

He looked down at her. "If it comes down to love or duty, I promise, you win every time."

EPILOGUE

It had taken two more months to clean up all the mess. And not just the literal mess that had been created within the Eagle Securities building, although that had been bad enough. They'd dealt with the police, the FBI, and the CIA and argued successfully that it had been their right to defend their property. Though it wasn't technically their castle, their home, it was their business, and they had a right to defend it against anybody who would try and take it or its contents from them.

Mac carried his coffee and laptop out on the balcony, savoring the warmth of early June, his favorite time of year. Delaney was still in bed, where she had spent most of the last three days recuperating from eight weeks of solid research and writing. Along the way, they'd seen the closure of both the chemical lab that had been manufacturing the drug Louisa had created and the research lab Louisa had been a part of. Best of all, Delaney had been able to connect the shell company behind the lab to Lemtov, who was finally behind bars awaiting trial. And with the support of a couple of cooperative assailants from the attempt to place Eagle Securities under siege, there were solid testimonies to back up his involvement. All of it due to Delaney's relentless focus.

During that time, Mac had returned to work and life had begun to take on a new kind of normal. He hadn't asked Delaney if she intended to keep living with him, and she hadn't asked him if he wanted her to go. But it was time to put a line in the concrete, a modified cliché that Delaney had once tried to use on him. If he was going to ask her to live with him permanently, he needed to move out of his brother's condo and find a place of his own. So, before he opened the laptop to read the article that was being run today that Delaney had put so much of herself into, he picked up his phone and called his brother.

"Hello," his brother said gruffly. "Any chance you could try to check your messed-up early-morning-early-riser military clock before you call on a Saturday morning?"

Mac checked the time on his watch. Seven a.m. Perhaps a tad early for the weekend. "I'm sorry, but there's just something I need to deal with." Mac heard bedding being moved around, and the shuffle of feet on the other end of the line. "I wanted to talk to you about the apartment. I'm going to ask Delaney if she'll move in with me, and I'm thinking it's time I should try and look for a place of my own, but I don't want to leave you in the lurch, so I'm curious what your plans are."

There was a pause at the other end of the line. "Yeah, so about that . . ."

The comment hung between them.

"What do you mean, *'so about that'*?"

"I'm not coming back to San Diego. That was never my plan. I have a house here."

Mac looked around the apartment and the way the water shimmered under the Coronado Bridge. "So what have I been house-sitting for? You should be renting this baby out. You'd make a killing with this view. I can get out of your hair as quickly as—"

"Shut up, Mac," Lochlan grumbled. "It's too early to listen to my big brother in problem-solving mode. You don't need to get out of the house because it's not mine."

Now Mac was really confused. "What do you mean 'it's not mine'?"

"Go to the office and get that big black box off the top of the closet."

Mac followed the instructions. "Is this some weird tax break for you or something?"

"Just get the box. There should be a black folder in there."

Sure enough, there was, and Mac pulled it out. "Got it."

"Open it up."

It was a legal document . . . with his name on it, and something about "transfer of ownership." "What is this?"

"Thank you for your service, brother. I bought that place for you."

Little dots appeared in Mac's peripheral vision. "What do you mean, you bought it for me? That's not a gift. A gift is a new pair of jeans from the Gap."

Lochlan laughed. "That's probably right if your net worth isn't slightly over the mid-nine figures. I knew you wouldn't let me buy a place for you, but if I told you it was mine, I knew you'd stay there, make a home there, fall in love with the place."

"Lochlan . . . I . . ." *Shit*. Words wouldn't come. He

choked on them as they left his throat. His baby brother had bought him an apartment, and a fancy one at that.

"Yeah, I know. You don't do emotion and shit, but everyone knows except you. Ma, Dad, everyone."

Mac wandered out into the living room that had started to become his and Delaney's over the past few months. The dining table was still Delaney's office, but plants had appeared, and some bright cushions. Lochlan was right. He *had* begun to fall in love with the place.

"Oh, and there's a trust for apartment fees. So, don't worry about that shit."

"Thank you," Mac said, his voice gruff.

"Yeah, whatever, dog breath. See you at Ma's in a couple of weeks, all right?"

"Fuck you with the dog breath, and yeah . . . It'll be good to see you again, Loch. Seriously . . . I'm—"

"Going back to bed." And with a click, Lochlan was gone.

He hung up the phone and wandered back out onto the patio. *His* patio . . . no, wait . . . *their* patio.

Thinking of Delaney made him open the laptop. Her article was live, and he started to read through it. It was nearly an hour later when Delaney padded out onto the balcony in one of his Navy T-shirts. It barely skimmed her thighs, and he could see her breasts bounce freely beneath it, always a good thing.

She grabbed his coffee and took a sip before making a face. "Bleurgh," she shivered. "I don't know when I'll learn that I don't like sugar," she said, sliding one leg over his knees so she sat astraddle his lap. Her shirt rose a little higher, revealing what he already knew and had zero complaints about, that she was naked underneath.

"How was it?" she asked. Despite the fact he knew she was asking about the article, he couldn't resist teasing her.

He rubbed his thumb gently over her clit, surprised when she jumped.

"Ah," she said, rolling back on his lap a little, revealing even more of herself.

Mac continued the motion. "As always, it's perfect," he said, pressing his lips to hers.

She began to grow wetter, but the balcony was perfectly private so he slid a finger into her, then another, savoring the way she always took what she wanted from him sexually. It was one of the many ways in which she'd grown, one of the many in which he preferred Delaney as she was now to the young Delaney he'd once known.

"Mac . . . mmm . . . that feels so good." She bit her bottom lip and rocked slowly. God, he wanted to get her off, and he wanted to get off too. But that would have to wait, because once he got started, that would be it for the rest of the morning. "I gotta stop, Delaney," he said, withdrawing his fingers, and sucking them clean.

"No," she insisted. "You really don't."

"Okay, two things," he said, lifting her into his arms. He could walk and talk, and then they'd be in a much better position to make love by the time he'd finished.

Delaney wrapped her arms around his neck. "What's that?" she asked as he nudged the door open to their room with his foot.

"First, your article was genius. If you don't win a Pulitzer, I'm gonna go find where that Pulitzer dude is buried, bring him back to life, and get him to give one to you."

She laughed. "You liked it?" For all the humor in her tone, he could hear the small part of her that was looking for approval.

He lowered her to the bed. "Yes, I loved it, and so did your readership, given the comments below the article."

"You read them?" she asked, incredulously.

Mac nodded. "Every single one."

Delaney sighed and closed her eyes, stretching her arms over her head, which only served to make her breasts stand proud, like his dick. "Good," she said finally on an exhale. "That's good. So, what's the other thing?"

Mac slipped her T-shirt over her head and then slipped off his own shorts before climbing onto the bed next to her. He reached behind him into the side table and grabbed a condom, which he began to roll on. He was always going to want her, would never get sick of it. As she climbed on him and slid down over his length, he groaned.

"I love you," he said, pushing her hair behind her ear while lazily grinding against her.

Delaney kissed him, a long lazy one with soft, sweet lips. "I love you more."

"Move in with me, Delaney," he said. "Officially. We've never spoken about it."

She fell forward, her hair tickling his face, and he used the opportunity to slide out and back in. He repeated the action as her mouth widened in a little O. "Yes," she gasped.

Mac grinned, and moved faster. " 'Yes' as in, *'Oh god yes, fuck me just like that'* or 'yes' as in 'I'd love to move in with you, Mac'?"

"Is it wrong if I answer yes to both?" she asked, answering his smile.

He pressed deep inside her, savoring the way she clenched against him.

"Never," he said, and set about proving just how right she was.

Read on for an excerpt from Scarlett Cole's next book

DEEP COVER

Coming soon from St. Martin's Paperbacks

Cabe stood and offered Amy his hand to assist her from the seat. It was the gentlemanly thing to do, plus, he just wanted to touch her once more. Her fingers gripped his, and for a moment, he thought she was going to keep hold. The sigh, followed by the slight frown, told him she was grappling with the two of them as much as he was, and she let go of his hand.

Given the late hour, he led them to the escalator that would take them to their rooms. The Nobu Tower's elevator required him to scan his room pass before entering, and Amy's room was just across the hall from his own. The doors slid open, and unable to resist, he placed a hand on Amy's lower back to guide her inside where they stood with their backs to the rear wall, almost shoulder to shoulder, but not quite touching. The elevator was devoid of people but filled with the same kind of tension that always happened when they were alone. The door slid shut painfully slowly, enclosing them in the small space. He could feel the heat of her skin close to his, and the nearness made the hairs on his arms stand on end as truly as if he were standing in the middle of an electrical storm.

He tried to focus on the reasons why she shouldn't have the effect on him that she did, but he couldn't list one of them. His mind and his senses were filled with only her.

"Do you feel that?" he asked hoarsely. Surely he couldn't be the only one who felt like he did.

After a momentary pause that felt like an hour but was likely shorter than the span of a heartbeat, Amy sighed. "I wish I could say I didn't, but I do."

He looked at the numbers, willing them to get to her floor before he did something stupid. But they took too damn fucking long and he couldn't help himself. He turned to face her, placed one palm on the wall behind her head, and cupped her cheek softly with the other. "Tell me no and I won't," he whispered. Perhaps she could be strong enough for the two of them. Perhaps she could see through the heat of the moment, see what it would mean for the op if he gave in to feeling instead of thinking for once.

"We shouldn't," she said, turning her gaze to his. Her eyes were wide, and she ran that damn tongue of hers along her lower lip. "But I'd be lying if I said I didn't want to know what it would feel like."

He pressed his forehead to hers, heard her gasp of breath. Took a deep one of his own. But the feeling didn't pass. It kept building, the heat cycling between the two of them, growing, burning, until it was all Cabe could do to hold her gaze. They had to be sure.

One second ticked by. Another.

But just as he felt as though he might be able to rein in his emotions, Amy tilted her head, the warmth of her breath tickling his skin. She was so close he was certain that if he so much as opened his mouth to speak, his lips would brush hers.

"Kiss me, Cabe," she breathed.

And he did. Slowly at first. She was a woman who deserved to be savored first and devoured later. Hopefully there would be time for both. He pressed his lips to hers as her arms reached for his waist and pulled him into the cradle of her body. His imagination hadn't done the moment justice. He'd not expected to feel the dizziness, the rush of blood . . . to his head and his cock. He'd not expected to feel this way about a woman, let alone a single kiss.

But she tugged at him in a way he couldn't explain. He trailed his tongue along the seam of her lips, groaning as she opened for him.

Then the elevator pinged and came to a halt.